CITY OF
STRANGERS

ALSO BY MARK WHEATON

Fields of Wrath

CITY OF STRANGERS

A Luis Chavez Mystery

MARK WHEATON

THOMAS & MERCER

Published by Thomas & Mercer, Seattle

www.apub.com

Amazon, the Amazon logo, and Thomas & Mercer are trademarks of Amazon.com, Inc., or its affiliates.

ISBN-13: 9781503935938
ISBN-10: 1503935930

Cover design by Damon Freeman

Printed in the United States of America

For Brother Andersen

PART I

1

The music started first, a folk number performed by a quartet shrouded in darkness alongside the outdoor stage. The dancers, illuminated by colorful footlights, followed seconds later in a slow-moving line. They were all women with their hair tied up in gold, wearing long pink shirts and traditional patterned *sinh* skirts. The women elegantly raised and lowered their right arms as they promenaded across the stage, fingers gently elevated in a pantomime of refinement. By contrast, their left arms were almost stiff to their sides.

The annual Thai Cultural Day festival, an all-day affair celebrating Thailand's rich and storied history, had moved to Downtown Los Angeles in the recently opened Grand Park. The dance being presented now, according to Father Chang's program, dated back to when Thailand was part of a larger empire that included Indonesia and Malaysia. As the number of dancers grew, little girls and even elderly women joined the line of brightly costumed women now snaking around on stage.

The audience was rapt. Chang, however, was not. For him the music was little more than a whine of tortured strings accompanied by an irregular drumbeat. It irritated his senses and reminded him of music he didn't miss from his own upbringing in Guangzhou. He rose from his perch alongside a large fountain opposite the stage and wandered to a row of food stalls, the smells of which had been calling to him all afternoon. He selected a vendor that seemed to value authenticity over décor and ordered boat noodles with beef and holy basil chicken over rice. When the proprietor passed it to him, Father Chang dressed the dishes with gusto from the stall's homemade condiments. The vendor nodded appraisingly when he made liberal use of the green curry.

"Are you Indonesian?" the vendor asked.

"No," Father Chang admitted. "Just spent a lot of time in Jakarta. Dressing it right makes all the difference, no?"

"Once you've done it the right way, there's no going back," the vendor agreed.

A few satisfied bites later, Father Chang glanced back at the stall to note the name of the restaurant it represented.

I should take Nan there, he thought. *And Suyin, of course.*

When he finished his meal, he left the festival and retrieved his car from the parking garage across the street. As he pulled his Lincoln up the ramp, he marveled at the park and all that had sprung up around it. Downtown Los Angeles, once considered a wasteland of street crime and derelicts after the sun went down, was evolving into something else entirely.

The old things passed away; behold, new things have come.

To return to his parish in San Gabriel, Father Chang cut through Chinatown. He typically avoided it not simply because of the plastic pagodas and faux-Buddhist iconography he found garish and offensive, but also for the reminder that at one time the Chinese in Los Angeles were considered as undesirable. Of course, almost any race had been thought of this way by Americans, and in some cases continued to be so.

And those are the kinds of injustices that get a priest up in the morning, he mused.

The heavily Chinese-populated city of San Gabriel lay just a few miles east of Los Angeles. Here, the signage was bilingual and most of the restaurants and businesses catered to a Chinese clientele. No builders mimicked out-of-date Chinese architecture or felt the need to create picturesque tableaus to backdrop tourists' selfies. The people who lived here were done living in China's imagined past. They were Americans now, though many had dreams of returning home once they'd made their fortune.

Father Chang didn't share these fantasies. Rather, he imagined one day retiring to Rome, perhaps becoming a chaplain at Thomas More College in Trastevere or teaching at some remote priory in Porto Venere.

Live like Lord Byron, but without the excess or scandal, he mused.

Maybe a *little* excess.

Chang reached St. Jerome's Chinese Catholic Church, located on the south end of San Gabriel's main thoroughfare, a moment later and parked in the spot closest to the rectory door. The church, built in the seventies, was perfectly round, with a spire that rose straight up from the middle like a Roman candle. The cross on top was so small, it looked like an afterthought.

Father Chang fumbled for his keys as he jogged the few yards to the rectory. He almost reached the door when he heard footsteps behind him.

"Father Chang?"

He didn't recognize the voice. He turned and found a wiry, middle-aged Chinese man behind him. His accent was thick and his facial hair in patches. His clothes looked pulled from a donation box. But it was the gun in his hand that Father Chang's eyes were drawn to, particularly as it was aimed at his heart.

"Can I help you?" Chang asked, his voice calm and even.

"You are a monster!" the gunman roared, though the words sounded awkward and rehearsed. "You are a vile creature who has no business wearing the robes of the clergy!"

This is for show, Father Chang realized. *He wants someone to hear.*

No sooner had this thought crossed his mind than four bullets tore through his chest. Father Chang was launched backwards, the weight of his body cracking the rectory's glass door.

As he fought for breath, agonizing pain pulsing through his body, Father Chang watched the gunman sink down into a cross-legged position and place the gun on the ground in front of him. He glanced at Father Chang as if only mildly interested in the priest's plight, then bowed his head as if in prayer.

Ego te absolvo, Father Chang thought.

━━━━

"A priest?" asked Michael Story, almost dropping the phone. "Somebody murdered a priest?"

Though it was well past midnight, the now–chief deputy DA of Los Angeles was still in his office, as he'd been for much of the past couple of months. The upcoming Marshak court case, a headline grabber which exposed corporate malfeasance and murder in Southern California's factory farm fields, had buried him in paperwork.

"This guy did," replied the detective, Doug Whitehead, on the other end of the line. "Shot him four times in the chest at close range. Then the shooter—name: Shu Kuen Yamazoe—put the gun down and waited on the wet pavement for officers to arrive. The first on the scene said he raised his hand in surrender before they even got out of the car. We think the killing might've been caught on a security camera."

"And he confessed?"

"Not precisely," the detective admitted. "He invoked his right to an attorney before they even had the cuffs on him. Arresting officer said it was clear he'd been rehearsed. By the time they got him to the station, a lawyer was waiting with a typed-up confession."

"Well, there's your premeditation, too. Sounds open and shut."

"Here's where it gets strange," the detective replied. "The lawyer is one of those back-of-the-bus, personal-injury-and-DUI types. Said he's never met Yamazoe but got an e-mail from him at around the same time as the shooting and came to the station immediately. Time stamp suggests Yamazoe hit 'Send' just as the priest pulled into the parking lot."

Hmm.

"And the lawyer just somehow knew it was time sensitive and didn't shove it off until tomorrow?"

"Oh, but of course," Whitehead replied. "The e-mail itself was in Mandarin Chinese, but the subject was in English. 'Time Sensitive. Read Immediately.' So he ran it through a web-based translator and came right over."

Double hmm.

"Want to hear the kicker?" Whitehead asked. "Yamazoe accused the priest of molesting his daughter on four different occasions over the past two months. The shooting was revenge."

"Oh Christ," Michael said with a sigh.

"We haven't informed the archdiocese yet, but there's no way this isn't going to be a public relations disaster for them, even if the allegations are false."

"Understandable," Michael said. "But I'm still waiting for the part where you need a deputy DA at this point. I'm pretty sure the department has its own liaisons with the diocese and the archbishop's office."

"Oh, we do. A bunch. That's not the problem. We can't find the girl."

Ah.

"Neighbors? Other relatives?"

"Getting a whole lot of nothing. If the parish pastor hadn't said he'd seen the girl a couple of times at Mass, we'd be wondering if she even exists. The confession explicitly states that she's been packed off to China to keep her away from any questions or trial. And you know if we reach out to the consulate, we'd only be asking to be strangled in red tape."

"Was he here legally?"

"Yeah. Resident alien. Arrived twelve years ago."

"And the daughter?"

"No paperwork whatsoever. When he applied for his green card, he didn't even list a family, though that's hardly uncommon. Just based on what we found in his phone, he did regularly communicate with at least some people back home. A wife, a mother, who knows? But as far as a daughter goes, we don't even have a name."

Michael tried to remember what he knew of Detective Whitehead. He was persistent but wasn't exactly well liked. If Michael didn't give him what he wanted, there'd be a dozen phone calls every other day "just to follow up" until he did.

"So, how can I help? You need a look at passenger manifests back to China around the dates in question? Help with LAUSD to see if she was attending any classes?"

The detective went quiet for a moment, as if unsure how to frame his request, but then bulled on ahead anyway.

"I don't think we're going to find documents tied to him. If she came in illegally, there aren't going to be any records, and if she left the same way, that's the case twice over. On top of that I don't see a scenario in which we get Yamazoe talking. I think he's said what he's going to say in the confession and that's it. So it's the neighbors and the other parishioners, but even if you're fresh off the boat and can't even open a checking account or get car insurance, you're still not going to talk to cops. So given the church angle, I thought maybe you could give your guy a call."

And there it was. Michael might have gotten all the attention and glory for the Marshak case, but here was confirmation of what he'd assumed: no one bought the narrative that this dogged, justice-driven deputy DA had acted alone. How much of the truth of Father Chavez's involvement was out there he had no clue, the priest having gone under-cover at great personal risk to expose the family's criminal machinations. But it was obviously enough, or Detective Whitehead wouldn't have bothered making the call.

"Let me think about it," Michael muttered, miserable.

II

The sun had barely cracked the eastern horizon when Father Luis Chavez was out the door of the St. Augustine's rectory and on the streets. There was an early-morning Mass at six thirty, which gave Luis about an hour for his morning run. He considered heading east toward the USC campus and its many jogging paths around the stadium and Natural History Museum, but the area would already be packed with students. Instead, he crossed the bridge over the I-10 freeway and headed for the south part of downtown, which he knew would be empty.

Though he could occasionally hear a car or truck a few blocks over, the city itself looked abandoned. Every block was depopulated, every shop locked up tight. The streets and sidewalks didn't get swept or the trash picked up here as often as elsewhere, adding to the apocalyptic feel.

Luis didn't mind.

So much of life at the church and at the neighboring parochial school, St. John's, was task driven. There was always something to do, always someone trying to get his attention. Even when in prayer it could feel as if he was stealing time from some other task that needed to be done. Out on the road he was able to open his mind, commune with God as he let his thoughts flow freely, and reflect on the days ahead.

The day before he'd gone out to the cemetery in Echo Park to visit the grave of Maria Higuera, a woman whose family had gotten caught up in the Marshak case, leading to the death first of Maria's brother and then Maria herself. Only her son, Miguel, remained. Though Luis tried to keep tabs on him, Miguel wasn't interested in what he had to say, preferring to spend time with newfound criminal associates. Of the many things he prayed over, this was one of the most frequent.

Once he reached the outskirts of the Staples Center parking lots, he circled back to St. Augustine's. He wondered if another reason he was attracted to running was that it was one of the only times while awake he was without his Roman collar. Passing a shop window, he caught sight of his reflection. His collarless appearance took him by surprise, making him feel like he was looking at some old photograph taken before he'd entered the priesthood. It wasn't so long ago, was it? But like an itch that needed scratching, he couldn't go too long without it on. He didn't feel like himself. He *wasn't* himself.

Like clockwork, whenever he began to feel like this, he knew it was time to head back to the rectory and start the day.

The sun was higher as the church came into view, the shadows of its spire and roof thrown long across the parking lot. Somewhere in that darkness near the chapel, Luis spotted the silhouette of a man trying first the doors leading to the administrative offices and then coming around to try the ones at the back of the building. People tried to enter the church at all hours of the day, so Luis didn't think much of it, until he saw the lone police car in the parking lot.

He froze. His instincts, formed in his pre-collar days, ran through the various scenarios. He hadn't likely been seen yet, so he could turn and go back the way he came. He should slow down, maybe cross the street at the nearest light. But where was the second cop? Could he have eyes on him even now, wondering what his next move would be?

"Excuse me! Sir? Could you come over here?"

It was the cop. He'd spotted Luis and was moving toward him. Luis's first thought was that he didn't have any ID on him, only the key to the rectory. The second was that he was wearing a St. John's sweatshirt and sweatpants and didn't look like someone you'd bust for loitering with intent even if it was the "quota time of the month."

"Can I help you, Officer?" he asked, walking over.

"Are you a priest here?" the officer asked, stopping and looking Luis over.

The officer's tone was suspicious. *Maybe I'm not above reproach,* Luis thought.

"He is," called out a voice. "One of our priests and teachers."

Both Luis and the officer turned as St. Augustine's parish pastor, Gregory Whillans, and a second officer came from around the side of the church. Though he'd only seen him the night before, Luis was still aghast at his pastor's appearance. In three short months the cancer that was laying waste to Whillans's body had diminished him to the point he was almost unrecognizable. Gone was the bombastic and imposing clerical figure Luis had so admired when they first met. In his place was a wizened old man who looked decades older than he was.

The first policeman relaxed as Whillans approached with his partner. Luis came over to take the pastor's arm.

"Is everything all right?" Luis asked.

"Well, no," Whillans admitted, glancing to both officers. "There's been a shooting. Father Benedict Chang at St. Jerome's. He was shot and killed last night in the parking lot. Though the killer was apprehended, the police—rightly so—have come to check on the other parishes."

Luis searched his memory. He didn't know Father Chang and barely knew St. Jerome's. Still, it was troubling news. People were killed every day in Los Angeles, but Luis couldn't remember the last time he'd heard of the murder of a priest.

"If you see anything, give us a call," the first officer, whose name badge identified him as Ybarra, said as he handed cards to Luis and Pastor Whillans. "This appears to be an isolated incident, but you never know."

Appears to be.

"Thank you very much, Officer," Whillans said, his hand weighing heavily on Luis's arm.

They watched the squad car drive away, then turned back to the chapel.

"Awful story," Whillans said. "It sounds like someone was waiting for him and shot him as he went to the rectory."

"A robbery?" Luis asked.

"No. The shooter sat down and waited for the police to come."

Luis could conjure no one reason somebody would shoot a priest. Rather, he could come up with a thousand.

"Well, we'll have to be on our guard," Whillans said. "But more than that, we'll have to make sure our students and parishioners feel safe. I'll write something up and let Erna circulate it. Will you tell the other priests?"

"Yes, Father," Luis said, guiding Whillans to the door of the admin wing. "Anything else right now? I need to grab a shower before morning Mass."

"Yes, in fact. Bridgette and I were talking about you last night," Whillans said, referring to the laywoman with whom he'd maintained a noncelibate relationship for the past twenty years, something Luis was still conflicted about. "It's the Feast of Saint Peter Claver this Sunday. I think—and she agreed with me—that it's time you deliver the homily at Mass. Is that something you feel up to?"

Luis was surprised. Since he'd become assistant pastor, Whillans had gradually increased his duties around the parish in order to help shield Whillans's condition from inquiry. Luis had thrown himself into these and learned quite a bit, but the homily? So soon? He knew that the other priests at St. Augustine's weren't likely to begrudge him, but this would be putting a novice out in front of the congregation as well.

"I think so," Luis said, hoping he sounded steadier than he felt. "What's the scripture?"

"Up to you," Whillans said. "But being Claver, maybe Jeremiah 25:5?"

"'Turn ye again now everyone from his evil way, and from the evil of your doing?'" Luis recited, feeling like he was back in faith formation class. "Mind reading a draft or two in advance?"

"Not at all," Whillans said. "One more thing. There was already a voice mail on the office phone this morning—Michael Story asking for you to give him a call. Any idea what it's about?"

Luis froze. Though some in the archdiocese knew of Luis's involvement sorting out the Marshak human-trafficking case that summer, only Whillans knew the whole story. Including that the ambitious and possibly venal deputy DA, to whom Luis had fed his findings, was not a person Luis thought he'd hear from again.

"No idea. Probably just some detail about the Marshak case."

"Of course," Whillans replied. "Just wanted to make sure you got the message. Let me know if it's anything else."

"I will, Father," Luis lied.

———

Dr. Suyin "Susan" Auyong stared at the headline in disbelief. Late for her morning shift at the clinic, she'd ignored the texts, e-mails, and voice mails from Nan that had her phone lit up like a pachinko machine when she'd woken from a less-than-four-hour nap following her last shift. It was her boss, the clinic's—well, unlicensed clinic's—chief administrator, Clover Gao, who'd brought the news story to her attention.

"Isn't this your friend?" she'd asked without feeling.

Priest Shot Outside San Gabriel Parish.

It wasn't even on the front page, didn't warrant more than a thousand words. Was that why she didn't take the news as hard as Clover wanted her to? Or was it that she had so long expected to see a headline just like this that when the shoe finally dropped, she felt only numbness rather than anguish?

"Yes, Father Chang," Susan acknowledged to Clover. "He was very charitable. We met because he would occasionally bring his parishioners here when they were in need. If they couldn't pay, he'd pay for them."

"Given the rumors I'm hearing about why he was killed, I think it best to say little of that association," Clover said in her infuriatingly Clover-like way.

"What rumors?" Susan asked.

"I won't spread gossip," Clover said airily before heading away. "Mr. Carreño is waiting for his pills in Room Four. Could you take care of that?"

Susan nodded as she sank back against the wall. She didn't want to deal with Mr. Carreño or his pills. For that matter she didn't want to do anything but go home, find whatever alcohol she might have lying around, and drink herself into a stupor.

Poor, poor Father Benny.

Then she remembered Nan. Dear God. She grabbed her cell phone and dialed a number.

"I'm so, so, *so* sorry I didn't call back," she said when it was answered. "Wherever you are, just come to meet me. You can stay in my office all day if you'd like. It's terrible, and I know you don't want to face the world right now. But I just don't want to think you're there all by yourself."

There were a few sniffles in response, a muffled sob of someone who'd been crying for some time now, then a grunt of acceptance.

"I'll expect to see you soon then," Susan said. "And I'll find someone to cover for me so we can go somewhere to talk about this. He loved us both so, so very much. 'We three vagabonds,' he called us, remember? Strangers in a strange land who'd found each other."

"He was . . ." Nan began but couldn't finish.

"I know," Susan said quietly. "I know."

As she hung up, still wondering how she would get through the next few hours, Clover poked her head out of her office.

"Mr. Carreño. Room Four," she said sternly.

Susan nodded and headed to the supply closet, where a delivery-man was stocking the shelves with boxes of pharmaceuticals, the unlicensed clinic being an unlicensed pharmacy as well.

In for a penny, in for a pound.

"What're you looking for?" the deliveryman, a pleasant-looking young man whose accent suggested he was also from Hong Kong, asked.

"Um . . . Hasix," Susan said, snapping back into work mode and pointing to one of the open boxes. "Thank you."

The deliveryman obliged, and Susan carried the box of pills down the hall. For all she cared she could be handing Mr. Carreño rattlesnake poison rather than his hypertension medication. She tried to comport herself before stepping into the examination room, but one thought kept playing itself over in her head. It wasn't a question of *who* wanted Father Chang dead but who *didn't*?

"Is Christianity based on the teachings of Jesus of Nazareth?" Luis asked his students. "Or the interpretation and expansion on those by Paul the Apostle? That is what we're going to tackle today."

Luis scanned the room. It was only the second week of classes, but he already had a sense of the group's comfort level. They liked a little boat rocking, particularly when he said something that flew in the face of something they'd heard at Mass. Too far, however, and they got uncomfortable, as if fearing for their souls should they hear something outright blasphemous.

"According to the historical record, James the Brother of Christ, also known as James the Just, may have been Jesus's designated successor," Luis continued. "But Paul, though he had never met Christ, had amassed a following based on his interpretation of so-called miraculous events authored by Jesus and what he claimed were Jesus's own words to him from the afterlife. It's hard enough having a conversation with a zealot. Now imagine if that zealot is countering your arguments with information he's saying Jesus is giving him from heaven."

Sure enough, a few students shifted in their chairs, while others cleared their throats as their parents might've done in church having heard the same thing.

"The study of the Gospels is a study in comparative literature," Luis said. "Why in the Gospel of Mark, which was written first, is he the Son of God but in Matthew he's described more like Moses, a teacher? Why in the Gospel of John are Christ's last words 'I am thirsty' and 'It is finished,' whereas in Luke he says 'Father, forgive them' and 'Father, into your hands I commend my spirit'? If the Gospels had been written by the apostles, they might be a very different thing. But as they were written by men who'd never met Jesus and had to set down their history by parsing stories passed down from the original disciples, and often through Paul's interpretation, context is key. Did you know that Luke was converted by Paul? That Mark was one of Paul's translators? There's a reason so much of the New Testament is made up of Paul's letters to groups of Christians. So again, is Christianity about Jesus? Or is it about Paul's interpretation of Jesus?"

In the back row he saw the first head bobbing downwards, sneaking a look at an iPhone.

Ah well.

Luis pressed on as best he could and even received a few interesting questions by the end. Just when he thought he would send them out on a high note for the rest of the day, someone raised their hand tentatively and asked if he'd known the slain priest in East LA. When he looked around the rest of the faces in the classroom, he realized it was all any of them had been thinking of.

"I didn't," he said. "But I'm sure he was a good man. I'm just glad the man who did it has come forward and admitted it, as there's now some hope for his immortal soul."

The answer was met with a few seconds of silence, before the bell, mercifully in Luis's opinion, rang to signal the end of the period. Once the students had evacuated the classroom, Luis gathered his books to head back to the rectory for his break period.

Instead, he found Michael Story leaning against the hallway wall, checking his cell phone. A small sticker identifying him as a visitor was stuck to his suit jacket's left breast pocket.

For a terrifying moment Luis imagined the deputy DA was here to tell him something about Miguel Higuera. But then Michael extended his hand and nodded, suggesting to Luis that he was here about something else entirely.

"Father Chavez, I thought priests were meant to lead with 'What the church believes is this,' or 'What we're taught is that.' You're more like 'Some people believe this,' or 'There are those in the church who believe that.' You don't think that confuses the issue?"

Luis shrugged, not taking the bait. "I believe the way we strengthen our beliefs is by allowing them to be rigorously challenged from all sides at all times. What do you believe?"

Michael grinned and extended his hand. "I believe it's been too long."

However dubious he was that Michael Story cared how long it had been, Luis shook the proffered hand. He peered into the deputy DA's eyes for any signs of remorse for past transgressions. He saw not a one.

"What can I do for you?" Luis asked.

"Can we go somewhere quiet?"

Luis led Michael out of St. John's and over to St. Augustine's next door. They were an unlikely pair: one a former teenage hood who'd traded that life for a path to the priesthood after his brother's murder; the other a onetime starry-eyed crusader for justice who had discovered, after joining the LA district attorney's office, that his ethical resolve was more pliable than he might've thought.

They reached a small courtyard, where there was a statue of Saint Francis alongside two benches. Luis sat on one and indicated for Michael to take the other. Michael remained standing.

"I'll get right to the point," Michael said. "You've no doubt heard about the shooting last night in the San Gabriel Valley. Did you know Father Chang?"

"Not at all."

"I didn't either, so I looked into him today. Seems like a good man actually. Cared a lot about his parishioners and the community around the parish as well."

"So, the shooter gave a reason."

Michael eyed him with a look that suggested he felt Luis may have missed his true calling.

"He did," Michael said. "But in a letter to his lawyer he also admitted the killing was premeditated. He says Chang molested his daughter."

Luis's face flushed hot. He knew he wasn't supposed to judge others, but he couldn't help the flash of anger and hate that coursed through his brain. The molestation scandals that had just about brought the church to its knees were such a raw wound, Luis winced at the possibility of another one.

"Is the girl safe?" Luis asked.

"We have no reason to believe not," Michael said. "The confession states that she's gone back to China. Just we can't get any kind of confirmation on that. We get a lot of 'yes' from people we talk to, only to find out it means 'Yes, I understand the question,' not 'Yes, I know where she is.' It's a cultural gap. Of course, we'd love to talk to her, but like you, her safety is our primary concern."

Luis could tell from Michael's body language that this last bit was a lie. He didn't care, though. The sooner he could get the deputy DA out of here, the better.

"So, why are you here?"

"We're getting some red flags," Michael admitted. "And given the recent scandals, including here in the LA archdiocese, we have to be right about this before the confession hits the press. No one wants to embarrass the archbishop, but no one wants to sweep something like this under the rug if it is true."

"What're the red flags?"

"It's just all so convenient," Michael said. "The daughter who doesn't leave a trace. The confession arriving at the station a moment after the shooter was brought in. The accusation of sexual misconduct at a time when everyone is primed to automatically believe it's true."

"What do you want me to do about it?" Luis asked, afraid he already knew.

"No one at that church is going to talk to the cops," Michael explained. "But they might talk to another priest. And you're good at this. You have an instinct for knowing who the bad guys are and the background to understand what makes them tick."

This tossed-off allusion to Luis's criminal past angered Luis even more. Michael didn't seem to notice.

"On top of that it's your own church's reputation on the line here. If anyone's motivated to get in there and get people talking, it's you. I want to get to the bottom of this as much as anyone. If it's a case of a molested daughter and a revenge shooting like he says, I want the truth of that to come out. If it's something else entirely and that's a smoke screen, I want that truth to come out. With you, I can get that done."

Luis eyed Michael for a long moment before rising to his feet.

"The answer's no," Luis said. "If you need someone to play mediator between you and Father Chang's congregants, the best person to ask is the parish priest at St. Jerome's or someone from the archdiocese. Not me."

"This is one of your brother priests," Michael protested. "Don't you even want to think about it?"

Luis considered a raft of responses to this. Instead of choosing, he turned and returned to St. John's.

|||

"This is amazing," Oscar de Icaza, small-time gangster and car chopper, enthused as he stared out the bay window overlooking Los Angeles. "You feel like the king of the city."

"It's what they mean by 'jetliner views,'" the listing agent, a middle-aged woman named Miranda, said. "You look down on everything as if you're in a—"

"Yeah, I figured that's what it meant," Oscar snarled, cutting the woman off midthought. "I'm not a five-year-old."

Miranda shot Oscar an aggrieved look, but when he offered no apology, she turned it on the third member of their party, Helen Story.

"Should we look upstairs?" Helen offered, acting in her official capacity as Oscar's realtor. "We haven't seen the rooftop deck."

"Yeah, let's see the *deck*," Oscar snapped, turning from the window.

He caught Miranda eyeing Helen with a strained look but didn't care. Helen raised a placating hand and followed him to the steps. When Miranda moved to come up as well, Helen stopped her with a smile. The agent got the picture and hung back.

"This is it!" Oscar announced once he reached the deck. "You can look back into the canyons, turn around and see all the way to Catalina, downtown, the beaches. This is dramatic. This is what he wants."

Helen smacked his arm.

"Who were you trying to impress with that cock-of-the-walk routine down there?" she asked.

"You, obviously," Oscar said, wrapping his arms around her and pulling her in for a kiss. "Is it working?"

"No," she said, scowling, then kissed him back. "Maybe a little bit, but we need Miranda."

"Oh, do *we*?" he asked.

"Yes. She lives in this neighborhood. This is her territory. There's never inventory up here, so you want to be that real estate investor she—"

Oscar cut her off with another kiss. He loved this woman. *Loved* this woman. Every ambitious, California, daddy-pleasing, white-bread, sun-kissed cell. But every so often he needed to remind her that he was the man, something he doubted her deputy DA husband-in-name-only ever did. As she shifted to acknowledge his hard-on, but without any real invitation to do something about it, he stepped away.

"Okay, so we make her happy," Oscar agreed. "How do we do that?"

"This house is way overpriced, but we go in at the asking price anyway," Helen said. "If it gets competitive, I'll confide in her what your top bid is and say I'll drop my commission to make it work without suggesting she drop hers. That's when I say 'cash.'"

"But won't we lose money on the resale?" Oscar asked.

"No, if you play it right you'll break even. But then you've got someone like Miranda slipping you leads in hopes of making another cash commission."

Oscar smiled and put his arms around Helen's waist. "How much time before she comes up here?" he asked, nodding to the rattan sofa on the far side of the deck.

"You're crazy," Helen said, brushing his hand away, albeit without much force.

"Come on," he cajoled. "We're about to pay three million dollars for this house. We should be able to use it once before handing the keys over to our new partner."

He slipped a hand under her shirt and felt her heart quicken. He knew the answer was still no but liked the effect he had on her body regardless.

"You're ridiculous," Helen said, voice barely a whisper, as she pulled his hand away. "But behave yourself and maybe—*maybe*—I'll come up with some reason why we have to come back and see the house on our own."

Goddamn, I love this woman.

———

"Are you hearing me?" the red-faced businessman, a Mr. Jim Jakey of Compass Bank of Fort Wayne, Indiana, thundered. "This was supposed to be billed to the company. When they reserved the travel, they should've paid for the room."

Zhelin "Tony" Qi, the hotel's front-end manager, smiled placidly in the face of the tantrum. Behind the businessman stood three of his junior colleagues, all of whom could not have looked more embarrassed. The trio obviously knew their boss had made a mistake. It was telling that none came to the man's rescue.

"The rooms were reserved by a corporate card," Tony explained without a hint of condescension. "But we were not authorized to charge it. We have a second company card, the one you gave us for incidentals when you checked in, on file. Would you like to put the rooms on that card?"

Mr. Jakey's chin jutted upwards, his knuckles whitening. Tony wondered how many times this performance had worked in the past.

"Why aren't you telling me anything different than her?" he said, nodding toward the young desk clerk who'd had Tony paged moments earlier when it seemed as if things might become violent. "I thought I was talking to somebody in charge."

The businessman's face was all contempt now. Tony straightened and reached for the phone.

"I apologize for wasting your time," Tony said. "It is my fault. I misinterpreted the situation."

Jakey tossed a smug look back to his surprised colleagues. They obviously wanted to see their overly entitled boss knocked down a few pegs. As he reached for the telephone, he hoped his next action didn't disappoint.

"Hello, this is Zhelin Qi, front-end manager at the Century Continental Hotel at 3021 Avenue of the Stars," he said when the call was answered. "We have a customer, Mr. Jim Jakey, at checkout refusing to pay his bill. The total is over eight thousand dollars. Yes, he is still in the lobby. Thank you."

Tony hung up. Jakey's look of bluster switched to one of confusion. "What was that?"

"Los Angeles Police Department's Commercial Crimes Division, Fraud Section," Tony explained. "They prefer we do not escalate these matters ourselves, particularly when the amount is equivalent to grand theft."

"The *police*?" Jakey roared, though through a cracking voice. "Are you crazy? Why would you call the police?"

"You are refusing to pay your bill," Tony replied. "I am trying to resolve the situation in a way that prevents loss to this hotel."

Tony allowed himself a glance to the desk clerk, Perla, who'd called him over in the first place. She not only seemed to be enjoying this, it appeared she was taking mental notes for the story she'd repeat a dozen times over the next few days to every worker in the hotel.

Oh, you should've seen unflappable Manager Qi take on that big, bad American asshole from Room 810.

As Perla was the hotel workers union rep for the Century Continental, it could not have gone smoother or more in his favor.

Tony Qi is a man who gets things done, she'd say.

And when down the line he needed her to, she'd follow his lead and make the others do the same. As a representative of the city's largest triad, Tony knew his reputation had to be sterling. The triad wasn't some murderous criminal organization like the Sicilian mafia, the Sinaloa drug cartel, or the Salvadoran MS-13. Rather, it was a political organization that operated outside the mainstream and worked to help those who similarly found themselves outside the political mainstream.

Or that was, of course, what Tony needed the workers at the Century Continental to believe about the sometimes-criminal organization. When they needed help and could turn to no one else, there'd he be. He just might need a favor—could be something as simple as a vote—somewhere down the line in return.

It took only a moment more for Tony to wrap up the matter with Mr. Jakey. Knowing the businessman had no recourse, he simply waited until he produced two credit cards for Tony to split the bill on and then left for the airport.

"Did you really call the police?" Perla asked once Jakey's shuttle pulled away.

"Absolutely. You should have the number, too," he said, writing it down. "This is a friend of ours in the fraud division. His personal cell. If you are ever in this situation and I am not here, call and use my name."

Perla had already appeared impressed. Now she looked awed.

"Thank you, Mr. Qi," she said, offering a slight bow.

"Of course," he replied, returning the bow and moving away. Tony had come over from Shenzhen via a so-called snakehead, the triad equivalent of the Latin American "coyote," when he was sixteen. His parents, grandparents, and even an uncle had chipped in almost everything they'd managed to save to pay the man to get Tony onto a container ship that docked at the Port of San Diego three weeks later.

When he was dropped off in the Gaslamp Quarter with only a crewman's ID, listing him as a Filipino national, he didn't blink. He marched into the first restaurant he could find and two days later he had a cash-under-the-table job as a busboy at a seafood place in Mira Mesa. Intent on making his way north, he looked for another job as soon as possible, finding a position as a poolside server at an Indian casino in the City of Industry. Over the next twenty years he worked his way to Los Angeles through several hotel jobs and wove himself into the fabric of the city, gaining citizenship and rising through the ranks of the San Gabriel–based triad, until he landed at the Century Continental. He didn't know if he would rise higher, either in the triad or in the hotel business. Those were the decisions best left to others. What made him happiest was continuing to further his reputation as an eminent and imperturbable problem solver.

The incident with Mr. Jakey turned out to be the only real fireworks of Tony's day. He did his rounds of the kitchen, the laundry, and the administrative offices. He spot-checked the ballrooms before the organizers of the Women in PR awards dinner arrived to oversee the setup. He then went outside to look over the grounds. All was in order and ready to be handed off to the night manager.

Tony went to the valet stand, where his car and keys were already waiting.

The traffic from Century City to the John Wayne Airport in Santa Ana was worse than he'd anticipated. Tony had hoped to stop somewhere and change. This was impossible now. He'd worn his blue Brooks Brothers suit to work that day, but it always struck him as officious. The gray regent-fit suit laid out in the garment bag in the trunk was more appropriate for the image he wished to cultivate to clients in his other job.

Particularly now.

Tony had two careers really, but only one employer. At the hotel he made sure the hotel workers union was kept happy. This meant providing jobs, bribes, and favors in return for a strong voting bloc, both politically and against hotel upper management when it came to supporting which outside vendors the hotel used for linens, liquor, and food supplies. Meaning: triad-owned ones.

Tony's other job for the triad, very much away from the hotel, was in the area of birth tourism.

The business of birth tourism in America had always been fairly skivvy and low end. It was rife with unlicensed doctors or midwives, seedy motels, and iffy paperwork that said it ensured American citizenship to those born on US soil but often did not. Somewhere along the line the triad had sensed a business opportunity.

As the Chinese economy surged, the desire among China's nouveau riche to have it all increased along with it. The idea that dual citizenship would make it easier for their children (well, their sons) to do business in America in future years meant they were willing to pay any cost. This led to high-end package deals—not dissimilar to ones offered by exclusive resorts—that included airfare, four-star accommodations, fine dining, and weekly in-home visits from a doctor fluent in Mandarin, Cantonese, or the language of the client's choice.

Clients weren't flown directly from Beijing or Hong Kong but to Hawaii first. Then they would board a separate plane that would land not at LAX but at the smaller John Wayne Airport in Orange County. The only time they would have to clear customs would be in Hawaii. It was not only foolproof, it was technically legal. This, Tony believed, appealed to the triad the most.

Once they arrived in the city, the client would be put up in a luxury condominium, complete with swimming pool, gym, and a twenty-four-hour concierge. For a little more money they could be put up in their own private house, one the triad owned for a short time, renovated utilizing triad-owned construction equipment and supplies, then flipped for profit afterwards.

After much internal discussion, it was decided that Tony Qi should run the operation. And the first thing he did was reach out to a trusted triad contact who'd dealt with them for years, shipping high-end stolen cars to Hong Kong, without being anything but a perfect gentleman and business partner along the way. Given that his "business" meant that he acquired an impressive knowledge of the city's poshest neighborhoods, Tony thought him an unimpeachable ally in this new venture.

Tony's cell phone buzzed.

Speak of the devil.

It was a text from Oscar de Icaza showing sixteen photographs, taken from various angles, of an amazing three-story house with views— jetliner views, an earlier text had promised—all the way to the Pacific from high over Sunset Boulevard. Even on his phone's tiny screen he could make out his hotel.

Again, he'd been proven right about Oscar. The house would work perfectly. He wrote back that they should acquire it right away and get it ready for their latest client. He didn't want to be too optimistic, but given his own commission on these arrangements, his time facing down irritating and boorish business travelers might be nearing its end.

Tony arrived at John Wayne Airport at a quarter to seven. He changed his suit in the United Club lounge and moved to the noncommercial gate. His airport contact, Shen Mang, was waiting.

"How was the drive, Mr. Qi?"

"As expected," Tony replied. The overly obsequious Shen wasn't his favorite person.

"I just heard from the tower. The plane is on its final approach. Ten minutes maybe."

Tony nodded. The client's name was Jun Tan. She carried the child of Kuo Kuang, a wealthy businessman and Hong Kong triad heavyweight who'd made his money only recently through a series of construction scams. He was married and had as many children as he did mistresses—six. Tony had heard through the grapevine that he'd planned to ditch Jun when he'd heard she was pregnant. But when he'd learned she was to have a son—his first—he'd had a change of heart.

Now she was arriving to spend the next two months in relative luxury before giving birth. Tony had no illusions that she would likely be cast off following this and hoped Jun had none, either. According to the San Gabriel Dragon Head, a friend of Kuang's who had arranged this, Jun was to be accompanied by her "aunt." Tony took this to mean a Kuang-approved minder/chaperone, not a blood relative, and he agreed to give them every consideration.

When the plane came into sight, Tony signaled the driver waiting in the bar to pull his SUV around to the hangar. Shen unlocked the security door that led out of the terminal and escorted Tony to a waiting cart. The hangar was only a hundred yards away, but Tony didn't wish to perspire.

"On the Internet it said that she was some kind of actress in the making," Shen offered. "Kuang saw her on television and demanded she be brought to him, as if he was some kind of feudal lord."

That's exactly what he is, Tony thought.

"You don't recognize her, you don't know her," Tony admonished. "She is the client. Therefore, she is your employer. Do you understand?"

Shen shrugged.

The private plane, a Challenger 605, landed on Runway Two and taxied slowly to the hangar, arriving at the same time as Tony and Shen. As a ramp agent hurried to put chocks behind the tires, Tony signaled the driver, who'd already arrived, to be ready to open the back door of the SUV. He then stepped alongside the plane, stopping where the foot of the air stair would soon be.

A flight attendant unlocked and lowered the door before stepping back. The next person to appear was Jun Tan herself. She looked cautiously around the hangar, a rabbit anticipating predators. When her eyes found Tony, she smiled. He returned the smile with a deep bow.

She wore peach-colored Capri pants and a matching blouse that mostly hid her protruding belly. Her hair was cut short, the back coming down just to her earlobes. Her eyes, brown as chestnuts, were wide and searching. She looked like every provincial Hunan girl that had ever washed up in Shenzhen.

"Welcome to California," he said. Not Los Angeles with its negative crime-related connotations; not America and its implicit threat. California conjured images of sunshine and movie stars.

Jun smiled and accepted Tony's hand as she stepped down the stairs. Her fingers were so light in his hands he worried he might crush them if he squeezed too hard or at all. Even her scent seemed chosen as emblematic of flowers native to where she was from.

"As you know, your house is being prepared for you right now," Tony explained. "For the first few days you will be a guest at the Beverly Hills Hotel in order to acclimate you to your surroundings."

In truth, it had more to do with making sure that if she just so happened to be followed by law enforcement, as some pregnant foreigners were, it would appear that she really was on holiday.

"Archie here will be your driver for the duration," Tony said, introducing the man now holding open the back door of the SUV. "I am Tony and will be at your disposal as well."

He took a cell phone from his pocket and was about to hand it to Jun when an older woman emerged from the plane, came down the steps behind her, and snatched it from his hand. She had a pinched face and was dressed in clothes that all looked a couple of sizes too big, as if she'd recently lost mass. From the way she eyed the phone, Tony wouldn't have been surprised if she'd taken a bite out of it. But then Jun took it away from her and checked the contacts list.

"Thank you," Jun said. "Yours is the only number programmed in?"

"It is."

"Fantastic," she enthused. "What am I to be doing these first five days?"

"Whatever you like," Tony replied. "Rodeo Drive is close by, as is the Beverly Center, the Grove, and the shops on Robertson. Some prefer just sitting by the pool."

"But what about other things?" she pressed, stopping just before the SUV. "What if I want to go elsewhere? Will you personally see to it that I get there?"

"Within reason," Tony said guardedly.

"No," Jun snapped back. "It was my understanding that everything was within reason."

"Of course," Tony said, not daring to look at the aunt. "What do you have in mind?"

"Disneyland," she said in a tone more akin to someone suggesting a bank robbery. "And I want to see the Los Angeles Dodgers. And the tar pits, where Tommy Lee Jones stopped that volcano. S'okay?"

Tony nodded and bowed.

IV

Luis's day had passed in a haze. He hadn't expected to be so angry about Michael's appearance. In truth, it wasn't so much anger as indignation. St. Augustine's was his sanctuary. To have it invaded by someone he found had no respect for the godly life made him livid. To do so under the guise of defending his church was even more insidious.

For even Satan disguises himself as an angel of light, Luis thought, recalling the words of Paul.

To clear his mind, he'd needed to pray, but the demands of the classroom kept him from doing so. And once class let out, Luis had to help Whillans with the evening Mass and hear confession for an hour after that. The unsated desire to hear from God was maddening, like waiting for the answer to an urgent letter. It wasn't that he wanted to petition for the Lord's guidance; he desired the cleansing feeling of being in the Lord's presence.

His last task of the day was a home visit to a young couple down the road in Crenshaw who were experiencing their first real marital problems following the birth of a baby and the loss of employment for the father. After counseling the couple to reach out to fellow parishioners to help with the baby, as well as to the parish itself for financial assistance should they require it, Luis even considered praying in his car before returning to the rectory. This was hardly practical, however, so he kept going, trying to obey as many traffic laws as he could.

When he finally reached the rectory, having challenged every yellow light and speeding as much as he dared, he hurried to his room, took off his shoes, got down on his knees, and forced the world from his mind.

God, I come to you for guidance, Luis prayed, opening his mind. *My understanding of my vocation is that I am here to act as your vessel on earth, to guide your congregation as you would. But there is a confounding soul in my path . . .*

There came a soft knock on Luis's door.

"Father Chavez?" said Father Passarella, the Argentine priest. "Are you awake?"

"I am," replied Luis.

"You have a phone call in the chapel office. They apologized for the hour but said it was very important."

Luis sighed and stood. Anything God had to say to him would have to wait.

Luis hurried from the rectory to the chapel to find Erna's lamp on next to the phone. He picked up the receiver and hit the blinking "Hold" button.

"Hello?"

"Am I speaking to Father Chavez?" a vaguely familiar voice said from the other end of the line.

"This is he," Luis said cautiously.

"I apologize for the late hour, but it's quite early here and we're all due downstairs to continue our progress with a breakfast at St. John in Lateran."

Luis's heart leaped. He tried hard not to afford the church's ecclesiastical hierarchy undue reverence, but when speaking to the archbishop of Los Angeles, this wasn't so easy. That His Eminence was calling from the Vatican, where he was traveling with the pope himself on a short tour of Northern Italy, didn't make it any easier.

The pope, Luis mentally intoned, hoping it sounded to him like any old word. Instead, the image of Saint Peter's keys on crimson slippers filled his mind.

"It's no trouble, Your Eminence," Luis replied quickly. "I had just returned from a home visit. What can I do for you?"

Why did I say that? Luis thought, beating himself up for trying to impress the archbishop with his diligence. *He would've understood if I'd merely said I was in prayer.*

"I have heard good things about you, Father," the archbishop said. "Your pastor and I go back several years. While we don't always see eye to eye, he is extremely adept at judging character."

"I am humbled to hear it," Luis said.

"He told me you were set to deliver your first homily this Sunday about Saint Peter Claver," the archbishop continued. "A great man. A man of humanity who condemned the slave trades as wretched and inhuman even as other Jesuits turned a blind eye. Apparently baptized over a quarter of a million slaves while serving in Colombia. Nowhere near as controversial as the problematic Saint Serra y Ferrer. Did you know Claver called himself the Servant of the Ethiopians?"

"I didn't know this," Luis said, wondering why Whillans didn't tell him he'd spoken to the archbishop.

The line went silent for a moment. Luis wondered if they'd been cut off. When he heard the archbishop draw in a slow breath, he knew the call wasn't simply for a pre-sermon pep talk.

"Benedict Chang was a close friend of mine, Father Chavez, going back several years," the archbishop said quietly. "A very good man beloved by his parishioners but also his community. His death is a terrible blow to the archdiocese, but also to those who benefited from his charitable works and deeds. He was a crusader for Christ."

"Yes, Your Eminence," Luis said when there was a pause.

"What compounds the tragedy are the accusations and rumors going around about the man after he can no longer defend himself. There was a time when the church turned its back on gossip it believed to be false or, worse, decided to sweep it under the rug. This is not something we can allow anymore. Too many people have been hurt. Too many lives destroyed. When I became archbishop, I had to strip my predecessor of all but his title, as he was one of the worst offenders when it came to aiding and abetting the accused and shrugging off the accusers. The church in America may not recover for generations."

Luis suddenly understood where the archbishop was going with all this.

"Which is why someone coming along to use those accusations to tar an innocent adds tragedy to tragedy. There is no benefit of the doubt. The accusation was all it took for his congregation to turn their backs on his memory. Now, I've been told that someone sympathetic to our cause, someone who also doesn't believe the rumors, has reached out to you from the district attorney's office."

An electrical charge burst through Luis's nervous system. He'd stepped into an open snare without noticing. How much had Michael told the archbishop? It wasn't as if he'd kept his past a secret from the archdiocese, but he doubted everyone knew.

And more than that, how might it affect his station in the eyes of the congregation if word somehow got to them?

No one who practices deceit shall dwell in my house; no one who utters lies shall continue before my eyes.

"I just wanted to let you know that you have the full backing and support of the archdiocese as you assist the city with their investigation. Normally, this would be considered too weighty a concern for a novice priest, but as Pastor Whillans has indicated his confidence in you by elevating you to his assistant, I think we can safely follow his lead and trust you as our representative."

If the archbishop had said this while sitting in the same room, or over the phone from the seat of the archdiocese at the Cathedral of Our Lady of the Angels, Luis could've found a way to navigate around this. "Our" might mean the archdiocese or even just the archbishop and, say, Pastor Whillans. But that the call came at the exact moment when Luis was most in need of the Lord's wisdom and that the archbishop was a few yards, if not a few steps, from the Holy Father himself imbued it with the full weight of the Holy See.

"Yes, Your Eminence," Luis said, already overwhelmed.

"God bless you and aid you, Father Chavez," the archbishop said. "Please keep me informed as your investigation progresses."

Luis was about to respond when the line was cut off. He sat down in Erna's chair and hung up the phone before turning off the lamp. Cast in darkness, he was finally surrounded by the silence and peace he'd chased all day.

But now he had no need. God had made his wishes clear as a bell. *All right, God. Let's get started.*

"Take the two pills in the pack right away, right when you get home with food. *Dos. Con comida,*" Susan explained, indicating the pills in the Z-Pak—well, at least its generic third cousin twice removed, albeit with the exact same active ingredients. "Then take the next five, one each day, with food. *Una cada día.* As I said, it's just an upper-respiratory infection. Should knock it right out."

Her patient, a seventysomething Guatemalan woman whom Susan knew had been sick for weeks and had to be cajoled into coming to the clinic by her two sons, nodded skeptically and pocketed the drugs. Susan had no idea if she planned to take them and made a mental note to call the eldest son the next morning and get him to make sure.

After the patient left, Susan checked her watch. It was already half past two. She'd been on shift for fourteen-plus hours. Well, except for the hour she'd spent eating lunch with Nan, who'd taken the bus over from USC, up around the corner at Barnsdall Art Park. Barnsdall had been a favorite spot of Father Chang's, and they'd decided to go there to honor his memory with a lunch of his beloved pho. Though it was small enough to walk from one end to the other in five minutes, Chang had never tired of leading Susan and Nan through Hollyhock House, the Frank Lloyd Wright creation that stood in the center of the park, and pointing out obscure features and Wright's architectural signature.

"He loved the view up here," Nan had said. "He could see the whole city."

Susan had agreed, though mostly she could see the rooftops of nearby Little Armenia. Still, it had been a beautiful day, not a cloud in the sky to remind them of the previous night's rain.

They'd spoken of so many things relating to Father Chang. How each of them had met him for the first time, how neither were particularly religious, which was why Chang had probably enjoyed spending his off-hours with them. They spoke of Chang's relentless curiosity and thirst for knowledge. They tried to come up with subjects that might not have interested Father Chang in the slightest, and couldn't come up with one.

"Watching paint dry," Nan tried finally.

"No, he'd go off on some tangent about the subtle spectrum of colors the paint arced through as it released its water and took its final form," Susan joked. "And by the end he'd have convinced us it was the most interesting thing ever."

They laughed over this. They moved on to discuss the funeral, though Nan hadn't wanted to talk about it. Susan didn't bring up the fact that when she'd called St. Jerome's, the parish pastor had said that no one from the church would be available to deliver the eulogy. As it had been so many times in life, it would be just the three of them at the grave, though one would stay behind.

The one thing they didn't talk about was who killed him. Not the identity of the shooter himself. That part wasn't important. Nor was the rumor going around that it had been linked to some kind of sex crime. No, what they really didn't want to talk about was who Father Chang, on one of his endless crusades against injustice, had pissed off enough to want him dead.

"He always said he'd be martyred, but I think he did it like people who joke about their plane crashing," Nan explained. "Say it enough times and it won't happen."

"I think you're right," Susan said dully. "He was too interested in whatever was going to come around next."

After seeing Nan off on the bus back to campus, Susan considered going home. But that would mean thinking about things, obsessing about things, and that would do no one any good. So she returned to the innocuous square two-story East LA shopping plaza that housed her clinic to throw herself into work. The clinic itself was rather small, with only four examination rooms, a tiny waiting area, a medication-filled break room that doubled as a pharmacy, and then an office Susan shared with four other doctors. All four had like Susan trained overseas but hadn't been accredited in the States yet due to immigration issues.

Susan didn't mind. When she spoke to friends of hers who worked in licensed doctor's offices and hospitals, the threat of malpractice and the bureaucratic nightmare that the HMO/PPO era had created made hers seem like a quaint neighborhood practice. Susan had gone into medicine at first because of parental pressure and expectation but then realized that she just genuinely liked helping people. One day, she hoped, she'd earn enough money to get away from Clover Gao, poach the best staffers, and set up a shop of her own.

But if the licensed practices did have anything up on the unlicensed ones, it was that they at least could operate out in the open, with signs on their doors. Susan had to walk up to what looked like an unmarked service exit with no handle and be buzzed in by a receptionist. Clover Gao was so afraid of being caught in a raid that she kept her office on the floor above the clinic, and even that was a single room in the back of a small tax preparer's office. For the first three weeks on the job, Susan had walked into the kitchens of restaurants, supply rooms, and almost got herself locked in the back room of a kitchen appliance wholesaler by choosing the wrong unmarked door.

"I'm going to knock off," Susan announced to the night receptionist as she gathered her things. "Be back around nine. Tell Clover, okay?"

The receptionist nodded. No sooner had Susan pushed through the outer door, however, than a harried-looking young woman hurried up to her in a panic.

"Dr. Auyong?"

"I'm off the clock," Susan explained. "But there'll be someone in there to help you."

"My father's a patient of yours. He saw you today?"

As that could be one of sixty to seventy people, Susan stared back blankly.

"César Carreño? I'm his daughter, Esmeralda. He was in for his hypertension medication."

"Of course. Has he had an incident? If so, you'll need to call 911."

"Oh, no, no. His blood pressure is fine," Esmeralda said. "But I think he's coming down with the flu or something. He's got a light fever, a sore throat. My son had it a few months ago, so I know the symptoms."

"Then you should also know that it's a virus and there's not anything we could prescribe for him," Susan said, trying to hide her exhaustion-born irritation.

"Isn't there something?" Esmeralda pressed. "He's in construction. He's terrified of missing work, as they replace them so fast."

Susan knew there was nothing, but she also knew that the young woman would persist until she was handed some kind of pill.

"Go in. Tell the receptionist you need two boxes of AnaPyr. It's a prescription-strength ibuprofen. It'll bring down the fever. Other than that you're on your own."

"Thank you so much, Doctor!" the woman enthused, and hurried past to the door.

"No problem," Susan replied, so tired she worried she'd fall asleep on the drive home.

———

Luis dialed Michael's number and waited. When the deputy DA finally answered, he sounded as if he had been pulled out of a deep sleep.

Guess that's what the normal people are doing at two in the morning.

"Hello?" Michael said.

"Hope I'm not waking up your family," Luis said.

"Nah, my wife's still out with her girlfriends," Michael replied. "You're not exactly someone I expected to hear from again."

"I heard from the archbishop," Luis explained. "Nice play."

"Thanks. I had to do something."

"If I do this for you, I get the option to walk away at any time, particularly if it begins to interfere with my work at St. Augustine's or St. John's," Luis said. "Is that acceptable?"

"Absolutely. Of course."

"Also, I don't want you calling me for updates. If I find something out, I'll call you. Good?"

"Perfect," Michael said. "What if I find something out?"

"Then you can tell me if and when I call. How long do I have before the letter gets made public?"

"I don't know," Michael said. "It's the kind of thing that leaks. And once it's out there, you can't put that genie back in the bottle."

"Got it," Luis said. "One more thing. You've been out to San Gabriel. There are dozens of lawyers out there. How come Yamazoe picks some *barrio abogado* like Caesar deGuzman?"

There was a pause. "I hadn't thought of that. I'll follow up. Thanks."

Luis hung up and sank back onto his bed. What bothered him now wasn't anything that Michael had said or the words of the archbishop. Rather, it was the feeling he'd received from God when he sat in prayer after the call. At first, there had just been a deep sense of foreboding like none he'd ever experienced. When the words finally came, they were simple and to the point.

This is only the beginning.

Michael put his cell back on the nightstand and stared up at the dark ceiling. He couldn't figure Luis out. He'd known contacting the archbishop was drastic, but it had worked like a charm. He had his secret weapon back and, knowing Luis, the priest wouldn't rest until he uncovered something, at least. Whether it was an unhappy truth about the late Father Chang or an actual motive mattered little. The case would be put to bed, and there'd be another feather in Michael's cap to show for it.

But it was his own ready acceptance that troubled him. This had gone from a quick favor to using an untrained outsider to investigate a brutal murder. Was there any part of him, however small, that relished putting the priest in harm's way?

One less person who would know his sins.

He quickly banished this thought. If Luis was somehow killed, his connection to Michael would be discovered, and only bad things could come of it. But that he'd even thought of it made him wonder just how corrupted his mind had become.

He glanced over to Helen's side of the bed, seeing only the silhouette of her bare pillow. He saw less of her these days, as her real estate business was starting to take off. *A high-profile client,* she'd said. He was glad of it, as she deserved success. It alleviated the guilt he felt over cheating on her. She wasn't pining for him; she was going out and doing things for her, which included blowing off steam with some of her friends at—what had she said tonight was? A nineties mash-up party at a dance club?

Whatever it was, he was happy if she was.

V

The five young men clad all in white—white hemp shirts and pants, white headbands, white sashes, and white straw sandals—crossed a narrow bridge made up of only two wooden planks and moved under an archway of swords. The Vanguard and the Incense Master, both in red silk gowns with red headbands, waited in front of the large statue of Guan Yu, the third-century general who helped establish the state of Shu Han. Smoke billowed from a cauldron, where a large fire burned.

"What abilities do you possess?" the Vanguard asked the first of the five initiates to the triad.

"Honor and loyalty to my brethren," the young initiate replied, using formal Mandarin and bowing deeply in deference to the older man.

"And what shall happen to you if you dishonor your Hung brothers?"

"I shall be killed with knives!" he shot back.

There was little light in the banquet hall set up for the initiation ceremony, but Tony didn't need to see to know exactly how the ritual would proceed. As he stood with the other members of the triad—ranking members in red headbands, but all in suits instead of silk gowns—he thought back to his own initiation ceremony with pleasure. He'd been nothing before, a mere Blue Lantern, the lowest on the totem pole as far as the triad was concerned. Then everything changed.

"If the police were after your brothers and offered you gold for information, would you be loyal to your brothers or take the gold?" the Vanguard demanded.

"I would be loyal to my brothers!" the initiate cried.

This time the Vanguard answered by slapping him across the back with a flexibly bladed sword. The initiate didn't flinch.

"Kneel," the Vanguard ordered.

The first initiate knelt and raised his hands in front of him, palms together as if in prayer. The Incense Master came over and placed five lit sticks of incense between his fingers.

"The oaths," the Vanguard said.

The initiate nodded as smoke rose around his head. Tony wondered if he'd managed to memorize all thirty-six oaths. It was hard to go first.

"I shall never betray my sworn brothers!" the initiate swore. "I shall not disclose the secrets of the Hung brethren! If I rob a sworn brother, I will be killed by knives!"

Tony's eyes traveled to the last of the five initiates. Though he was sure the young man, Billy Daai, had memorized the oaths, arranging for him to go last so he could hear the others say them first just to be sure hadn't been difficult. Billy was his godson after all, and there was nothing he wouldn't do for him, which of late had included securing Billy's new job with one of the liquor distributors that delivered to his hotel.

Billy was a good boy and a quick study. He understood that learning about the products was as important as being able to anticipate the needs of both client and vendor. On nights he had off he moved across the city trendspotting in clubs and restaurants. He was handsome and lean with a gregarious nature he put to good use insinuating himself into any group or situation. He was always the first to know what was gaining popularity in the city and provided this information gratis to those for whom he served as a go-between. Even better, he used longer holidays to travel to New York, Miami, Las Vegas, and London to see and experience those scenes as well.

"I'm worried that he's caught up in the lifestyle," Billy's uncle, Lichun, told Tony at one point. "He's always buying fancy clothes and going to parties. You see he's driving a Maserati now."

"He's not driving a Maserati," Tony had gently corrected. "He has one leased that he keeps in a garage. During the week he's either in his Sentra or in the delivery truck. The clothes are like the Maserati—part of the uniform that gets him into places of exclusivity. I have never seen him drunk. Not once."

Tony reflected on this as his godson's turn came and he kneeled to recite the thirty-six oaths. What Billy then said took everyone in the room by surprise. Well, not what he said, but how he recited it: in an older, more classical pronunciation of Cantonese.

"I shall not cause discord among my sworn brothers by spreading rumors, or I will die by five thunderbolts," Billy announced. "After entering the Hung brethren, I will forget all grudges I may have previously held against my brethren, or I will be killed by five thunderbolts."

As Billy went through the oaths, there were a few murmurs around Tony. He imagined some were critical of Billy for wishing to stand out, but others would understand it as a sign of deep respect for triad tradition.

When Billy finished, the Vanguard moved down the line with a needle, pricking the fingers of each initiate. A wineglass was produced and the drops of blood were collected from each. Tony heard the clucking of the live rooster, albeit a heavily sedated one, as it was brought into the room in a basket by two other men in traditional dress. Tony stepped forward and handed over a knife, his tiny walk-on role in the pageant. The rooster was cut under its chin, and the blood added to the glass.

"On this date these Blue Lanterns have died and passed over," said the Vanguard, reading from a scroll he'd kept in a leather pouch at his side for the duration of the ceremony. "They are now reborn through binding righteousness into the Society of Heaven and Earth."

This scroll was added to a cauldron in front of the statue of Guan Yu, and the embers soon rose to the rafters. When the last bit was burned to ash, the initiates were allowed to stand and be recognized by the others with applause.

"Congratulations, Billy," Tony enthused, taking his godson's hands in both of his.

"Thank you, *zūnjià*," Billy replied, bowing deeply. "I am glad you could be here to take part."

"Your father will be so proud," Tony said, his tone turning more serious. "You honor him today."

Billy nodded. His father had begun serving a twenty-year sentence in Lompoc prison for heroin trafficking three years earlier. His sentence had been extended, however, due to bloody altercations with the Mexican mafia and various other prison gangs, from the Aryan Brotherhood to the myriad incarnations of Crips and Bloods. Though the senior Daai had been a fairly low-level member of the triad when outside the prison walls, he'd quickly become a unifying and stabilizing presence within the organization on the inside.

As his reputation as a prison leader increased, respect for his son did as well.

"I heard about the Indiana businessman," Billy said. "At the hotel."

"What are they saying?" Tony asked.

"A couple said they would've kicked the guy's ass right there in the lobby. Everyone else said you achieved the same result without lifting a finger."

Tony Qi, the outsider. Tony Qi, the street hustler who'd gained the respect of the most powerful Chinese businessmen in Los Angeles. Tony Qi, the triad's number-one fixer.

"Good. Maybe they'll follow that lead and stay out of prison."

He knew his words were a mistake before they even left his mouth. Even if he hadn't, the look of disgust and anger that flashed across Billy's face drove the point home. Though it disappeared just as quick, Tony straightened himself and bowed.

"I'm sorry. I didn't mean that how it sounded."

"No, I know what you meant," Billy replied. "And you're right. These hotheads will end up in prison for nothing one day. But maybe your example will help."

Billy excused himself. Tony became flushed. What had he been thinking to demonize prison to a young man whose father was incarcerated? Slights could go unforgiven for years, if not lifetimes. How could he have ruined the young man's day in that way?

Of course, he knew what he'd been thinking about. She'd been the only thing on his mind since he'd met her twelve hours before. She'd been so merry on the drive, so full of life and mischief, that he'd found himself delighted in her presence.

Tony wasn't insane. Making an overture to Jun Tan of any sort was outside the realm of possibility. In fact, it'd be the quickest way to find his head and hands separated from his body. But he hadn't met anyone quite like her in some time, if ever. It was as if she knew the role she was meant to play and had decided to subvert it, at least while she was in America.

How curious and clichéd of him to find attractive someone who couldn't be more his opposite.

The previous night Tony had been under strict orders to take Jun from the airport to the hotel with no stops. But as they cruised down the Sunset Strip, Jun had announced that she wanted to stop and get out. There were small packs of young people moving up and down the sidewalks toward the various restaurants and clubs. She wanted to be among them and cloaked the request by saying she was hungry.

Archie had shot a look first to Tony, then the "aunt," whose name had been revealed as Chen Jiang. Jiang looked at no one directly, but Tony saw that she was watching him carefully in the reflection of her window to see how their host would handle this.

"Most of the restaurants along here are booked up this time of night," Tony had announced, producing his cell phone. "But if you see one you like, I can call and find out if they'll make an exception."

Jun had smiled. It wasn't a smile of relief at hunger soon to be satisfied, but one of gratitude. He'd chosen her over the dictates of some faraway keeper. She'd soon spotted a tucked-away place with a courtyard surrounded by trees. Tony made the call, and they turned around to pull up to the valet station a moment later. Though Archie was clearly uncomfortable with the breach in protocol, Jun lightened him up with her tales of Hong Kong's wild nightlife and the adventures she'd had before the child in her belly tied her down to Kuang. Before their entrées arrived, the driver was eating out of her hand.

Tony tried to speak to the aunt, only to discover that she was not from Hong Kong but Jinan. She was an old hardliner still waiting for Mao to self-resurrect and punish the degenerate capitalists. He wanted to tell her that the late Communist Party chairman secretly lived a life more decadent than any of China's new money vulgarians could even imagine, but he doubted it would go over well.

So he let her stew and had enjoyed Jun's stories late into the night.

As he turned to leave the Blue Lantern ceremony, his thoughts returning to how he might erase the implied insult to Billy's father, he spotted one of the triad's most prominent lawyers, Jing Saifai, entering the back of the small restaurant in which the triad held their observances.

As a woman she had no place at triad functions. Even more so, as a prominent attorney she could hardly be seen at such a place. Tony idly wondered how long she'd waited outside. A passerby might've thought it odd seeing such a well-dressed woman standing outside a closed restaurant at this hour.

The biggest surprise, however, came when she approached Billy Daai, bowed, and leaned in close to speak to him. The show of deference was likely due to it being a special day for the young man, but the intimacy of their conversation that followed was unusual. Tony didn't even know the two were friendly.

She must have something to do with one of Billy's endless new schemes and businesses, Tony decided. *He was always looking for that new marketplace to exploit.*

He averted his eyes for fear of offending Billy twice on this day and moved away.

"He was filth, plain and simple," declared Father Ian Siu-Tung, the parish pastor of St. Jerome's. *"Filth."*

Luis was kneeling beside the door to St. Jerome's Chinese-American Catholic Church's rectory, staring at the two bullet holes in the frame. Though forensics had come along to pry out the fragments, he could still make out splinters of lead.

"I don't know if he was even liked by the congregation," Siu-Tung continued, as if unhappy with Luis's lack of response. "He could be arrogant and self-righteous. That's not me talking out of school, either. He'd say that to your face. He was far more interested in the secular world than most priests I've known. He had his own money, you know, and would go on these trips and retreats, only to come back frustrated with the way we did things in Los Angeles."

Luis put his hand on the concrete. It was already warm from the early-morning sun, giving him the sensation that Father Chang's body had only just now been lifted away.

"Did you know he even had his own apartment in the city? He didn't think we knew about it. That's where we believe he must have had the assignations with that poor girl. I guess he thought he knew better than God as to what a priest was allowed in this life, particularly when it came to the promise of celibacy."

Luis finally turned to the priest with a cold eye. Celibacy wasn't the question. Statutory rape was. And murder. Luis was starting to believe that Father Chang might've been right to be frustrated here.

"Celibacy in the priesthood came about in 1139 at the Second Lateran Council," Luis corrected. "It was never an edict of God."

Luis didn't admit he knew this only because his own parish pastor used it to justify his long-term affair with a laywoman, but he enjoyed the derogatory look on Father Siu-Tung's face regardless.

"Impudence," Siu-Tung added, waving away Luis's correction. "That was something else that branded Father Chang. Impudence."

Luis rose and pointed to a parking space.

"That's where he parked?"

"Yes. It was towed away by the police to check for forensic evidence," Siu-Tung explained. "We should get it back in a few days, they said."

"A parish car?"

"Again, his own. He bought it used a few years ago. Perfectly acceptable by the rules of the parish."

The way the pastor said this last part told Luis exactly how he really felt about one of his priests having his own car. Luis reconstructed Father Chang's path, exiting the driver's-side door and moving toward the rectory. He glanced around, looking for where Shu Kuen Yamazoe might have hid.

"And no one saw Yamazoe before?" Luis asked.

"No, but most had gone to bed long before Father Chang returned from his party."

Thai Cultural Day festival.

"So it's possible he'd been hanging around?"

"It's possible."

"Any chance the shooter could've ridden in the car with Father Chang?" Luis asked. "It would explain why no one saw him. Also, why the police towed it to look for forensic evidence."

From the look on Pastor Siu-Tung's face, it was clear he hadn't considered this at all.

"I don't know. Father Minxuan and Father Yali were the only witnesses," Siu-Tung said, pointing up to two of the rectory windows overlooking the parking lot. "But then they heard, not saw. Both said they heard one car door open and close before the young girl's father—"

Not "the killer." Not "Father Chang's murderer."

"—called out Father Chang's name. Then they heard the shots. They both came downstairs and saw Yamazoe sitting in the parking lot, legs crossed, the gun a little away from him. He was soaking wet. It had been raining that night."

No car ride, Luis thought.

"Then what happened?"

"Father Minxuan called an ambulance. Father Yali woke me. We couldn't find our first aid kit, so we took the one Father Chang kept in his trunk and tried to save him, but he was already gone."

Luis nodded to a camera over the rectory. "Did the police take the original or a copy?"

"Father Chavez," Pastor Siu-Tung said, now annoyed, "I appreciate the archdiocese wanting a full report, but I cannot see how watching a man die is either respectful or appropriate."

"You haven't had a respectful word for him since I arrived," Luis said. "Why start now?"

The look on Siu-Tung's face soured even more, but he seemed to understand that the sooner he did what Father Chavez asked, the sooner he'd be gone.

"We can watch a link in the office. Come along."

The security camera footage, as viewed on the church secretary's iPad, was taken from such an awkward angle that Luis doubted it could be used at trial. Neither Father Chang nor his killer were identifiable in the few frames in which they appeared, though the image did go white with muzzle flash four times as Father Chang's body almost immediately dropped to the pavement and convulsed. It was some time before the other priests cautiously emerged, but Luis could tell that the pastor was right. Father Chang was already dead.

Though they were alone in Pastor Siu-Tung's office, the older priest had kept glancing away from the computer showing the footage, as if fearing they'd be caught. When it came to Father Chang's death, however, he made a show of looking away. Luis didn't have the luxury.

Even as the priests buzzed around him, Yamazoe sat stock still after the killing, as if meditating. Though Luis couldn't make out his face, nothing about his body language suggested he even took notice of what was going on around him.

Pastor Siu-Tung came into view, checking Father Chang's car for the first aid kit, coming out first with a box before putting it back and taking the first aid kit.

"What was that?" Luis asked.

"Nothing. Prescription medication. I saw the cross on the side of the box and mistook it for the first aid kit."

"He carried prescription medication in his trunk?"

"Our insurance, as you must know, makes us receive medication for ongoing conditions through the mail. Father Chang had hypertension and was on beta-blockers for it."

Luis nodded. He'd become intimately familiar with the archdiocese's medical insurance plans due to Pastor Whillans. "Was there anything else in the trunk?"

"No, just his dry cleaning, a box of dual-language Bibles like the kind we give out, and a couple of boxes of flyers for his causes."

"Like?"

Pastor Siu-Tung glanced around until he spied a bulletin board out in the hall. "A couple of them are still up. Community outreach stuff. Low-income housing mostly. A couple of marches. That kind of thing."

Not your kind of thing, Luis surmised.

"Can I see his room?"

Pastor Siu-Tung led Luis to the rectory. Father Chang's room had been locked but not sealed. Inside, the space was as familiarly spartan as Luis's own room at St. Augustine's. There was only a bed, a small chest of drawers, a wooden crucifix hanging on the wall, and a bookshelf. Luis opened the closet door and found clerical clothing and three pairs of shoes. The chest of drawers contained underwear and socks.

"He only ever wore the collar?" Luis asked.

"His uniform day and night," Pastor Siu-Tung said, the first words he'd spoken about Father Chang that weren't negative.

Under the pretense of pushing the clothes aside to see if anything was tucked behind them, Luis went through the pockets. They were empty.

"How about the bathroom?"

As with the rectory at St. Augustine's, the priests shared a bathroom on each floor. Continuing his search, Luis opened the small medicine cabinet above the sink and, sure enough, was able to identify Father Chang's personal effects by a bottle of prescription eyedrops on the second-to-lowest shelf. There was a safety razor with extra blades, deodorant, toothpaste, a toothbrush, and a comb. Alongside all that were two bottles of a prescription for Lozol.

"What about the apartment you mentioned?" Luis asked as he stepped back into the hallway. "The one he kept in town. Do you have the address?"

"No. We only know of it because there were times he didn't stay the night here."

"He couldn't have been with friends or at a hotel?"

"He'd return in fresh clothes."

"And these are things he couldn't have brought with him?" Luis asked.

The corner of Pastor Siu-Tung's lip curled and fell. He looked Luis up and down reproachfully.

"I still can't for the life of me understand why the archdiocese would enlist an outsider to help in their investigation," Siu-Tung said.

Outsider. Now there's a word that can be taken many ways, Luis thought.

"I imagine the archbishop didn't mean to impinge on you during your time of grief," Luis said. "He and Father Chang go way back, and he doesn't want to believe these allegations."

"Which is why you don't, isn't it?" Siu-Tung asked.

"I don't think I have enough information to form an opinion," Luis replied.

"But you have anyway," Pastor Siu-Tung said, though his tone had softened.

"I only have one more question," Luis said. "Then I'll be out of your hair."

The pastor raised a hand as if to say there was little he could do to stop him.

"The girl. Yamazoe's daughter. I know the police have a lot of questions about her. But you seem to be one of the only people who actually saw this person. As the entire case hinges on it, I think confirming her identity becomes pretty important."

Pastor Siu-Tung fell silent for a long moment, looking down to the carpet as if weighing his words carefully before giving them to Luis. When he looked up, Luis was surprised to see a sad smile on his face.

"First of all, you're wrong. Plenty of people saw the girl. She was in the congregation every Sunday for the past several weeks. Maybe people don't like talking about it or getting involved in a murder case, but they saw her. If they don't remember her, it's because she was so slight, so clearly uncomfortable and unhappy, that she did everything she could to disappear into the pew. What angers me and, perhaps to my discredit, provokes my disrespect for Father Chang's memory is that I saw that and prayed for her. He saw that and took advantage. I wish I'd known then what it was that caused her such displeasure to be in the house of God. But if it had been revealed to me, I'm afraid I might've done what her father did, and we'd be having a completely different conversation right now. She's real, Father Chavez. And now she's gone. Whatever the circumstance, it's just one more person this church has managed to fail. So, pardon me if I try to alleviate some of my own guilt in this by venting my anger at the late Father Chang."

Luis extended his hand. "Thank you for your time, Father."

"If you find her, please tell her I'm sorry."

Luis nodded and headed away.

VI

In the age of Google Maps and Waze, addresses in a big city like Los Angeles should have been the easiest things to find with a smartphone in hand. So why was it, Michael thought, that he couldn't locate the law office of Caesar deGuzman, Yamazoe's attorney?

He'd called to make an appointment, the receptionist registering surprise to hear that a deputy district attorney was coming in to meet her boss.

"Of Los Angeles?" she asked to confirm.

"Yes," Michael had replied with relish. "Can he see me?"

But now, as he made his way up and down the stairs of what looked like a courtyard apartment converted into offices, including one that had the logo of a recently canceled television series on it and two more for a so-called wellness clinic, Michael wondered if he was even in the right part of the city.

"Mr. Story?"

Michael turned. A young woman with hair so unnaturally red it looked less taken from a bottle and more from the side of a fire engine waved a hand at him from a doorway across the courtyard.

"That's me," Michael said, striding over. "Couldn't find the place."

"Oh, that's Koreatown for you," the woman said, pointing to one of three placards alongside the door that listed deGuzman's name under several others. "We're all on top of, under, and behind everybody here."

Michael resisted uttering the single entendre that entered his head as he followed the receptionist inside. For someone who spent thousands placing ads on the back of every bus and phone book in the city, the firm's actual office space was no larger than that of the two-bedroom apartment deGuzman's place of business now occupied.

"He'll be with you in just a moment," the receptionist said, taking a seat behind a desk which sat, Michael imagined, in what had at one time been the kitchen.

He'd just picked up an aged copy of *Popular Mechanics* when a squat man with a long black ponytail and bushy facial hair emerged from a back room. At first, Michael took him for another client. It wasn't until he extended a hand that he recognized him as the man from the bus ads, just an additional forty pounds and at least a decade further along on his journey through life.

"Mr. Story," deGuzman said, eyeing the deputy DA through thick glasses.

"Thank you for seeing me," Michael replied, shaking his hand.

"Come on back," deGuzman said. "And tell me how I can be of assistance to the great city of Los Angeles today."

Though the ads and trappings read ambulance chaser, what Michael saw in deGuzman's obsidian eyes was someone who in another life could've been a law professor or Supreme Court justice. He looked shrewd, and his eyes missed nothing. He folded his hands and sat at the head of a small conference table as he waited for Michael to speak.

"It's about Shu Yamazoe," Michael said.

"So you told Irma."

Michael decided that was the receptionist's name and pressed on. "I'm just curious as to how you and he came to know each other."

"You can't believe I'd actually have a conversation about this with someone from the prosecutor's office," deGuzman said. "I assume you thought I was someone who might wish to curry favor with a deputy district attorney by hanging a controversial client out to dry, but that's incorrect."

"No, I'm actually acting in an unofficial capacity at the behest of the Los Angeles archdiocese. They are concerned that Yamazoe's confession—"

"They should be," deGuzman interrupted. "So, they're already looking to discredit my client, are they? I guess I would be, too."

"No, they've just made mistakes in the past, so they want to approach this case as a model of what to do right next time."

"Because with the Catholic Church and statutory rape there's always a next time," deGuzman said.

Michael sighed. He wasn't getting anywhere with this man, who clearly enjoyed thumbing his nose at an office that he'd likely sat across from in contentious situations for decades. Michael realized he'd probably have had more of a shot if he'd announced himself as a ditch digger or trash collector. Saying he was from the DA's office meant deGuzman was more than prepared to stonewall and toy with him for as long as he sat there.

But then something occurred to him.

"You called Yamazoe your client. When did that become the case?"

"What do you mean?" deGuzman replied quietly, though his face said he was rapidly searching back over his words to check for miscues.

Not quite a Supreme Court–worthy poker face there, Counselor.

"I've read the confession. He didn't ask you to be his attorney. You only inferred that from the fact that he sent you the e-mail. How did you know he didn't send it to twenty lawyers, hoping one would show up?"

DeGuzman shrugged. "I didn't."

"But when you spoke to officers you called him by name," Michael said. "You said that you were there because of *Shu Kuen Yamazoe*. Correct?"

"Yes," deGuzman said warily.

Michael took out his iPhone and found the copy of Yamazoe's confession that had been sent to him by Detective Whitehead. He stared at it for a long moment before looking back up at deGuzman.

"How did you know his name?" Michael asked simply.

"It was at the end of the letter."

Michael held up the letter on his screen in the original *hanzi*. To a native Mandarin speaker, he was sure it looked just fine. To someone familiar with the Roman alphabet, it looked like Chinese logograms. But unlike a letter written by a Westerner, there was no real signature. Shu's name was simply the last three letters on the page.

"There are about a dozen words here that don't properly translate when plugged into a translation app. How did you know the difference between the ones that were actual mistakes and then the ones that were your soon-to-be-client's full name?"

DeGuzman said nothing, choosing to merely eye Michael through his thick glasses as if waiting for the younger man to continue. Michael simply sat back in his chair.

"So, you can either tell me how you came to know Shu Yamazoe's name," Michael said. "Or I can get a warrant from a judge to search your offices and suspend your license."

DeGuzman took off his glasses and placed them on the conference table. He rubbed the bridge of his nose, sighed, and leaned over the table toward Michael.

"I guess you'll just have to go see that judge then."

———

Luis had believed finding Shu Yamazoe's house wouldn't be easy. But then a simple search of the archdiocese's parishioners' mailing list database during his off period revealed an address of an apartment in Monterey Park straightaway. This was unlucky. A house he could've probably broken into if he needed to get a look around. An apartment meant a building manager and likely a sealed-off door.

Rats.

Still, at the end of the school day he hurried to take out a parish car to check out the space before he had to return to help with evening Mass. He had told Pastor Whillans in vague terms what he was doing. Whillans gave his equally vague approval.

"If you get arrested, say you were impersonating a priest," the pastor had said.

Luis had considered wearing street clothes when he went to the apartment. The problem was, he more often than not felt this invited trouble, as if announcing that he was denying the Lord in some way, which in turn would make the universe deny him. So he kept on the collar, drove to Monterey Park, and parked in front of the building.

All he really wanted was that one piece of evidence telling him that the girl, whatever her name might be, had stayed with her father at the apartment—it could be an article of clothing, a second bed, a book, a keepsake, *anything*—so that he could erase the skepticism of her existence from his mind. So when he arrived at apartment 12B and found the front door wide open, he was about to say a quick prayer of thanks to God when he suddenly noticed that the place was completely empty. No furniture, no wall hangings, *nothing*.

A middle-aged man pulling a commercial steam cleaner stepped out from a hallway. When he saw the priest, he stopped short, as if doing a quick self-assessment to see if he was in the process of sinning.

"I heard this guy was a crazy killer, but did they really call for an exorcist?"

Luis grinned. "New city requirement. Apartment vacancies have to be exorcised whenever someone's broken a lease. Heading to jail counts."

"Hope the archdiocese is getting a big cut of that," the man said with a laugh.

"Oh, they are. Big-time. Bonus if we have to fight demons."

The man laughed and extended a hand. "Jerry Bunker."

"Luis Chavez."

"Are you looking at this place? I'm just finishing up. Building manager is around somewhere."

"No, I was just—"

"Oh crap," Jerry said, paling. "I knew this guy was a killer but didn't realize it was the guy who murdered the priest."

"Yeah. That's right."

"So what? You coming around to bless the place? That's kind of weird."

"No, no. The shooter was a parishioner, and he had a daughter. We just wanted to check in on her."

It wasn't a lie, but it wasn't the truth, either. Luis hated himself a little for putting it out there. To make it worse, Jerry nodded reverentially.

"That's something," he said. "That's very Christian of you. Ain't no girl here now, though. I don't know the story, but the place is getting cleaned out and ready to be rented again. Anything that was left behind I took to the Dumpster."

"Was there much?" Luis asked.

"Nah. Trash mostly. Contents of the kitchen. Somebody had already come for the furniture. Which means the building manager probably sold it. Sinister business this."

"I agree," Luis said. "Nothing of the daughter's?"

"Not a damn thing as I could tell. Sorry."

Luis turned to exit, then glanced back. "Which Dumpster, by the way?"

There were three at the back of the building. Jerry had said he'd tossed everything in the one closest to the back door. Sure enough, Luis found two garbage bags of food pulled from the cabinet. As they were dry goods, he considered yanking them out to take back to the church's stores, but then relented. They already smelled of the Dumpster, and there was no telling how long their contents had been in Yamazoe's cabinet.

Under the garbage bags, however, were a handful of pint glasses, a couple shattered, all with the logo of a bar, Old Taipa, including the address, a place down in the City of Industry. Each also featured a different animal and year. Luis realized they were commemorative glasses of some sort tied to the Chinese New Year.

"Hey, did you pull these from this apartment?" Luis asked Jerry after carrying a couple of the surviving glasses back up.

"I did," Jerry said, nodding. "Tried not to break them in the Dumpster, as some trash digger might come along and get some recycling nickels out of them. Think I was only half-successful. If you want those, they're all yours."

"Ever heard of this bar?"

"Oh, of course!" Jerry said, smiling. "It's not really a bar, though. Why? You feeling lucky?"

———

Susan had slept for ten hours straight. She'd blown past the time she was supposed to be back on shift but surprised herself by not feeling guilty.

Oh well.

She got dressed, realized she didn't have a single clean lab coat left, and made a pile of all her used ones to trade at the dry cleaner's for the ones she'd dropped off the previous week. Even when they'd handed her the ticket and said, "Tuesday after five okay?" she'd grinned, knowing it would be days after that before she'd finally have time to come back.

She checked her phone, was perplexed to see no messages from Nan, then hoped that meant he'd managed to get some sleep, too.

As she drove from her tiny duplex in San Gabriel toward the clinic, she scanned through the radio stations looking for news but found none. She took out her cell phone and while in traffic flipped through the websites of the local TV news stations and the *Los Angeles Times*, looking for updates on the Father Chang murder. She wondered what it meant that there hadn't been anything new reported in the past twenty-four hours. Weren't people interested?

Nan had shown her where, in comments sections and on social media, people had hinted at the priest being a child molester. At first, she thought it was just unspecific anti-Catholic venom. Cracks about molester priests were omnipresent. But then they got more specific, referencing a teenage girl, suggesting the shooter was a relative, and so on.

So they're killing you twice, she'd thought.

Susan put her mind to the murder now, trying to remember the last protest march or rally or sit-in Benny had attended. She usually found out after the fact, as he seemed to know which ones she'd try to talk him out of. There was the one against the state for potentially using eminent domain to kick poor people out of their houses to make way for a high-speed rail line running up to San Francisco. There was another following the police shooting of an unarmed teenager down in Watts. Then there was that teachers union that staged a silent protest outside schools for better pay.

In one way or another he'd been involved in all of them. But so were a lot of people, and he was hardly the driving force. He was a presence. A presence in a Roman collar with all the baggage that came with it, but a presence nevertheless.

When she arrived at the dry cleaner's, she was surprised to find no one at the counter. It was a family-run joint that prided itself on service. Whoever was closest to the front would drop anything they were working on as soon as a customer walked through the door.

"Hello?" she said, arms full of lab coats.

That's when she heard the commotion coming from the adjoining room. Though primarily a dry cleaner's, they also employed two tailors to do alterations and repairs. One of them, Rabih Chamoun, a charming old Lebanese gentleman, was a patient at the clinic and traded his services in the form of coupons to the doctors who looked after him.

"Are you guys okay?" Susan called, hearing chairs scraping, people talking quickly back and forth in panicked voices, and then the rasping cough of an old man.

She dropped the coats and hurried around the counter. Pushing past the hanging clothes, she found the owner's daughter, Celia, kneeling beside Rabih as he lowered himself to the floor. His face was bright red, and he clutched his chest as he coughed. Another worker, whose name Susan didn't know, spotted her and looked relieved.

"Dr. Auyong!" he said. "We just called 911. I think he's having a heart attack."

Susan rushed to Rabih's side. She wasn't his primary physician but frantically tried to remember anything of his medical history. She thought he had high cholesterol and heart disease. But when she touched his skin, it was hot and clammy, indicative of a fever.

"It's not a heart attack," Susan said, mainly to herself.

But then Rabih coughed once more, sending up a gob of blood. As he continued to cough, bracing himself against his sewing table, more blood emerged. Susan grabbed the nearest article of clothing, wadded it into a ball, and shoved it under his head.

"Mr. Chamoun, can you hear me?" Susan asked.

"*Ya allah,*" Rabih said, though his eyes wouldn't focus.

"Mr. Chamoun. An ambulance is on its way. Please relax. Short deep breaths."

"But I . . . can't breathe," Rabih replied. "I can't—"

"Yes you can," Susan said. "If you can speak, you can breathe."

She took his hand. Less than a minute later it went limp. And no matter what Susan did to try and resuscitate him, Rabih Chamoun was gone. When the ambulance finally arrived, Susan explained what she could, holding back the information that Chamoun was a patient at her clinic. The paramedics half listened, then had to make a few calls of their own.

Susan consoled Celia for a moment, then took her dirty lab coats back to her car, only to find that she was blocked in by the ambulance. When her cell phone rang, she saw that it was Clover Gao and picked up anyway.

"I'm stuck at a trauma scene just down the street," she explained, hoping to sound distressed. "It was one of the clinic's patients, Rabih Chamoun. I should be there in a moment, though."

In the silence that followed, Susan wondered if Clover actually gave a damn. This *was* historic.

"Well, there's a coincidence," Clover said. "I was just calling you about another patient of ours. You saw César Carreño yesterday, did you not?"

"Um, yes. He came by to pick up his pills."

"But you also saw his daughter a few hours later?"

"I did," Susan agreed, though she barely remembered the encounter.

"Carreño just about died in our reception area," Clover said impassively. "His daughter brought him in saying he was in great distress, but he toppled over before we even got him into an exam room. We called an ambulance, and they rushed him to Kaiser."

What? Susan was flabbergasted.

"He was perfectly fine yesterday!" Susan declared. "The nurse did the usual—blood pressure, temperature, et cetera. He didn't complain of anything. Eyes and ears were fine."

"From the looks of it he had pneumonia. If he'd died here, that would've meant real trouble. There would've been an investigation. We would've been shut down. As it was, I had to get Esmeralda to let us move him into the parking lot for when the paramedics arrived."

You are an awful, awful human being, Susan thought but didn't say. *The worst.*

"Not that she'd sue us, given her immigration status, but that could've been really bad news," Clover said in a chastising tone. "Now, I know you received a real shock yesterday, but I need you to put the patients first, or I can't have you working here. Is that understood?"

"Of course."

"Good. Now, see that you get here soon, and make sure you call the daughter just to check in. Could go a long way toward smoothing this over."

Susan was about to reply when Clover hung up.

It was then that Susan remembered something Father Chang had told her once: "All of us are dying." He'd tossed it off as a breezy literalism, referring, she thought, to the title of a book or even a poem. But it came back to her now with surprising force.

All of us are dying.

VII

Tuesday evening's Mass was a sparsely attended affair, but that just made it more appealing to Luis. Though Whillans officiated over the Mass, Luis greeted the congregants at the door, passed out bulletins, and prepared the sacraments.

On Sundays St. Augustine's could appear cavernous, the sea of faces stretching from the altar to the back doors until they became a single mass. During the week it was more intimate, more like the Masses Luis had celebrated in New York when he'd been a seminarian. With a group this small it was easier to unify everyone in a way that allowed the Holy Spirit to be much more apparent in the room.

A larger group could often make the priest feel as if he was preaching at rather than preaching to. And when that happened there was a disconnect—people began to fidget, and those who came were there out of a sense of duty or habit rather than a deeply felt desire to commune with God in the Lord's house, attended by his servants on earth, the priesthood.

Eh, you're just scared of giving the sermon on Sunday, Luis chided himself as he moved to the confessional.

After an hour he allowed himself to be replaced by Father Pargeter and informed Pastor Whillans as to where his travels would take him that night. Whillans raised an eyebrow, but Luis assured him again why this was necessary in the eyes of God. With that he went to his room and switched out his collar and clerical outfit for the nicest clothes he could find in the donation bin.

He needn't have bothered.

Having only seen Las Vegas casinos on television and in the movies, he figured the Golden Dragon Casino would be about the same. Dimly lit gaming tables, noisy slot machines, roulette wheels, and masses of people in motion, from players to dealers to cocktail waitresses.

Instead, as he stepped from the Dragon's impressive foyer to the gaming floor, Luis found himself in a place that more resembled a large bingo parlor. Rather than a few tables tastefully arranged around the room, the ones here were lined up in tight rows, as if to scrunch as many into the space as was physically possible. The overhead lights were bright fluorescents, the walls the calming beige of an asylum. The stained carpet looked as if it had been purchased from a rest home's fire sale, and the tables resembled lawn furniture.

Despite all of this and the fact that it was a Tuesday night, Luis could see that every stool around every table was filled. The customers, almost uniformly men, were dressed casually, some in ball caps and shorts. A number of them looked as if they'd been playing hand after hand of poker for hours, even days. Food and drinks were placed beside them on flimsy trays by an efficient waitstaff as dealers kept the cards coming.

"Help you find a table, sir?"

Luis turned as a young Asian woman sidled up next to him. He shook his head and immediately changed his posture to affect the street swagger of his youth. When he caught a glimpse of himself in a nearby mirror, however, he was immediately embarrassed.

"Sorry, I'm meeting someone in the Old Taipa bar," he said, straightening. "Can you tell me where it is?"

"Of course," she said. "All the way in back. It'll be pretty full right now, though. There's a game on."

"Thank you."

As soon as he began walking toward the bar, he realized he had no plan. He didn't have a photograph of Yamazoe to use to "ask around" like in an old crime movie. He also didn't have the faintest clue whether Yamazoe himself came here or had merely gotten the pint glasses from someone else. Heck, maybe he bought them at a garage sale.

He felt foolish for a moment, then angry at himself for being so prideful that he thought he could pull this off on his own. It wouldn't be that easy. Still, he'd come this far, so he might as well check it out.

As the young hostess had indicated, the bar was packed. Everyone was watching baseball and seemed passionately behind one team or the other. Luis realized, given the time of year, it must almost be the play-offs.

He stood around for a moment, considered ordering a drink, then stayed back. Others pushed past him, flagging down the bartender, then paying or opening a tab. As several did so, they handed over a thin white card with the casino's GD logo on it that the bartender slid through the reader of the touch-screen cash register before ringing up the bill. Each time he did, the customer's photo and information came up on the screen, connoting they were part of a "loyalty program."

When one customer claimed he didn't have his, the bartender asked for his phone number, and they looked it up.

Piece of cake.

Well, piece of cake if the phone number Shu Kuen Yamazoe used with the church is the same he did with the bar.

Luis took out his phone, found the information he'd used to locate Yamazoe's address, and hastily memorized the phone number so he could at least reel it off without seeming as if it was a number he'd learned one minute before.

"Hey, I just wanted a round of drinks for my table," Luis said, squirming through the cheering customers as someone on the television hit into a double play. "But I forgot my loyalty card. Can I give you my phone number?"

The bartender, a woman this time, turned to the machine and nodded. "Go ahead."

Luis rattled off Yamazoe's number, and as soon as she typed it in, there was Yamazoe. Almost as soon as the profile appeared, Luis had the wherewithal to realize if he could barely memorize a phone number, he'd have a bear of a time with everything on the screen. So he lifted his cell phone, took a fast photograph of the screen, and just as quickly put it away. The bartender turned back to him, shaking her head.

"I think I typed it in wrong," she said, indicating the photo.

"Oh, it might be under my old phone number," Luis said, the lies coming easy now. "Hang on a sec."

He moved away from the bar and disappeared into the throng. He made his way to the nearest men's room, moved into a stall, and checked the photo. Though some of it was blurry from the haste with which it was taken, the salient information was right there. Not only was Yamazoe a longtime customer of the casino dating back several years, he'd also had all of his privileges suspended. There was even a note that if he entered the casino, he was to be immediately escorted out.

"Huh," Luis said aloud before pocketing the phone.

Luis may never have been to a casino, but he did understand those who profited from gamblers. There was seldom one incident that blackballed a longtime customer. Someone with that level of addiction was useful, as they would beg, borrow, and steal to move money from their pocket to yours. Though they eventually exhausted the goodwill any friends or relatives felt toward them, up until that point they were the *last* customer you blackballed.

As Luis exited the men's room, he almost ran into a tall Asian man in a suit.

"Excuse me," Luis said quickly, and moved to go around him.

Only when he did he found himself facing another Asian man, this one younger, also in a suit.

"Can we help you find something?" the first man asked, stepping into Luis's path.

"I'm just leaving," Luis said.

A third man took Luis by the wrist.

"We need to have a quick word off the floor," the first man explained. "Please come with us. If you don't, it will be a matter for the authorities. But I think we can clear this up ourselves, don't you?"

Luis froze. He'd seen the pit bosses and managers. They all had name badges and pins with the casino's logo. These men had nothing that identified them as employees.

"We're private security," the first man said, following Luis's eyes. "There are the ones for show"—he indicated the uniformed guards at the doors and the cages—"and then there's the real thing."

Luis looked from man to man, then fell into step behind the leader when he walked away.

———

"All right, just one more push," the doctor, Martin Soong, was saying in a soothing voice. "I have the baby. It's coming right now."

As Tony watched, the sweat-covered young mother on the hospital-grade medical bed gave one final push and the doctor pulled the baby free.

"Perfect!" he exclaimed. "Nurse?"

A nurse hurried over to take the child as the doctor moved to help the mother. "See? Piece of cake."

The mother laughed a little as the nurse cleaned the baby before holding him up. "Can I hold him?" she asked.

"In just a moment," the doctor said. "We need to cut the cord, weigh him, then put him on the baby warmer a moment to get his temperature up. When he's all wrapped up, we'll give him right to you."

The doctor turned to Tony. "You want to do the honors?"

Tony stared at the cord in amazement, then bowed to the mother. "Is that all right?"

"Of course, Tony," she said kindly.

As the doctor clamped off the section of cord for Tony to cut, Tony retrieved the scissors. He was always present at the births in case something needed to be done or an emergency arose, but was seldom in the actual room. This particular woman had come to the States on her own, a surrogate for a politically connected family in Anhui, and had asked for Tony to be in the room for the delivery as a source of moral support. As the family in Anhui wanted to be certain the baby wasn't switched at birth or the victim of some other funny business, he was required to be there anyway, but was glad it would seem as if it was her choice.

When he cut the cord, he stared into the baby's eyes and realized that though much of this business was dollars and cents, occasionally it could be about something greater.

Your first breaths are in this country, so they will forever welcome you as one of their own, even make you president, he thought, eyeing the baby boy. *What a strange old belief it is that your allegiance would be to the land you emerged in rather than the one in which you were raised. Americans and their birth mythology.*

He remembered the name of the boy was to be Qingquan. He smiled up at the mother, who looked more relieved than overjoyed. He knew she was being very well paid but heard a rumor, likely from Shen Mang, that part of this payout was due to the two abortions she'd been made to have earlier when it was discovered that she was carrying girls. He hoped this wasn't true.

"So, I went by the hotel today and dropped off prenatal vitamins and folic acid for Miss Tan," said Dr. Soong a few moments later after mother and baby were resting.

"How is she?" Tony asked.

"Good. Everything's progressing well. She takes good care of herself."

Tony bristled at this remark. He didn't think it was proper that a doctor should take notice of such a thing, then realized it was meant without lascivious intent.

"She asked about you, by the way," Dr. Soong said.

"Did she?" Tony asked, genuinely surprised.

"She admires you," the doctor said simply. "Apparently you told her something of your past."

"In passing. She's talkative."

"She is. But I think a part of her wishes she'd had the guts to do what you did. Come over when you're young. Make a life for yourself here. Become a success."

"She said all that?"

"In not so many words, but yes. You have a fan, Tony Qi."

The doctor grinned and finished packing up his things. As Tony showed him to the door, he glanced back at the large Silverlake house, the last one Tony had bought before bringing Oscar into the picture.

"And how much of a profit do you think you'll see on this one?" the doctor asked.

"We'll know after the renovations are complete," Tony said dismissively. "Thank you again, Martin."

As the doctor left, Tony stared out into the starry sky.

You have a fan, Tony Qi.

Luis was brought into a small office that looked like an unfinished movie set. There was a desk and chairs, but nothing had been decorated or lit yet. Nobody could possibly use it. But as the special security men indicated for him to sit in the chair in front of the desk, Luis realized it was the opposite. It was probably used all the time.

I wonder if Shu Yamazoe sat in this chair.

"Truthful answers will make this fast," said a young man from behind Luis. He came around to the desk and sat on the corner.

"Okay," Luis agreed.

"The license plates of your car say it's registered to a church. What're you, a thief? A volunteer?"

"A priest," Luis said.

The man raised an eyebrow. Luis didn't think he could be much older than twenty, but the other men in the room clearly respected him. He, too, was Asian and had a shock of spiky black hair jutting up from his scalp like porcupine quills. His suit was not only expensive, it was immaculately tailored. Still, he hadn't seen him out on the floor.

"Why are you using a crooked man's phone number?" he asked. "A mistake and you could've gotten by. But you took a picture of it? That got our attention."

"Yamazoe may be a bad guy," Luis said evenly, "but he was a parishioner, and there's a concern in the parish for his child."

The man eyed Luis long and hard, then shook his head.

"I don't like priests," he said. "We're in the same business—taking the money of fools hoping for a better life—but somehow I think we're more honest about it."

Luis actually found this analogy intriguing but had to save it for later. "Do you know where Yamazoe's daughter is?"

The man rose, moved close to Luis, then slapped him so hard that Luis tumbled from the chair. The slap stung Luis's skin but didn't do any real damage that he could feel. He righted himself but stayed on the floor.

"Not his daughter," the man said simply. "Got another question?"

"Is she safe?"

The man slapped Luis again, but this time on the other cheek. Luis wasn't ready, and his head snapped back, his neck crashing into the chair leg. This sent a jolt down his spine. As his head throbbed, his fingers and toes burned, as if he'd touched a live wire.

"Of course she is. She's back with her family. She did great, don't you think? Any more?"

"How much was Yamazoe into you for?"

The young man balled up his fist and fired a right into Luis's face, sending his head into the carpet. Blood trickled from Luis's nose and mouth. By now the pain was coming in from so many directions that his body twisted and reeled as if to escape it.

The man considered the question, then shook his head. "Not answering that one. What else?"

"If the girl wasn't Yamazoe's daughter, why did he kill Father Chang?"

The young man straightened to his full height and indicated for the special security men to lift Luis and put him back on the chair.

"Hold him there," he commanded.

He punched Luis twice, a quick one-two to the face again, more blood smearing across his hands. "Another question? Go ahead. Ask anything."

"If the girl wasn't Yamazoe's daughter, why did he kill—?"

Before Luis could finish his sentence, the young man boxed him in the ears. The twin blows affected Luis's equilibrium to the point he almost threw up. He still righted himself, however, and stared up at his tormentor as if asking for more. He was obliged with three swift blows to the head.

One of these knocked the delirious Luis unconscious. When Luis came to, he was being dragged to the parish car. Even the slightest movement sent darts of pain through his system, so he hung as limp as possible. One of the security men unlocked the driver's-side door, and the other shoved Luis behind the wheel. His keys were tossed in his lap and a pistol placed to his temple.

"If you come back here, priest or not, we'll kill you. Understand?"

Luis managed to nod, the motion practically bringing tears to his eyes. The security men moved away. Luis felt around in his pockets, then leaned out of the car.

"My cell phone. You still have my phone."

The security men looked back at him incredulously. The taller of the two plucked Luis's phone from his pocket, turned it on to delete the photo of Yamazoe's loyalty customer screen, then threw it as far away into the parking lot as he could, a star quarterback's amazing field-long Hail Mary of a pass.

Then the two security men walked away.

It took ten agonizing minutes of staggering through the parking lot to find his phone. When he discovered it behind the rear wheel of a Datsun, the screen was cracked, but he could still dial. He immediately rang Michael Story, only to get voice mail.

"Yamazoe was a big gambler. Lost a fortune to, I think, the local triad. The girl worked for them in order to establish some kind of cover story. So it was either the triad who wanted Father Chang dead or someone who hired them. That's all I got."

He hung up, turned on the ignition, caught sight of his monstrous reflection in the rearview mirror, and grimaced as he thought about how he'd explain this away in front of the congregation on Sunday.

VIII

When Michael listened to the message from Luis, he couldn't call Detective Whitehead fast enough.

The triad? No one could touch the LA triad. It was understood they existed, sure, but they kept themselves so far from the spotlight and politically insulated that they were practically untouchable. Even the tiniest foothold into their operations was worth taking a run at.

He arranged a sit-down with Yamazoe first thing the next morning and headed over to the Hollenbeck station.

"What do you have?" Whitehead asked when Michael entered the building.

"Nothing remotely actionable or concrete," Michael said. "Which is why I need to work him alone."

"You can't talk to him without his attorney," Whitehead said.

"Wrong. I can't talk to him about the shooting of Father Chang without his attorney," Michael said. "But I can ask him about an unrelated crime."

Whitehead eyed him curiously. "This your guy working?"

"Maybe, maybe not."

That didn't sound good enough for the detective, but Michael knew he'd have to accept it anyway. Whitehead arranged to use one of the interrogation rooms and had Yamazoe brought in from the cells. As the prisoner hadn't eaten breakfast yet, he was grumpy about being interrogated so early. When he saw Michael and Detective Whitehead waiting for him instead of deGuzman, he got downright irritable.

"Where's my lawyer?" Yamazoe demanded.

As if having been waiting for such a prompt, Whitehead rose and moved to the door. "I'll go see if he's here yet."

After Whitehead exited, Yamazoe turned his dull-eyed attention to Michael, who sat down opposite him.

"Who're you?"

"That depends."

"On what?"

"On you, asshole."

Yamazoe scoffed. "You think that's how you get me to talk?"

"Not at all."

Yamazoe sighed and glanced around the room. It was claustrophobically small. Michael knew it had been constructed that way on purpose.

"All right," Michael said. "Let me ask you something."

"You can't ask me anything without my lawyer present," Yamazoe said.

"There are two things wrong with that statement," Michael said, leaning back in his chair. "First, I sure can ask you questions without your attorney present; it's just inadmissible in court. Second, why don't you listen to the questions first before deciding you don't want to answer?"

Yamazoe smirked but said nothing.

"Oh, come on."

Yamazoe crossed his arms and eyed Michael as if challenging him to stop wasting his time.

"Okay, but let's just pretend for argument's sake that you're a big gambler and that you are actually into people for a lot of money."

Yamazoe didn't so much as twitch. Michael almost laughed. When someone was working that hard to betray nothing on their face, well . . .

"And let's just say that you're also a big loser. And I mean across the boards a big loser. Sporting events, horse tracks, cards, you name it. In fact, the one thing you're actually successful at is getting idiots to float you as you rob Peter to pay Paul to the tune of the low- to mid-six figures."

While it was true Luis had only mentioned the one casino, Michael was able to use this information to extrapolate the next few steps. A contract killing from a nonprofessional was a huge chunk of change. To get somebody to do that implied a debt that had gone so far outside of Yamazoe's control that his desperation took over. It had become mortal.

Do this or die.

To Michael this meant a lot more money than a casino, particularly a Los Angeles card room, would ever allow a player to get into the hole to them for. Yamazoe probably owed the Golden Dragon guys somewhere in the low five figures. But knowing inveterate gamblers, he imagined the casino was only one of the places Yamazoe had found to lose money.

The triad aspect threw Michael a little. He hadn't dealt much with Chinese organized crime in the prosecutor's office. He knew it existed, sure, but the main number he always heard was that they made their bones controlling 70 percent of North America's heroin trade and then on moving illegals into the US—the birth hotels bust of a few months back had been just that, a bust, as zero charges came out of it.

But Luis knew the city's criminal element better than Michael did, particularly the ones that didn't get caught. If he said the casino was triad-run, he believed him.

"Let me be frank," Michael continued. "The people who put you up to this probably targeted you early on. They like nothing more than to cultivate marks with an impossible level of debt. In fact, they like to go around to the people you owe money in order to consolidate that debt, like a reverse loan shark. Yeah, I'll bet some of your debtors would've been just as happy to break your legs, but when the triad comes along—"

This time there was a flinch.

"—and they're offering to pay the full amount to assume the debt, well, then you're really screwed."

Yamazoe seemed to fold on himself, like prey trying to make itself a smaller target. Michael knew he'd rattled him.

"Now, maybe you'll answer a few questions."

"Not without my attorney present," Yamazoe said weakly.

"The one the triad set up for you? The one that, when he hears the kinds of questions I'm asking, will report back just how much we know to the local Dragon Head? I'm not entirely sure that's how you want this to go."

Yamazoe's knee bounced up and down. As soon as he realized he was doing it, however, he made it stop.

"But then there's the version where your attorney knows that no one in law enforcement or the prosecutor's office would be stupid enough to jeopardize a murder trial by talking to you without your lawyer present. Which means if I'm able to act in any small way on anything you say, no one will believe it came from you, right?"

Yamazoe said nothing, but his eyes found Michael's. He opened his mouth and exhaled so hard Michael thought he'd deflate.

"If they find out I said anything, I'm dead," Yamazoe said quietly. "Not 'my time in prison will be hard.' Not 'they'll find the judge that'll make sure I never see the light of day again.' They'll just kill me, and no one'll care. Not you, not Detective Whitehead, nobody."

Michael was too giddy to realize he should've countered this, but Yamazoe plowed on.

"And I get it. I was dead to them already when they gave me this shot to keep breathing. I knew it was a sucker's bet, but I didn't have a choice. They said you'd never be able to link it."

"That's because they're not as smart as they think they are," Michael said. "But if you tell me what I want to know, I can't promise you leniency, as there's no doubt you pulled the trigger on Father Chang. What I can do is take your case to the Justice Department and get you into protective custody. You'll be so gone, I won't even know where you are. Understand?"

Yamazoe considered this. Michael doubted the gambler trusted him, but he knew his options were dwindling. There was also the possibility that if Michael could tie him to the triad in a matter of days, someone else could, too.

"All right," Yamazoe said. "What do you want to know?"

———

Susan checked her phone for the hundredth time in the past half hour. It was fifteen minutes before she had to leave.

"I can see one more patient," she told the receptionist as she turned over the billing information for her last appointment. "Then I have to go. Try to make it someone who won't ask a lot of questions."

The receptionist nodded and sent back a fiftysomething Hispanic man who didn't want to be there in the first place. Only, he'd let some kind of ear infection go so long that it was now affecting his balance and speech. Susan felt around his swollen nodes and recognized an out-of-control infection, but one that could be handled with antibiotics. She retrieved the boxes of pills from the supply closet, explained how to take them, and then sent him on his way. He seemed relieved to be done so quickly.

"I'll be back in a few hours," she announced on her way out the door.

Not wanting to answer questions, Susan changed into her black dress in the backseat of her car rather than in the office. She'd already tempted fate by printing a couple of photos of Father Chang on the office printer, which she knew Clover would find a reason to complain about. This was a bad enough day already.

The photos had actually been an issue, though. There were practically none of just Father Chang. All were either Benny and Nan, her and Benny, or, in a single instance, the three of them together. She tried to remember the occasion, then realized it was taken at some art opening and later e-mailed over by their host.

What made the photo all the more interesting was how it illustrated just how unlikely a trio they were. On one side there was her, short and stocky, in her midthirties with her thrift-store fashion. On the other, Nan, tall and thin with a perpetual slump, barely into his twenties, wearing his perpetual dark corduroy pants and gray-green sweater. Then in the middle, with his arms around them both, was Benny, in his midfifties and well preserved, if not a little rotund, his equally perpetual Roman collar the focal point of the image.

The smile on Benny's face reminded Susan of why she enjoyed his company. Sure, he could be something of a depressive who medicated himself with alcohol and sleeping pills, making him manic, paranoid, and horrible to be around. But when he was clean, his sense of wonder and curiosity made him a boon companion. He was always reading the new book, listening to the latest music, or taking in the most modern art out of a sense that *someone* had to, or the world might as well hand itself over to the barbarians.

And he felt the exact same way about people who couldn't fight for themselves. In fact, there was nothing quite so unstoppable as Father Chang when he decided an injustice was being done. She remembered that he'd even been teaching himself Thai at the time of his death, his sixth tongue, in order to better communicate with a group of locals in the garment district he thought could benefit from his activist support.

Though she assumed Benny knew how much she respected him, she was never really sure where she stood with him. He used her—to pick up scuttlebutt from the various communities that utilized the clinic, as a sounding board for his latest schemes, but most of all for Nan.

They'd go to a movie or attend the opening of an art exhibit and be mistaken for God knew what. As a Catholic priest, the obvious—that Father Chang was literally their father—was likely ruled out. Besides, Nan and Susan could not have looked more different, so siblings was out. The process of elimination then had it that Nan and Susan, despite their age difference, were somehow a couple, and Father Chang their benevolent friend and chaperone.

What no one ever suspected was the truth.

"You said ten o'clock," Nan scolded as he climbed into her car seconds after she pulled up to the steps of the biochemical engineering building. "I've been waiting half an hour carrying these."

He indicated a bouquet of white lilies. She couldn't understand why her lateness was such a crime but didn't blame Nan for being so touchy, given the week he'd had.

"Check your texts," Susan said, turning back onto the road. "I said ten thirty. I said it twenty times."

Nan didn't check but simply folded in on himself. She touched his arm.

"It doesn't matter anyway," he huffed.

No, it doesn't.

———

The cemetery was on a flat stretch of ground just off the 110 freeway. Cars whizzed by, and the suffocating stench of diesel fumes choked the area. Susan thought Nan might criticize her for allowing the priest to be buried here, but he said nothing. He probably knew there hadn't been much choice.

"Over there," she said, pointing to a van alongside an open grave.

They hiked up to the spot and saw three men in work clothes alongside a fourth in a suit.

"Dr. Auyong?" the suited man asked. "I'm Walt Broderick. We spoke on the phone."

"Yes," Susan managed, unable to take her eyes off the simple cherry-wood coffin sitting nearby.

Her friend. Her lively, rambunctious, fatally stupid friend.

She glanced at Nan. His eyes were fixed on the highway. He seemed to have the exact opposite problem. If he acknowledged the coffin, it would mean Father Chang was really dead.

He's so young, she thought.

The funeral director shot a glance at the grave diggers to make them move away. The three of them wandered to the other side of the van, but Susan could still hear them chatting amiably, as if being within earshot of a recently and brutally murdered man was an everyday occurrence. She wondered if it was.

"The priest just went to his car," Broderick said, nodding to the vehicle-lined road that passed along the east side of the cemetery. "He'll be right back."

"Priest?" Susan asked. She hadn't expected this. "From Father Chang's parish?"

Broderick shrugged and shook his head. "No idea. Thought you'd invited him."

Susan scowled and turned to Nan, figuring he'd share in her anger. She was surprised instead to see him wiping a steady stream of tears from his cheeks. She moved to his side and put her arms around him. He kept his at his side but leaned into her.

"I'm so sorry, Nan," she whispered.

They stayed like that for a long moment. Susan heard footsteps. Broderick raised his arms as if in relief that he could turn the situation over to someone more qualified.

"Father Luis Chavez," the funeral director said, indicating a nearing priest. "This is Dr. Susan Auyong."

Susan broke away from Nan and eyed the young Latino priest. Though she was hardly a regular at St. Jerome's, she'd been around enough to recognize the other parish priests. She didn't know this one.

"I'm deeply sorry for your loss," the priest said quietly.

"Bullshit you are," snapped Nan, head turning so fast he flung tears. "I know what you're saying out there about Father Chang. You believe he was some kind of criminal."

Susan expected the priest to be put off by Nan's attack, but Father Chavez didn't move. Instead, he nodded and raised his hands in supplication.

"I've heard the same rumors that you have," Father Chavez said. "But the archbishop was an old friend of Father Chang's and doesn't believe them in the slightest. He asked me to look into it while he's away. Though I have only begun, I have found nothing to substantiate the stories whatsoever. I fully expect the diocese to repudiate the charges in the strongest possible language when the inquiry is completed."

Susan had expected a diplomatic response. This sounded like an honest one.

"Then why aren't any members of his parish here?" she asked. "No congregants, no priests, not even his pastor. This is a joke."

"No, this is fear," Chavez said simply. "But right now let's concern ourselves with not what has brought us together but who. Recriminations can wait."

Even Nan seemed pacified by this. Broderick signaled the grave diggers, who came over to lift the coffin from the bier to the casket-lowering device positioned over the open grave. Father Chavez shook his head and looked to Susan and Nan.

"Maybe we take him the rest of the way ourselves?" the priest asked.

Nan broke away from Susan and moved to the side of the coffin without a word. Susan followed, wondering if the three of them could lift it. Chavez drew up behind her as they all gripped a handle.

"On the count of three?"

The coffin was heavy but manageable. They carried it the short distance before placing it gently atop the casket-lowering device, the green nylon webbing bending gently under the weight.

With this done, Susan placed the photo she'd decided to bring, the one of all three of them, even if tradition called for a photo of the deceased alone, on the casket. Nan added the lilies.

"May I lead us in prayer?" Father Chavez asked as he moved to the head of the coffin.

Susan expected something Catholic and reverential. Instead, the priest prayed for God to give her and Nan strength in the coming days but also to help get justice for Father Chang. He implied that Chang had met his fate head-on and didn't run, showing courage in the face of his own mortality. He even suggested that in time Father Chang might be seen as a martyr for his beliefs.

"Amen," Father Chavez concluded before turning to Susan and Nan. "Would either of you like to say anything?"

Susan considered it. But she'd already said everything she'd meant for Father Chang's ears in her mind over the past twenty-four hours and didn't feel the need to repeat it for Nan's or Father Chavez's benefit. Nan, however, stepped forward.

"Father Chang hated the church but loved God and loved people," he began. "He thought he could change the church and make it into what God and the people needed it to be. That's what got him up in the morning. He wanted to lead by example. He wanted to change things. He wanted people to know that Jesus was about love, and that was it. That every single last one of Jesus's teachings came back to that simple fact. Love one another as God loves. That's it."

As Nan stepped away from the coffin, Susan's eyes met Father Chavez's. He seemed as impressed by Nan's diatribe as she was.

"Then let that be Father Chang's legacy," Luis said. "Go forth in love."

The funeral director, who'd reappeared next to the van, surprised Susan with a hearty "Amen."

"Let's get out of here," Nan said as the grave diggers climbed into the grave to strip off the ropes.

Susan nodded and turned to head back to the car. The priest was beside them almost immediately.

"Thank you for those words," he told Nan. "Father Chang meant a lot to you?"

Nan side-eyed him but said nothing.

"When you say you've found nothing to substantiate the stories, what did you mean?" Susan asked, changing the subject.

"No witnesses who ever saw Father Chang and the alleged victim together for one thing," Father Chavez said. "The parish pastor had a story that Father Chang kept an apartment outside the rectory but didn't know where it was."

I wonder if he meant my apartment, Susan thought. *He stayed there a few times when we'd stayed up late drinking wine, listening to music, or whatever else we'd get up to.*

"Yeah, but the cops have a confession, right?" Nan said. "And don't cops go with the line of least resistance?"

"Normally so," the priest agreed. "But the archdiocese has been in contact with the district attorney's office, and there's a full investigation underway. I don't think they'll just take the word of the shooter without evidence. In fact, I think it will come out sooner than later that he was contracted by someone else."

Susan stared at Father Chavez for a moment with new eyes. If this man had already found all that out in such a short amount of time even as the police seemed to know nothing, maybe he was someone worth speaking to.

"Do you have any idea who hired the killer?" Susan asked.

"I may be getting close to the who," the priest said. "But not the why."

"Will you let us know?" Susan asked. "Father Chang did mean a lot to us. Being a priest was part of who he was, probably the most important part, but there was more to him. This week I'm starting to think we might've been two of the only people who were privy to that. Feels like a blessing and a curse right now. Do you understand?"

"I do," Father Chavez agreed.

"Do you?" she pressed.

"I'll keep you updated with everything I learn," Chavez replied.

Susan nodded and took Nan's arm. That's when she realized that Nan hadn't taken his eyes off the priest once as he spoke. She led him away.

———

Luis waited alongside the grave, watching as the pair made their way back to their car. They were three or four yards away when the boy glanced back. From the look on his face, the torment he was feeling over Father Chang's death wouldn't be disappearing any time soon.

Luis wanted to counsel the boy against harboring vengeful feelings, particularly given who might have been responsible for Chang's death. But it was a day to grieve. Looking for the way forward could wait until tomorrow.

IX

The question-and-answer session between Michael and Shu Kuen Yamazoe lasted less than thirty minutes. If the Los Angeles triad was behind the killing of Father Chang, it had done a good job of insulating Yamazoe from the truth.

"Who approached you?"

"I never knew their name."

"Where was the approach made?"

"They were waiting at my apartment when I came home from the track one day."

"What'd they say?"

"'You know who we are and why we're here. Don't try anything.' They then dragged me to my bedroom and put a noose around my neck. They hung me from a hook they'd drilled into the ceiling. They even had a note listing my debts that they placed on my bed next to my driver's license and passport."

"And you started to die?"

"I was suffocating. I blacked out after less than a minute. When I woke up, I was on the bed. They told me I had to kill Father Chang, or they'd kill me for real. I said I wouldn't. They hanged me again. When I came to, they showed me the weed killer I'd drink, which would take two days to eat through my stomach and organs. Then they showed me a photo of the girl who'd be my 'daughter' for the next three months if I'd shoot Father Chang."

"What was her name?"

"I was never told. She was from a small rural area and only spoke Xibe or Manchu. I can barely remember my Mandarin most days."

"She was a prostitute?"

"They meant her to be, but it never became that. She moved in with me. She cooked and cleaned. I made her stop. We were supposed to be seen here and there to establish that she was my daughter, particularly at church. We spent every moment of three months together. They wouldn't let us leave the city, so I took her to every corner—the beaches, the hills, the parks. She learned a little English. I think her father did something to the local triad back home. She knew she was under some kind of sentence. We made the best of it. They gave us money, so we ate at nice restaurants. We went to the movies. I bought her clothes."

"And then what happened?"

"I came home from the grocery store on what she managed to tell me was her birthday after she was able to decipher the calendar here. I had a cake. She was gone. In her place was the gun."

"Do you think she's dead?"

"Yes," Yamazoe said, tearing up a little. "I could tell in the way they were with her. They felt guilty about it in advance. She was going to die for her father's sins."

"They could've just put her on a plane."

"If somebody got her to talk, it could jeopardize the cover story. That's why I figure I'm a dead man, too."

When Michael exited the interrogation room a few minutes later, he found Detective Whitehead standing in the hallway opposite.

"I don't know the how and I don't know the who, but Yamazoe's lawyer just showed up in the lobby demanding to speak to you."

"To me? Not his client?"

"It's not deGuzman. It's Jing Saifai."

Michael stopped cold. This was not only unusual, it was downright unheard of. It was a murder case. A salacious one due to the victim, but the press was done with it in a day. For one of the most powerful corporate attorneys in the city to roll up saying that she was now representing Yamazoe was madness.

Michael had no idea how someone like Saifai would've come to represent a man like Yamazoe any more than he knew how she'd known he was there interrogating him. She was a partner at a big white-shoe law firm, not a criminal defense attorney, much less someone who chased high-profile cases.

But who told her I was here? Michael wanted to find out more than anything.

He considered slipping out a side door but was more concerned with how that would look to Detective Whitehead and the other cops than Saifai. In the end he composed himself and headed out to greet her, hoping he could bull his way through any confrontation.

"How are you, Mr. Story?" Jing said from across the lobby the moment he walked through the bullpen door. She extended her hand and walked out, her heels clicking smartly on the tile, all clipped political aggression. "I don't believe we've met."

"Indeed. What can I do for you?"

"Not a thing!" she said. "My firm is taking over the defense of Mr. Yamazoe, and I'm here to see him."

Oh, I'm sure you are.

"You were just speaking to him, were you not?" she continued.

"I was," Michael said, deciding she must've been tipped off by someone in the department.

"Did he or did he not invoke his right to have an attorney present?"

"This was about another crime. LAPD hasn't even brought the case to the DA's yet, and I doubt I'd be assigned anyway."

It was a good lie. Jing saw through it like it was cellophane.

"What was the crime?"

"I can't say quite yet—"

"Oh, I think you can!" She smiled in a way that reminded Michael of why star athletes make such great motivational speakers. For a moment he was actually moved to want to make this person happy, if only to have that smile shine on him a little longer.

"Suffice it to say that Yamazoe has been on our radar for a long time. There are a number of open investigations that I believed he might be able to shed some light on for us."

"Okay then. I will still require a full transcript of the session to make sure that was the case."

"I'm afraid you'll need a court order for that," he replied lamely.

"Not a problem," she said, the smile now that of a shark seconds from consuming its prey.

———

Luis returned from Father Chang's funeral with more questions than he'd had before. But at least he now felt his view of the late priest was more well-rounded. Those closest to him not only believed in his innocence, they also cared deeply for him and mourned his loss as if he'd been a family member. It was only a prattling parish pastor who didn't seem to like Father Chang in the first place who'd had a bad word for him. Luis's instincts told him to put more stock in the estimation of the archbishop and the pair at the funeral.

When Luis finished teaching his classes for the day, he walked back to St. Augustine's and poked his head into the main office.

"Do you mind if I use your laptop?" he asked Erna.

"Go ahead," she replied. "I'm off to run some errands."

Luis took a seat and began searching the Internet for stories relating to Father Chang's crusades. There were plenty of articles, plenty of quotes, but if he was expecting the rhetoric of a fire-and-brimstone activist priest, he came up short. Sure, there were endless photographs of Chang appearing at this event or that alongside community leaders and organizers, but he was never at the microphone himself. And whenever a reporter quoted him, he never mentioned himself, only that he was there to listen to the views of others.

That's when Luis figured out what Chang had been doing. He was a presence, not an instigator. He legitimized the various events, marches, and rallies with his mere attendance while never suggesting even offhandedly that he was there representing the church or its interests. But time and time again there was his name next to the quotes—"Father Benedict Chang of St. Jerome's Chinese-American Catholic Church."

He was like some kind of guardian angel letting those in opposition know that they would be held to account. His quotes more often than not cited scripture. They weren't controversial passages, mostly a lot of "Whoever is generous to the poor lends to the Lord, and he will repay him for his deeds," or "The exercise of justice is joy for the righteous." But the insinuation was clear. Those he stood with were doing the Lord's work.

Luis took out a pad of paper and began to sort through the presumed villains in each case. There were corporations, the city, planning commissions, government officials, big-box retailers, and so on and so on and so on. Any number of people who didn't like being told no if there was a profit to be made. Only, it wasn't clear that if Father Chang was removed from the situation it would do anything at all.

He turned his attention to a handful of international stories that mentioned Chang. The articles detailed his visits to churches and Catholic communities overseas, places where Christians were often in the minority if not outright discriminated against, particularly in Asia. These were even less controversial than the ones in the local paper. In photo after photo Chang smiled as he stood near other priests and congregants in traditional clothing in large cities and small villages alike, always identified as a Chinese-American priest of the Los Angeles archdiocese.

It was all so innocuous. Father Chang's schedule for the past few years had been packed, but with things that were fairly above reproach. Was it some kind of cover? What if all those overseas trips had been somebody using him as a courier? That would explain the money, the possibility of an extra apartment, the need to kill him once he'd outlived his usefulness. What it didn't explain were the boy's words at the funeral or why he'd continued to keep up appearances back home, like attending that festival the night of his murder.

Who knew he was going to be there?

Now there was a question.

How had Yamazoe known Father Chang was going to return from something alone that Sunday night? He couldn't have been following him, could he have? He had been lying in wait. He *knew* where Father Chang was, just as he knew that it was late enough at the rectory that he wouldn't be chased off. It was the perfect window in which to murder a man. But if Chang had been as guarded as Pastor Siu-Tung seemed to imply, who would he have told, except perhaps Dr. Auyong and the young man?

Then he realized there was a way.

Luis opened a browser and went to his seldom-used e-mail account. He logged in, opened a new letter, and typed the briefest query he possibly could. He knew it would likely go ignored, as every other query he'd sent Miguel in recent months had, but he still had hope. He reread it quickly, considered deleting it altogether, then simply hit "Send."

———

Michael knew something was up by the time he reached the car. His phone was buzzing with multiple e-mails, texts, and voice mails. As this was hardly typical, he assumed it must be tied to his interview with Yamazoe. When he saw that several were from DA Rebenold's office, he called her back first.

"Let me explain," he said.

"You don't have to," the city's district attorney said. "This is too reckless even for you."

"I don't know what she told you, but—"

"She didn't have to tell me anything," Rebenold said, cutting him off. "I got a call from the office of the director of the FBI. I was informed that due to questions of citizenship in regards to Mr. Yamazoe and his daughter, the Chinese government has taken a strong interest in this case. Jing Saifai is their acting liaison."

Oh crap. Crap . . . crap . . . crap . . .

"They then went on to say that Yamazoe was being questioned at this very hour by a member of my staff. Do you have any idea how embarrassing it was to have to admit I had no idea what they were talking about?"

"I'm sorry, Deborah. I received time-sensitive information this morning regarding the case. To my knowledge the only other person who knew was Detective Whitehead. Someone from inside LAPD must've leaked the information to Saifai."

"What is it with you and international incidents, Michael?" DA Rebenold continued with a sigh. "Part of me wants to chalk it up to restlessness. You got a huge upswell of support from the Marshak case, but now that's calming down and you're looking for your next big victory. Well, this isn't it. The Chinese ambassador has requested—wait, no, *demanded*; that was the word he used—that you have no further contact with Mr. Yamazoe or those investigating the case. Do you understand?"

"What if I told you that the killing was a triad-ordered hit he took on to pay off gambling debts?" Michael stated evenly. "That there never was a daughter? That they're using the sexual abuse angle, as they know everyone'll buy it and won't look too deep? What if I told you that I got Yamazoe to admit to all of that, and the appearance of Jing Saifai at the division office only seems to confirm what has long been suspected about her—that she's a legal counsel to the Los Angeles triad and uses her political muscle to keep them from ever being prosecuted?"

There was a long pause. Michael tried to imagine how the DA would spin this.

"He said all of this to you?"

"He did."

"And he'll testify?"

"If we can rope in the Feds to get him some kind of protection, yes."

Another silence. "You know, they want me to suspend you."

"I'm sure. But if we can prove the LA triad was behind the murder of a local priest, we could suddenly get a toehold into one of the most entrenched and elusive organized crime outfits this side of the Mississippi. We might never get a chance like this again."

"All right," she said, as if finally realizing the potential political capital that could result. "Be in my office in ten."

———

"*This* is the house?" Jun asked as Tony led her inside. "It's wonderful!"

Tony knew she'd like it but didn't think her reaction would be that strong. As she flitted from window to window, taking in the sights, he could tell she was overjoyed.

"What's beyond those hills?" she asked, pointing to the eastern view out the back window.

"The San Fernando Valley," Tony replied. "Beyond that the Mojave Desert. After that? Las Vegas."

Jun smiled. "I've always wanted to see Las Vegas. Though I'm sure nothing there can compare to the opulence of Macau. Have you been, Mr. Qi?"

"No, I traveled the province so little when I was a boy," Tony said, shaking his head. "Leaving my village to come to Hong Kong was the first real jour—"

"No, silly!" Jun said, cutting him off. "Not Macau. *Las Vegas*. Have you been *there?*"

Tony admitted that he had. Jun demanded to hear all about it, clearly seeking stories of liberal excess. Without ever implying he took part, Tony reeled off tales of parties and events, show openings and galas, high-stakes gambling tournaments, and even Chen Jiang had to work hard to feign disinterest. She moved around, as if checking the different rooms for things to disapprove of, but was always in earshot.

Whenever he glanced at Archie, however, he saw a smug grin on the big man's face. It wasn't as if Tony didn't know why. The driver had likely attended as many gatherings as Tony described, but also as a member of someone's staff—hardly as the invited guest or bon vivant that Tony was painting for Jun.

"I wish I could go there on this trip, but I'd look absurd," Jun said, patting her belly. "When you're at home or going about the city you live in, you can dress however you like. But in a place like Las Vegas you want to look your best from the moment you wake up until you go the bed—and maybe even then, too!"

Tony found himself wondering who he'd have to be for someone like Jun, functionally a kept woman for a gangster, to want to be with him. He was no Kuo Kuang or Jim Jakey, wealthy businessmen with no morals. He'd known plenty of men like that. They regarded women as naturally inferior, something to possess and discard. Tony wanted an equal partnership like, strange as it was, the one he'd observed between Oscar de Icaza and Helen Story. They were ambitious. They had common goals. They complemented each other. Together they made a formidable team. That was the kind of relationship for him.

"Now that I'm through being an actress, I think I'd like to go into cosmetics," Jun was saying.

"As a model?" Tony asked.

Jun laughed merrily.

"No, as a businesswoman!" Jun corrected him. "I've seen how these companies push junk on women, mass-marketing inferior products and herding women into flashy mall shops. I'd individualize the customer experience. Your beautician would be like your hairdresser or doctor. As fashions change, you would come to trust this person, and they would guide your look over time. Nothing screams 'old woman' like someone holding on to something that hasn't worked for decades."

"If you're serious about it," Tony said, though he heard Chen Jiang stiffen in her seat, a noise that even he knew meant he must proceed with caution, "I know some people here in Los Angeles who work in that industry. These connections are ones I've made strictly in an official capacity through my hotel, so they're hardly personal and they owe me no favors. But if after the baby is born and you begin to establish yourself in Hong Kong—"

He was interrupted by a knock on the door. Jun's face was frozen. Tony could see immediately that he'd gone too far, had made too bald an attempt to curry favor, and that she was already mustering a firm you're-too-kind refusal that would close the door to further embarrassing back-and-forths like this one. The knock on the door just might be enough for Tony to save face and pretend he had said nothing.

"Mr. Qi?"

The man in the doorway was Dr. Martin Soong, dressed sharply in slacks and a tie. Tony eyed the younger man unhappily. The doctor was quick to smile and easygoing. He was also a doctor. If there was anyone Jun would actually be attracted to in this scenario, it would be him.

"Come on in, Dr. Soong," Tony said. "We're just getting acquainted with the new house."

Martin shook Archie's hand, warmly greeted Chen Jiang, who made an almost imperceptible head nod, and then bowed to Jun. She bowed back, then kissed him on the cheek.

"Welcome to my estate!" she exclaimed, indicating around. "It's something, isn't it?"

"Very much so," Martin agreed. "Tony outdid himself this time."

Martin glanced around for the nearest bedroom and pointed. "Shall we go in there for your checkup?"

"Of course," Jun replied, nodding.

Tony moved to the door to exit, but Jun hurried after him and took his hand. She pulled him close and gave him a peck on the cheek.

"Thank you so much for finding such a great house," she said just loud enough for Chen Jiang to hear before dropping her voice to a whisper. "And if you really know anyone in cosmetics, I'd be dying to meet them to explain just how we all could make a fortune back home."

She broke away, flashed her smile, and followed Martin into the bedroom.

We all. It was unambiguous.

"Good night, Archie," he said, patting the big man on the shoulder as he left.

Outside, the midday sun bathed the city in gold. Tony walked to his car, the impression of Jun's fingers still in his hand, her scent still in his nose. When his cell phone rang, he imagined that Jun had forgotten something, couldn't bear to be away from him for so many seconds. When he saw it was Billy Daai, however, he became all business.

"Hello, Billy. What can I do for you?"

"Hey, Tony. There's been some trouble. I need your help."

Tony was relieved. He hadn't forgotten his careless words from that morning. But Billy was calling him in need. Tony was more than happy for the chance to atone.

"Anything at all, Billy. Anything at all."

X

Luis was stunned. He didn't know what he expected to hear, but this wasn't it. "I don't know what to tell you," Michael said, his voice distant and harried, not helped by the fact he was on his car's speakerphone. "Sometimes these cases are downright impossible and it's nothing but dead ends, and then other times, like this one it seems, you get what you need early on and then it's just miles of paperwork from here until sentencing."

"I don't understand," Luis said, surprised. "He just . . . caved?"

"He did," Michael said. "That's the real world of criminals for you. The triad might've put the fear of God in him—no offense—but sometimes they go and rat on you anyway. It happens."

Luis remembered his first time behind bars as a young man. Detectives had sweated him for three days even though he was underage. He hadn't said one word about the gang he'd been affiliated with at the time. His reward? A vicious jumping-in initiation ceremony at the hands of his comrades and a full membership he rejected following the murder of his brother.

"It's too easy," Luis said. "They covered their tracks well. A lot of planning went into this. They're not going to let him live."

"No kidding," Michael said. "Which is why the DA immediately signed the order putting him into protective custody. He's already on the move. He'll be surrounded by armed deputies in an undisclosed location 24-7 from here on out. But just to make sure, they're going to swear him and begin the deposition process tonight."

"They'll use someone you don't expect."

There was silence on the other end of the line. Finally, Michael sighed. "Father? Can't you be happy about this? It is almost *impossible* to make a case against the Los Angeles triad. They're so protected and legit in all the right ways they're practically untouchable. But thanks to you we just might get a few of them on conspiracy to murder. That's the kind of thing that sends a message. Suddenly they don't look so monolithic. Makes finding witnesses who'll testify the next time that much easier. If that's not the Lord's work, I don't know what is."

"What was the motive?" Luis asked. "Why did they want Father Chang?"

"We don't know yet," Michael admitted. "The fact that their lawyer, Jing Saifai, showed up was our first real confirmation of their involvement. Yamazoe wasn't on the inside, or they wouldn't have used him. So, he's got no clue. Once we start to follow the money back, however, I'm sure we'll come up with something. Any more questions?"

Luis had plenty but didn't think he'd get the answers he wanted. There was one bugging him, however.

"The triad targeted Yamazoe not because he was a gambler but because they could establish a motive, since he was in Father Chang's parish. Do you know if anyone in the church might've helped the triad find their mark? Chang was not well liked in the parish, it seems."

Michael started to say something, then stopped himself. Luis figured he'd readied a quick reply, then realized Luis might have a point.

"That's a good question," Michael finally replied. "If I find out anything, you want me to tell you first or the police?"

"Don't you have to tell the police first?"

"We're partners, Father Chavez. It's the least I can do."

———

When Michael got off the phone with Luis, he called back Detective Whitehead, who'd rang every five minutes for the last half hour. He'd invited the DA's office in as a courtesy, but now they were lifting away his suspect to use in a conspiracy case. His frustration over not being a part of the decision-making process was palpable.

"I brought you in on this," Whitehead repeated for the fourth or fifth time. "I'm the lead detective. You're the guy I make look good in court. Hopefully. One day. But now I've got deputy sheriffs and the FBI and the Marshals Service pretending to treat me with deference while really looking for any way possible to shunt me to the side."

"We're all on the same team, Detective," Michael protested. "This isn't about credit, though you know the DA's office is all about shining a positive spotlight on the LAPD."

"I don't care about credit. This priest, it turns out, had a few friends in the community. Not business owners, not politicians really, but people from the neighborhood who come up to our officers and ask about the case. They liked him and don't buy the rumors about this daughter, and they're starting to hammer us about it. They want that tamped down before it becomes the story. You bury Yamazoe in some plea-bargaining cage for the next several months, and those stories don't get refuted. They become the facts. Help me out here. Let me at least make a statement."

"If it gets out that we're thinking this is some kind of hit, they'll know we didn't buy the cover story, and the real villains could go to ground," Michael said. "I'll see what I can do, but no promises."

There was a pause. "You'll see what you can do? Well, screw you, Michael Story."

The line went dead. Michael gave himself a once-over to see if he cared and came up dry. Trying to make everyone happy was a good way to send everyone home mad.

The car clock read 7:22, which meant he was only a little late. Traffic from downtown to the Palisades, usually a nightmare, had cooperated. He had forgotten all about his oldest daughter's science fair tonight until he'd gotten a text from Helen reminding him to come early, as there wouldn't be much parking. George R. Clark Elementary might have been one of the best public schools in the city, but as it was tucked into a tiny exclusive neighborhood among the highest property taxes in LA, the one thing it couldn't afford was enough land for a parking lot.

Michael finally found a spot eight blocks from the school. As he climbed out the car, his cell phone buzzed to announce a text. It was a selfie from Jillian that included her siblings and, in the background, Helen, with the caption, *Where are you?* He texted back that he was just parking and hurried down the sidewalk.

Things were stabilizing with Helen, he thought. The murder of his—he hated to call her his mistress—but the murder of *Annie*, the do-gooder lawyer who had first brought the Marshak human-trafficking case to his attention, had led him to reassess aspects of his life. Part of that meant being more attentive toward Helen. Though she wasn't all that receptive to him in the bedroom, something he chalked up to her being tired from balancing her job and the kids, as well as the waning libido of a woman approaching forty, she did seem happier these days. Calmer. More centered and at peace with herself and him. There were other ways to be close than just sex.

He was almost certain that Helen didn't know about his affair. Still, he performed little acts of contrition and penance, asked for or not. Some of that included showing up at events like Jillian's science fair even though he had to work early, as he knew it made things that much easier for Helen, who then wouldn't have to juggle three kids.

He plucked the phone back out of his pocket and looked at her photo. Helen was beautiful and smart and a great mom. Her family was wealthy, and one day they'd inherit the kind of fortune that would keep them comfortable for life. He'd won the lottery marrying her.

A silhouette approached on the sidewalk. Michael pocketed the phone as he recognized the man as Jeff Lambert, the father of one of his daughter's classmates, who worked as a political consultant. From time to time he'd cornered Michael to take his temperature on political matters, but Michael was in a hurry tonight. He accelerated, readying an excuse, only for Jeff to stop short and block his way.

"Just the man I was looking for," Jeff said, extending a hand. "How are you, Michael?"

Michael shook Jeff's hand. "Good. Late for the science fair."

"I'll only take a second of your time then," Jeff replied, gripping Michael's hand. "Heard you had quite a day."

"I don't know what you've heard," Michael said, pulling away, "but if I know my office, it's probably two parts hogwash, three parts bunk."

"At first we thought it was coming from Deborah herself," Jeff said, scoffing. "Not that it'll do her any good. That ship has sailed."

We?

As if confusion was the very reaction he hoped to reap, Jeff smiled. "It's about next year's election," Jeff said. "Deborah's been looking for ways to impress us into supporting her reelection bid. But we've made our decision."

Now Michael was confused. He hadn't thought twice about next year's political cycle. The mayor was as strong as ever and was a shoo-in for reelection. There were no challengers to the DA's post that Michael knew about, despite the fact that the district attorney's office was supposed to be a nonpartisan position.

"What're we really talking about here?" Michael asked.

"The opposition is quietly floating Antonio Ramos, which is about as good as announcing he's going to be their guy."

Michael knew the name. Ramos was the DA in Orange County. He operated at the pleasure of local potentates, which included any number of big businesses and wealthy political donors. Ramos liked headlines, but he also liked being the sheriff of Disneyland. Michael had never heard even one word about Ramos having political ambitions on the LA side of the 605.

"He's a joke," Michael said. "No one's heard of him. He's never done anything. If you think Deborah wouldn't wipe the floor with him in a general election, you're insane."

"If he was on his own or Deb was a decade younger, maybe, but the barons of the OC want one of their own in the governor's mansion. They've decided that road passes through the LA DA's office, and Ramos is the horse to back. They're going to paper the town with his name. Massive TV buy, a poster on every signpost, endless public appearances. They're going to have him at Dodgers games, Laker games, Galaxy games, Angels games—"

"Good thing Deb's a Clippers fan."

"This isn't a joke!" Jeff said, still smiling. "We can't match their spending, especially for a nonpartisan spot. And we've done the polling. Deborah could lose, and that destabilizes us all over the city. We can't risk it."

"So, what do you want from me?" Michael asked. "Are you looking for recommendations?"

"No, man. We want *you*."

Michael laughed out loud. "I'm not just being humble here, but you really have the wrong guy. I don't have the experience. I've never run for office. I'd be the youngest and least qualified in the city's history."

"That can be handled, even used to your advantage. What we can't handle is losing the DA's office. And what our polls tell us is that thanks to that human-trafficking case, your media profile is already through the roof. We pour a little fuel on that fire, particularly in the form of this triad business, and the election's yours. And don't worry about Deb. Gene Cuellear is retiring next year. We're offering her the Thirty-Seventh Rep District as her consolation prize. Makes it look like Congress has always been her ambition."

When Michael said nothing, Jeff leaned in close. "You think you're not ready. That's great. That'll play. By the time anybody's ready for this it's generally too late. In your case you could be up against a powerful incumbent or already out of that office after Ramos sees what a comer you are. Just think about it, okay?"

Jeff released Michael and moved away.

"My answer won't change," Michael said.

Jeff laughed. "Talk it over with Helen. Call me tomorrow."

Michael watched Jeff disappear, then thought to commit all this to memory for some future interview or memoir.

When did you know your life was about to change, Governor Story? Oh, you know, I was on my way to my daughter's science fair one autumn night . . .

———

Life for Shu Kuen Yamazoe had never been so exciting. He'd been a gambler his entire life, getting to the point he lived for the high and nothing else. That is, until Chunling was brought into his life. As he'd told the deputy DA, they'd become friends. She snapped him out of his addiction so fast that he couldn't quite believe the person he'd been the week before could've inhabited the skin he did now.

He didn't even want to think what had happened to her. It was like a cruel joke. Convince him that maybe he wasn't so disposable after all, then prove that he was. He knew as soon as the DA walked in that he'd give up the triad. If they'd given him some sense of hope, some belief that he'd see her again one day, if only to go to the planetarium, visit a farm out in the Valley, or even ride a rented pony in Griffith Park, he would've toed the line forever.

But they'd miscalculated and taken her away for good. He didn't care what happened to himself now.

What he hadn't expected was for the feeling of his old vice to return. Since he'd been dropped off in front of St. Jerome's, he'd been waiting for the bullet to hit. No, *daring* it to hit. He constantly bet against himself. Would the cops shoot him? Was it better to simply kill himself? Did the triad have a shooter off-site who would do the job for him to make sure his mouth stayed shut?

But it never happened. He was printed, photographed, and booked. The lawyer came and went. He was interrogated by detectives. He was placed in a cell. Guards changed shifts. Prisoners passed him in the halls. He expected every pair of eyes that glanced his way to be those of his assassin, but it didn't happen.

Which was why he talked to Michael Story. He knew this feeling would only get worse. He'd bet against himself, calculate down to the second the likely moment of his death, then roll the dice again if it didn't happen. Talking to the deputy DA meant peace of mind. Meant a life sentence still, but hopefully one where on occasion he'd be called into a courtroom, made to give a deposition or testimony. There'd be something to do as opposed to sitting in a cell staring at a wall waiting for any anomaly in his day he could gamble on.

"Prisoner, extend your hands through the slot," came a voice on the other side of his cell door.

He'd been expecting this. He was going to be moved. He rose and went to the door as the slot was opened. He pushed his hands through, and handcuffs were placed around his wrists.

"Step back."

Yamazoe complied. The door was opened, and two sheriff's deputies entered and placed his ankles in restraints as well before chaining them up through a belt and to his wrists.

"Wow," Yamazoe said, expecting commiseration.

"Quiet, prisoner," one of the deputies said before coming up to eye level. "You shot a priest, man. Ain't no Chatty Cathy-ing here."

Yamazoe nodded. The deputy DA had barely mentioned the fact that he was a killer, focusing almost solely on his gambling and manipulation by the triad. Yamazoe liked feeling understood, even in those small moments. Once the story was out, he figured the guards would treat him differently.

"Prisoner. Step out of the cell and move down the hall."

His inner gambler came out again. He looked to each cell door and each deputy, wondering which would be the one that took him out. Would it be one of the escorts? Would it be the one who buzzed them through the magnetic locked doors into the booking area? Would it be the older deputy seated nearby, who seemed to be waiting to come on shift? Would it be somebody on the other side of one of the three doors in the room?

The older deputy rose and switched out the handcuffs and ankle restraints with a new set, handing the old ones back to the guards. The right cuff was actually sticky, either from something spilled on it or, Yamazoe thought, grimacing, the sweat of a previous prisoner.

"Loading out prisoner," the deputy said.

There was another buzz, and the outer door opened. Yamazoe held his breath. It was as if he were in a haunted house on Halloween and a ghost was sure to jump out from behind the door.

He walked the short distance from the jail to a black van with the symbol of the sheriff's department on it. The back door was slid open by the driver.

"Prisoner, step up into the van."

Yamazoe did so, though his foot slipped. He felt dizzy, as if the cuffs were cutting off the circulation to his brain instead of just his hands and feet.

"Sorry," he offered, though no one replied.

He raised his foot enough to gain purchase in the back and swung himself onto the row of seats. The driver indicated for him to sit in the middle. The deputy leaned in and now removed the ankle restraints and handcuffs in order for the driver to lock him into the restraints built into the van.

It felt bizarrely inefficient to Yamazoe, but he figured there was a reason. The older deputy carried the cuffs and restraints back into the station, and the driver got behind the wheel.

"Short ride tonight, but a longer one in the morning," the driver said. "Taking you to a courthouse around the corner to ask a couple of initial questions. That'll be about an hour. Then you're heading down to Laguna Niguel for the next couple of days while everyone gets organized. You behave, this'll be easy on all of us. You don't, and you'll quickly find out the hundred little ways we can make your life hell. We good?"

When the driver didn't hear an answer, he turned around in his seat. Yamazoe's tongue, already turning from purple to black, hung from his mouth as his eyes bulged from their sockets. The veins in his neck looked ready to pop.

By the time the driver was out of his seat and around to the back of the van, Yamazoe was dead.

———

Luis sat up in bed. His pillow was soaked with sweat. He tried to remember what his dream was about as he reached for the phone and checked the time.

He's dead.

The thought struck him as if blasted from a loudspeaker.

He's dead.

He texted Michael Story. If there was no response, maybe he was crazy. But he knew Michael would be among the first they'd call. A message came back a second later, a confirmation of what Luis already knew.

Yes, he's dead. No, we don't know how. Somebody got to him.

That this ended the communication suggested to Luis that Michael's night was going far worse than Luis's. But that was when he remembered the rest of his dream. Or more accurately, the second part of the thought.

He's dead. And many will follow.

PART II

XI

"Goodness me, Father," Whillans exclaimed as Luis approached him in the chapel at daybreak. "You look like something the cat dragged in. You know you're not supposed to look worse than me, right?"

Luis took in the frail figure, this man he'd thought would be his spiritual guide for years to come, and dropped his gaze.

"That better be self-pity," Whillans said, feigning annoyance. "If it's me you're feeling sorry for, I might have to kick your ass."

Luis scoffed, eyeing him ruefully. "Somebody murdered Father Chang's killer while in custody."

"Another prisoner?"

Michael had called Luis once he'd gotten more information. The working theory was some kind of poison on a pair of handcuffs. But when they'd searched the officer whose handcuffs they were, including tossing his locker and car, they came up bone dry.

"Doubtful. They were suspicious of one of the corrections officers, but that's how the triad seems to work. They never authorize a murder without providing law enforcement with a suspect."

Whillans put a hand on Luis's shoulder. Though he appeared almost infirm, his grip was as strong as ever.

"The Lord has called you to the priesthood, not to the rank of detective. You can do what you can do, but no more. You may one day understand how you fit into his greater plan, or you may not. What's important is that you allowed him to guide you in this case, and justice may be served."

"But a man has died because of me."

"Yes, he has," Whillans admitted. "But not before he confessed his crimes. And you don't need me to tell you how important that part is on any path to redemption."

Luis didn't. Whillans indicated the door.

"Ready for our field trip?"

Though Whillans had managed to keep the severity of his deteriorating condition from the archdiocese, he knew it was only a matter of time before a parishioner, layperson, or visiting clergy passed word back. All it would take was a simple "Is Pastor Whillans quite all right?" and some interfering agent from the archbishop's office might swoop in with pronouncements about getting Whillans "the best care," and he'd be gone. Such an intervention would likely try to exclude Bridgette, whom Whillans was almost entirely reliant upon, and he wouldn't have that.

So whenever they left St. Augustine's for his biweekly chemotherapy treatments at Good Samaritan Hospital, Luis was careful to take Whillans out a side door and straight into a waiting car. This way as few people as possible would see Whillans in his pre-chemo fasting condition. Though with his dazed expression, hollow cheeks, and skin becoming more like parchment by the day, it wasn't a secret that could be kept much longer.

"How's your sermon coming?" Whillans asked once they were in the car.

"It's not," Luis said. "I've been working on this Father Chang case."

Whillans nodded with only faint disapproval. "I understand, but I'm wondering if you do. I know you see working on these cases might make you feel better about the crimes in your own past, but I also think that's too simplistic. Whether you admit it or not, I think you miss that life, and this gives you a window in allowing you to stay with us the rest of the time."

Luis shrugged. It wasn't something he thought about, and he wasn't happy that Whillans brought it up so casually. This was a life he'd put behind him and had nothing to do with the present.

"I'll finish the sermon," Luis said. "It won't be as good as yours from this past week, but it'll be better than whatever your first one was."

Whillans laughed. It was a merry sound until it was strangled off by choking coughs.

"That wouldn't be hard," Whillans retorted. "Particularly if you knew the extent to which I was making it up as I went. I researched and researched, read and read, and took them on a tour through scripture like they'd never seen. It was when I learned to pray first and say what my heart already knew that I became worth a damn as a priest. What do you know right now about Saint Peter Claver?"

"He was from Spain, he came to Colombia, and he baptized hundreds of thousands of slaves brought over from Africa. He saw slavery as wicked, as did the papacy at the time. He took it as his mission on earth to convert as many slaves as he could."

"You left out the part about him dying penniless and physically abused for years by an ex-slave hired to see after his care."

Luis shook his head. "Never believed that part. Felt too much like your typical racist demagoguery. 'Look what a mighty servant of Christ he was. He could've chided this ex-slave, but he chose to endure it instead. What a good soldier.'"

Whillans eyed Luis with such a look that Luis feared he might've overstepped. He hadn't meant to sound so cynical.

"My, my, Father Chavez," Whillans said. "With priests like you around, maybe the church really will survive the next thousand years. That is, if you don't leave it first."

When they arrived at the hospital, Luis parked, jogged to the entrance to retrieve a wheelchair, and rolled it back to the car. Whillans was already flagging from hunger and couldn't go much farther under his own steam.

"Thank you, Father," Whillans said, settling into the chair. "Now let's get this over with."

The fifth-floor oncology wing was as silent as the chapel at midnight no matter how many people were there taking their drip. Whillans had told Luis he'd originally thought it would be social, everyone in the same boat, but he soon found that everyone kept to themselves.

"There are Stage Ones who don't want to imagine they belong in the same room as the Stage Twos, Stage Twos who are terrified of looking at the Stage Threes or Fours and glimpsing their future, then Stage Fours who are clearly going through the motions for the benefit of their families. They're ready to die."

"And you?" Luis had asked.

"I'm the guy willing to make a four-hour commitment in hopes it buys me an extra five hours of life. Five hours I can spend with Bridgette, the congregation, with you, and, simply, in the enjoyment of living in God's miraculous creation here on earth."

Luis had no idea what he'd do when Whillans was gone.

A nurse approached to take charge of the pastor. Luis leaned down to him, inhaling the familiar scent of Whillans's aftershave. His own father had never worn aftershave, so he figured this smell would be one he'd only ever associate with the pastor.

"You'll be okay?" he asked Whillans.

The pastor held up a battered old copy of *Ulysses.*

"Just getting to the play script," Whillans said. "Been saving it. Funniest part of the whole book."

Luis nodded. When he'd first met Whillans, the priest had told him that everything he needed to know about God was in the Bible, and everything he needed to know about man in Joyce's *Ulysses*. So far he hadn't managed to get past the third or fourth page.

Someday.

With one last glance back at Whillans, Luis headed down the hall toward the parking lot. He had just enough time to get back to St. John's before his first class. Bridgette was the one who'd have to deal with the hard post-session nausea Whillans would endure when she picked him up four hours later. Luis said a quiet prayer for God to overlook the pastor and Bridgette's romantic transgressions and help them through these hard times.

He'd just said a mental "amen" when a doctor ran past him. A second person, this one some kind of administrator in business attire, followed a moment later. Everyone in the hall looked at everyone else for an explanation. A phone buzzed at a nurse's station. The nurse blanched as she listened to the voice on the other end.

Luis had to get to his class. He wasn't a doctor any more than he was a detective.

So why was the voice in his head practically demanding he follow them downstairs?

Knowing he would regret it, Luis turned on his heel and headed for the stairwell he'd seen the administrator disappear into. He'd waited too long to hear fading footsteps so knew he'd have to try the door to each floor. The fourth-floor hallway was a desert. The third floor was busy but there were no signs of alarm.

The second floor, however, was all alarm. Orderlies were closing patients and visitors off into rooms. Security guards were in the hall, as were multiple doctors. Everyone wore face masks. Luis exited the stairwell just as two orderlies, also in face masks, rushed a similarly masked woman on a gurney to the one open door in the hallway.

"In here!" a nurse commanded.

The orderlies hurried the woman inside. As they did, Luis caught her wild-eyed gaze, which became fixed on him. She tried to speak but was gone before she could get the words out.

Luis moved determinedly down the hall after her. The doctors were already consulting each other as he pushed past to the door.

"Father? You can't go in there!" a nurse barked even as he moved inside. "Father! For your own health, please step back."

"She needs to see me," he said simply.

"Security!" the nurse exclaimed, but Luis was already through the door.

The tiny room was packed with people. The woman on the gurney was being transferred to an examination bed at the same time that an isolation tent was being erected around it. A nurse attempted to affix two small disk-shaped sensors to the woman's body to remotely monitor vital signs, but the patient kept thrashing around.

"Should we sedate her?" a nurse asked.

"No," one of the doctors said. "We have to stabilize her first. If that's even possible."

Through the cacophony of overlapping voices, Luis could pick out the woman's. She was crying and calling out for her son in Spanish. Her voice was ragged and wet. Her words simple and repetitious.

"Padre?" the woman asked.

Luis glanced back to the doorway. A security guard stood there now, but as soon as he glimpsed the chaos inside he took a step back. He wasn't wearing a mask. Luis ignored him and moved toward the bed.

"I'm here," he said quietly in Spanish.

Anyone in the room who hadn't noticed his presence now turned to him in surprise. The woman's eyes found him again and she began to settle. Though the first instinct of the medical staff had been to kick Luis out, now they took advantage of the quiet beat to examine the patient. A cuff was wrapped around her upper arm, her blood pressure taken, and an oxygen mask brought down over her face.

"My son," she said between gasps. "My son needs the doctor now. Please."

The woman's skin color had gone ashy and white. Her eyes were milky, and mucus ran from underneath the mask. A tremor shook her body. But still her eyes beckoned Luis closer.

"Please find my son," she repeated. "You have to save him. Please, Father. Help him."

One of the doctors, as if finally recognizing the danger to the priest, nodded to an orderly, who took Luis's arm.

"I'm sorry, sir, but you cannot be in here."

"Where's your son?" Luis asked, reaching for the woman's hand, though he was blocked by the isolation tent wall.

"He's with his babysitter, Mrs. Gomez," she managed to say as she struggled to breathe. "Our doctor will know what to do. Please find him. Take him to her."

A nurse who'd been listening to this exchange turned to Luis.

"Tell her she needs to tell *us* where he is. She might be right. He might be in serious danger."

"Tell these doctors where he is—" Luis began.

"No!" the woman cried. "There'll be police. *You* find him. *You*."

Luis was about to reply when two masked security guards came in the door behind him, grabbed his arms, and led him out of the room.

"Are you crazy, Father?" one of them asked. "A stunt like that can get you dead *quick*."

XII

If there was anything truly unexpected Michael had learned from his beat as a deputy DA, it was that the human body was a monstrous thing. Standing in the morgue looking down at Shu Kuen Yamazoe's corrupted form, his skin blackened and his face so bloated and puffed out to be virtually unrecognizable, he felt this maxim was being proven all over again.

"What happened to him?"

Michael glanced to DA Rebenold as she stood on the other side of the metal table, eyeing the corpse.

"The human body is ultimately a very toxic environment," the county medical examiner, Dr. de la Loza, said. "Once it stops functioning, gases and fluids build up, everything becomes compressed, and, well, in cases like this you get extreme bloating of sacs, membranes, and even the protrusion of the tongue and bulging of the eyes. Usually that takes days, however. In this case it was a matter of hours."

Michael's eyes traveled down to Yamazoe's wrist. The black festering ring was as telltale a sign of where the toxin had been introduced as a scorched plug after a house fire.

"What did this?" Rebenold asked.

"Nothing," the medical examiner said. "As far as the autopsy shows, there is no sign of a single obvious external factor in Yamazoe's body. The poison relied on his own internal chemistry to start this chain reaction. It makes you wonder how many times it gets misdiagnosed as some kind of overdose, heart attack, or extreme allergic reaction."

Nah, I'm perfectly comfortable not wondering that at all.

The medical examiner could see that Rebenold wanted to be alone with Michael and found something else to busy herself with.

"I signed the transfer order," Rebenold said softly. "It was as explicit as I could make it without calling even more attention to the case. I was worried they'd get him in the courthouse, which is why I had them convene at night. How did they know?"

Michael eyed his boss. She was taking it pretty hard. He wondered if she was still holding out hope that her reelection possibilities could get back on track with this case. She must know now that it was all over.

"Did anything show up on the cameras?" Michael asked.

"Not a damn thing. The deputy used his own cuffs. We're pretty sure the poison was applied when he was at home. We checked the cuffs of everyone else on shift, and his were the only ones that had been tampered with. They clearly didn't care if he died, too."

"No," Michael said.

"'No' what?" Rebenold asked.

"Wearing latex gloves is practically procedure these days for anyone that has direct contact with inmates. They must've known that. He wouldn't have actually touched the poison unless he had a reason to take the cuffs out before he went on shift."

Rebenold stared at him. In that moment Michael felt her taking his measure. He was the better investigator of the two. He had the instincts.

"Any word from the Chinese government?" he asked.

"Of course!" Rebenold said, throwing up her hands. "There are already endless newspaper articles filled with speculation and quotes about the 'tragic situation,' selling Yamazoe's 'suicide' as an 'honorable man acknowledging his guilt.' They're talking him up like he's a hero, a man of great sacrifice avenging a crime against his family by a vile Western priest."

"Jeez."

"But you know the best part? The detail that won't ever come out really but will keep me awake for years to come?"

Michael waited to hear it.

"A Hong Kong paper was among the first to run the story online. It hit about twenty minutes after we announced the death to the press. There was a quote by some minor government functionary expressing sympathy for Yamazoe's family and how his suicide restored the honor of his name after the murder."

"Random."

"Right, but it was very explicit, very thought-out. So I searched for the guy online. It turned out that he's one of those types that's drawn to a television camera like a moth to a flame. He was, in fact, on a talk show the entire time, from the announcement until his quote ran."

"Live? Not pretaped?" Michael asked.

"Live. If anyone asks, I'm sure they'll say his office provided the quote, not him. But he has deep ties to the Hong Kong triad. He must've known what was about to happen. And if he knew, a lot of people knew. I'll never be able to prove it, but I'll never not believe it." Father Chavez had said something like this about a misdeed of Michael's not long ago. Michael thought he'd even used the exact same words.

"You talked to Jeff Lambert last night," Rebenold said.

It wasn't a question. Michael looked over at Rebenold to see if she was hunting his face for a lie, but she wasn't looking at him. He knew she'd be able to tell from his voice anyway.

"I told him no," Michael said.

Rebenold scoffed and turned to him. "Look, I was initially pissed off that they made the decision without consulting me," Rebenold said. "It was an ambush, it couldn't have happened in a vacuum, so I started looking around for who might have been on it. For a time I thought that included you."

"I had no—"

Rebenold raised a hand to silence him. "I know. But once I realized the fix was in and I was out, the idea of moving to DC began to reveal its appeal. Burt has family back there. Baltimore. Frederick. And there's nothing worse than hanging around when everyone's waiting for you to show yourself to the door."

Michael said nothing. He didn't necessarily care what Rebenold had to say about all this, but he knew better than to do anything but let her say her piece.

"So, if you magically 'think about it some more' and decide to run, you'll have my full support. Cool?"

Michael hadn't expected this. When he'd postulated the various scenarios that ended up with him on the election trail, one of the big what-ifs was how it would look to the public if his former boss didn't endorse him, much less campaign for him. Now, if she was out there waving signs and giving speeches, this just might work.

"I appreciate it, but I don't know if I'm ready. What do you think I should do?"

Rebenold laughed so loud and with such vicious incredulity that Michael wished he could tuck himself into one of the morgue's cold chambers.

"You're going to have to do a lot better than that if you want to win a political election, Michael," she chided. "Your silence was enough. Trying to ingratiate yourself when you already know damn well you're going to run is just déclassé. Make this all about you on your own time, Michael."

With that, Rebenold exited the postmortem examination room. Michael took one last look at Yamazoe's body, plucked his cell phone out of his pocket, and dialed a number.

"Yes, Mr. Lambert's office, please. Thank you."

———

Luis was escorted from the sick woman's bedside directly into an isolation room of his own. A security guard was stationed outside.

"You're being quarantined for your own good," a nurse told him. "We don't think there was any exposure, but part of this is because you were a real jackass back there. Got it?"

"Got it," Luis said.

As soon as he was alone, he took out his phone and ran the name he'd seen on the paramedic's form: Esmeralda Carreño.

For a moment he thought he'd come across the wrong person. The woman whose Facebook, Instagram, and LinkedIn pages came up was a larger person who looked about twenty years younger than the woman in the isolation tent. But then he recognized the eyes, and it horrified him even more. How quickly had she disintegrated?

Beyond the photos and a résumé, there wasn't much to go on. No address, no son's name, no link to a Mrs. Gomez. He wasn't sure what he expected, but he had less than nothing to go on. He wished he'd waited to see if someone brought in her purse or ID, but that might've been risking a call to the police.

He had tried to make his case to the two security guards on the way to the isolation room, but they weren't having it.

"If she's got a sick kid out there, the cops'll take care of it," said one of the guards. "You don't understand. Two days ago we started getting weird calls like this one. People who shouldn't be getting this sick from what looks like a summer flu are dying."

"What're you talking about?" Luis asked.

The guard shrugged. "My girl is on the night shift here. She said people are talking. Doctors have been told to look for certain symptoms. They're not letting the information go wide, because they know it'll start a panic. But something's going on. You saw how fast those masks went on in there."

Luis had, but he hadn't thought much of it. It was a hospital. People were sick. Masks seemed smart. Whatever.

But once he was in the room alone, he couldn't think like that. Ms. Carreño had found him, had asked *him* to do something for her. She obviously knew she was dying. Her only thoughts were for her son. This was not something he could take lightly. God wouldn't have put it in front of him if he'd meant for his priest to look the other way.

So Luis raised his phone and dialed a number he'd probably called three dozen times in the past two weeks alone. He prayed the voice mail wouldn't be full when it clicked over. When it beeped, he spoke as quickly and as plainly as possible.

"This is a matter of life and death. Not mine. A woman at Good Samaritan named Esmeralda Carreño was just brought in at death's door. She's worried that her son is infected, too. He's at a 'Mrs. Gomez's house.' That's all I have. I'm afraid that if he doesn't get to a doctor soon, he may end up here, too."

There was so much else he wanted to say, but he knew better. He hung up and hoped for the best.

For the next half hour Luis alternated between praying and searching the websites of local LA news outlets for word on the other deaths. He found nothing to substantiate what the security guard had said. But that didn't mean anything.

When his phone rang, the caller ID read 310-111, not even a real number. He answered immediately.

"Miguel," Luis said.

"The son's name is Federico," said a voice, distant and flat. "Mrs. Gomez is Abigail Gomez of 3432 Sierra Street in Montecito Heights." Then he gave a phone number.

As there was no paper or pen in the isolation room, Luis put the phone on speaker and quickly typed the number into his notepad.

"Thank you for this," Luis said. "I really appreciate it."

The silence that followed went on for so long that Luis thought Miguel might've hung up. He wouldn't have blamed him. But then he heard the young man shift his weight.

"Are you still there?" Luis asked.

Miguel said nothing. Luis pressed on.

"I sent you an e-mail about the murder of a priest. Somebody paid off his killer. I think it was the LA triad. I was wondering if you could look into any bank records or—"

The line went dead. Luis cursed himself for using this opportunity to speak to Miguel for something like a case rather than to find out how the young man was doing. Pastor Whillans was wrong. He was failing the young Higuera boy every chance God provided him.

Luis dialed the number Miguel had given him for Mrs. Gomez. She picked up, thankfully, after two rings.

"Bueno?"

In Spanish, Luis identified himself as a priest, explained where he was, and quietly informed Mrs. Gomez about what had happened. He expected perhaps hysterics, but she was cool and collected. He realized that this wasn't likely her first time dealing with a tragedy.

"I will call the boy's father right now and tell him what you said," Mrs. Gomez replied. "It should be him that informs his son."

"Yes, I agree."

"He's going to have to be a man now," she said. "His grandfather passed only a couple of days ago, too."

Alarm bells went off in Luis's head.

"Had he been sick?"

126

"Not at all," Mrs. Gomez replied. "He was a hard worker. Then one day he went to bed and didn't get out. It sounds like that's what happened to his daughter, too. Do you think they had the same illness?"

The thought sent a chill down Luis's spine. He needed to tell one of the doctors in the hospital.

"Who's the boy's doctor? Was it Esmeralda's doctor, too?"

"Oh, she's everyone's doctor," Mrs. Gomez said. "The whole neighborhood goes to her or her clinic. Hang on. I've got the number on the refrigerator."

Mrs. Gomez stepped away from the phone. Luis could hear cartoons in the background and pictured the unsuspecting Federico enjoying the last moments of innocence his life would know. He said a silent prayer for the boy and then added Miguel.

God, please be a guide to the motherless sons.

"Ah, I have the number right here," Mrs. Gomez said, returning to the phone.

She read it off. Luis again typed it into his phone.

"And the name?"

"Dr. Susan Auyong. She's in San Gabriel."

There it is again, Luis thought, *the everlasting proof of the Almighty's hand.*

"SARS?" Tony hissed into the phone. "Are you kidding me? Who's saying there's a SARS outbreak? That's the kind of thing that makes it into the news."

"There's some emergency directive from the FAA and the CDC that just hit," Shen Mang said quietly, the noise of the airport in the background. "They're trying not to panic anyone. But there have apparently been three deaths already. They're now testing other suspicious deaths from the last twenty-four hours or so."

Tony didn't know what to think. There were flu outbreaks, the measles outbreak tied to the antivaccination crowd. He'd even heard of the occasional listeria or scarlet fever epidemic. But SARS was a boogeyman akin to Ebola or bird flu. People sat up and took notice.

"Right now they're just talking about posters for incoming passengers, but there'll also be screenings for anyone coming in from an Asian country or carrying an Asian passport. If you have anyone arriving in the next few weeks, you're going to have to get word to them of what they can and can't say to Homeland Security, or they'll be pulled aside and really questioned."

Just when things were starting to look up, too.

"Keep me informed," Tony said. "If I don't hear from you by this evening, I'll call back."

"You got it, Mr. Qi."

Tony hung up and glanced around the office for solutions. He knew in an instant what a SARS outbreak could mean for both of his businesses and those of his brethren. The losses could be staggering.

He had to get out in front of it.

Picking the phone back up, he dialed the cell of the hotel's general manager, Garth Rinker. It was the middle of a workday, so Tony figured he was on the links at the Hillcrest Country Club around the corner.

"Sir? It's Qi. I need to put something on your radar."

Twenty minutes and several brief conference calls later, the hotel's corporate office in New York had confirmed with the Los Angeles city government that a press conference announcing the quarantine of patients with SARS-like symptoms would begin momentarily. The crisis communications group they had on retainer was looped in, and a strategy was outlined in broad strokes.

"When SARS hit Toronto, the losses to the hotel business were in the tens of millions," said one crisis manager. "I think with the proper response we can greatly reduce our exposure to something like that. In the short term you need to tell your front-end managers like Mr. Qi that the staff needs to lead by example. Guests are going to have questions immediately. We're not going to have all the answers. What we can provide is calm."

"A good thing we have Qi in place then," Rinker said. "Nobody's calmer in a storm than he is."

Tony beamed. "Thank you, sir."

"All right," the crisis manager said. "The press conference is getting underway. Let's all watch and circulate questions. Mr. Qi, please keep us in the loop as directly as possible. We'll help you with any responses or special cases that arise. And when it comes to cancellations there'll be a lot of reactionary ones, and we have to just let that go. The better we handle things on that end, the better they'll feel about coming back when this all blows over."

Everyone hung up. Tony unmuted the television he had on across the room as a man in a gray suit with thinning hair was introduced by no less a personage than the mayor of Los Angeles as a representative from the CDC.

Why did it have to be SARS? Tony fretted.

Though it stood for something else entirely, Tony didn't know a person who didn't think the SA stood for "South Asian" the way the ME in MERS stood for "Middle East." Because it was thought to have come from Asia, it might as well have.

"SARS is contagious only through direct contact with bodily fluids, such as mucus or other respiratory secretions emitted during sneezing or coughing from an infected individual," the CDC rep on the television was saying. "Washing your hands and avoiding contact—"

Tony's cell phone rang and he lowered the volume on the TV. He figured it was his general manager calling him back. It turned out to be an assistant to Wanquan Yang, the San Gabriel Valley's Dragon Head.

"There's going to be an emergency meeting tonight. Your attendance is mandatory."

"I'll be there," Tony said.

As photos of Esmeralda and César Carreño, Rabih Chaumon, and then a fourth victim, a five-year-old girl named Meredith Boyers, flashed on the screen, Tony sank into his chair. If the bosses were already calling an emergency meeting, it might be worse than he knew. If SARS in Toronto hurt the hotel business that bad, what about all the businesses that kept the hotels supplied? And Asian-owned businesses in general?

He thought about this for a long moment. But then a plan—a wide-sweeping, almost mad but amazingly complete plan—formed in his mind.

He grabbed his cell phone and made what he hoped would be the most important call of his life.

XIII

"You're very lucky, Father," a doctor, who'd introduced herself as Dr. Sohmer, chided as she examined Luis. "You never touched her. You weren't masked, but that hardly matters with SARS, unless she sneezed or coughed directly into your face."

"I'm in the clear?" Luis asked.

"I've learned to never say never, but there's another matter at play here," she said. "The media knows there was a priest who ministered to a very sick woman at personal risk. As we let people know about how SARS spreads, using you as an example of someone who had safe contact is helpful."

"I apologize for all that. I'm not sure what came over me."

"Of course you are," the doctor said. "Everybody in the room saw. It was compassion. I'm sure you converted more than your share in that moment. Did you find the son she mentioned?"

"I did."

The doctor's eyes widened a little. "And?"

"The boy's father is taking him to the doctor immediately."

She clasped his hands together. "That was a very good thing you did. Thank you."

Luis listened attentively as the doctor proceeded to give him a list of symptoms and informed him that if he felt any of them, even ones he assumed were born from suggestion, he should come back in. She then told him he was free to go.

But as he went to the door, she moved to him tentatively.

"Will you maybe pray for us? Say a blessing or whatever it is you do? This could be nothing, an isolated incident, or it could be very bad for a lot of people. We don't know yet."

Luis nodded. He blessed the doctor and her hands. He blessed the hospital. He prayed for the other doctors, nurses, and orderlies. Then the two of them prayed against the disease.

As Luis made his way to the parking lot a few minutes later, he passed an orderly pushing a frail old woman in a wheelchair. She glanced up to the priest in surprise, then took his hand. She said a few faint words that he couldn't understand until he leaned closer.

"Got hot zikh bashafen a velt mit klaineh veltelech," she said in what Luis recognized as Yiddish.

God created a world full of many little worlds.

"He did indeed," Luis replied, patting her hands. "He did indeed."

———

Oscar had been scouting a new house with Helen when Tony called. It was a magnificent four-story affair in the Palisades with a trail leading to a beach and a breathtaking view of the ocean from the fourth floor. What more could anyone want?

"If you're eight months pregnant, you don't want to do the stairs," Helen had said, leading Oscar away from the eager realtor, who'd seen the gleam in Oscar's eyes. "So the view's irrelevant. The view out the back windows on the first two floors is of the base of the embankment a dozen yards away, like looking at the wall of a prison. I vote no."

Oscar had fumed. This was the first house he had found rather than having to rely on Helen. That he'd missed all of this made him feel embarrassed in front of the one person whose opinion he cared about. But sensing this, she'd moved into his eye line and touched his hand.

"That's why I'm here, Oscar," she'd said lightly. "That's why we're a team. But so you know, I'm not interested in being with someone who makes me feel like I have to worry about hurt feelings every time I say something that might stroke his ego in the wrong way. If you want somebody to just shut up and do whatever you say, tell me. I can probably point you to the right person. But it won't be me."

Oscar had stared at her, wanting to take her up into his arms and kiss her, but had refrained, as he'd heard the realtor's soft footsteps in the hall.

"You're right," he'd finally said.

"I know," Helen had replied, leaning in to kiss him on the lips even though the realtor had walked into view.

As they'd pulled away, Oscar's cell phone had rung. It was Tony Qi asking if Oscar could meet him in about an hour. He was to come alone. When Oscar agreed, Tony had texted him a map point of an area called Shadow Hills, a remote location deep in Auyong Valley. Oscar had immediately feared some sort of trap but had no idea what Tony would have against him.

Contrary to his better judgment, Oscar drove out on his own.

When he got to the spot on the map, he thought what it chose to designate a "road" was overly generous. It was more of a sandy trail marked by ATV tracks and the hoofprints of horses.

Now I know it's a trap, Oscar thought.

He checked the pistol in his glove box, the one in the magnetized holster under the driver's seat, and a tiny and an ineffectual-at-best .22 two-shot Derringer he kept in the sunshade, and pressed on. But then he saw Tony Qi's car parked up ahead and its owner sitting alongside an old and twisted tree. It was just about the only thing that broke up the vast empty vistas. There was clearly nowhere to hide an ambush, unless they'd tunneled underground or would drop from the sky.

Oscar parked and climbed out of his car, his feet sinking into the soft sand. Tony rose and came to meet him, extending his hand. Oscar shook it.

"Tony Qi," Oscar said by way of greeting.

"Thank you for coming all this way to meet me," Tony said. "I thought you'd enjoy seeing this tree."

Oscar thought Tony must be joking. When he realized that he wasn't, he shrugged.

"Okay."

Tony led him over to it and patted the trunk. "This tree is five thousand years old. It is literally one of the oldest living things on the entire planet. It predates not only most of what exists in this region but civilization as we know it."

Oscar was already bored. The sum total of his knowledge of China was formed by watching Jet Li and Jackie Chan movies. He figured this must be some kind of Chinese honor thing tied to tradition. He also expected a long speech of some kind. He'd given up a quickie with Helen on some side street in the Palisades for this? Maybe he was the one who was there to shoot Tony.

"I asked you here to negotiate an alliance," Tony said.

"Don't we have one?" Oscar asked.

"One that extends far beyond our agreements relating to the houses we're buying," Tony explained. "It is one between my society and your organization."

Organization?

Oscar scoffed. "I'm not sure who you think I am, but you should know that it may not be who you think I am. There is no organization.

There's me and my shops, my guys, a few affiliated crews, but that's it. Maybe a hundred men."

"No, I have a clear picture," Tony said. "A hundred men is precisely what I need. About a hundred of yours that can replace a hundred of mine. And quickly. Very quickly."

"Wait, what's this about?" Oscar asked, alarmed. "I don't want to get in the middle of some kind of power struggle."

"It's not that at all. Necessity makes strange bedfellows, as they say. But perhaps we can build to something mutually beneficial. You see, it's about to be open season on Asian businesses in Los Angeles. Boycotts, picketing, possibly even violence, though I doubt it'll get that far. And the businesses I'm related to can't afford that."

"Whoa," Oscar said. "That's crazy. Are you guys paranoid or something?"

"Have you heard of SARS?" Tony asked.

"Yeah, it's like bird flu. You guys invented it, right?"

"Therein lies the problem. An hour ago the CDC confirmed a SARS outbreak here in Los Angeles. Two Hispanics, a Lebanese man, and a young Caucasian girl have already been positively identified as carriers. All four have died."

"So you think they're going to look at you and not a bunch of Hispanics or Lebanese people? I mean, they're not going to look at white people, of course. But you're crazy if you think they're going to go after Asians."

"All right, then let me be crazy," Tony said. "My motivations aside, would you consider deepening our relationship?"

"Are these illegal businesses?" Oscar ventured.

"Not at all," Tony said. "Food deliveries, restaurant supplies, linens, liquor distribution, and so on. I need a few people in warehouses, but more importantly, I need different trucks, different drivers, and different men carrying the boxes into these businesses."

"Different as in non-Asians?"

"Yes."

Oscar thought about it. His commission for rounding up a bunch of guys to drive around the city to make a bunch of paranoid triad guys happy would probably be significant. Also, the fact that Tony had brought him out to some five-thousand-year-old tree as if to imply the strength and longevity of this new agreement meant that, aside from being a drama queen, he was also desperate. This meant Oscar was in the catbird seat.

"One big caveat," Oscar said. "I can't have my guys involved with narcotics. That's a deal breaker. If I'm not willing to do the sentence for a crime, I'm not going to send my guys out to do it. And heroin's a bad, bad rap. Also, we'd start running into territorial issues with some of our own."

"No drugs, I assure you," Tony said, shaking his head. "It is only a question of perception. When news of the outbreak reaches far and wide, no restaurant can allow its customers to see our deliverymen. It's that simple. Perception, Oscar. That's all. And if it wasn't for decades of 'yellow peril' racism associated with incidents like this, I might agree with you about being paranoid. But if there's any constant in this world, it's that people are always looking for ways to be exclusionary and xeno-phobic, as pack animals do, and this is a golden opportunity."

As much as he didn't want to admit it, some element of what Tony was saying rang true. He nodded.

"I'll do it for the money, but I don't want this to be a temporary stopgap," Oscar said. "We keep your trains running on time, we get to keep a couple of routes after this SARS deal blows over. We have the pack mentality, too, and if it's our people in our neighborhoods mak-ing the delivery money, I'm sure I can get a few restaurants added to your list. Maybe even in areas of the city you haven't been able to crack. What do you think?"

When his counterpart didn't reply, Oscar wondered if he'd over-stepped. Then Tony rose and offered a solemn handshake.

"If my associates agree," Tony declared, "maybe this will turn out to be a blessing in disguise."

Oscar nodded amicably. He'd worked with a lot of people in his day. But this Tony Qi guy took the cake.

———

Susan had been Federico Carreño's doctor for more than half his life. She'd seen him through ear infections, a broken finger attributed to school sports (which the doctor would later learn was a result of a wrestling match with his drunken father), and a handful of other childhood illnesses. But she'd only really ever thought of him as a name on a chart. He'd come in, she'd look down to remind herself of who he was, then ask him about school, summer vacation, or plans for Christmas break, depending on the season. If forced, she doubted she could pick him out of a lineup.

But now she was faced with determining whether he carried a disease that had already decimated his family.

"And did you come over to the house after your grandfather fell ill?"

"I did. With Mamá."

"Did you see him?"

"She made me stay downstairs," he recalled. "She didn't want me to miss any school."

Thank heaven for small miracles.

"And your mother? Did she make you stay away from her, too, after she got sick?"

The boy's father shifted in the examination room doorway. Federico sniffled. Tears formed in his eyes. Susan kicked herself for not finding a better way to frame the question.

"I'm sorry," she said quickly. "I know this is hard, Federico, and you are being very brave."

What she didn't want to say, what she *couldn't* say, was that she needed to know all this to determine if he might be infected, too. But that was too much to put on this boy's mind. If he was sick, there wasn't much she could do. There were no antibiotics, no vaccines, no cures. The only thing to be done was to try and keep the infected patient's organs functioning long enough for the virus to pass through the body.

"When she came back from the hospital after *abuelo* died, she was really sad," Federico said. "She climbed into bed with me. She wasn't coughing, though, not like *abuelo*."

Susan froze her features so the boy wouldn't see how far they'd fallen. Esmeralda had thought to keep her son safe from her father but not from herself. She'd had no idea she was sick. It was potentially devastating news.

"Thank you, Federico," Susan said, moving away from the exam table. "Everything's going to be okay. I'm going to go talk to your dad now. We'll be right back in."

Susan led the boy's father, Pablo Ochoa, into her office.

"Is he sick?" Pablo asked.

"He's definitely been exposed," Susan said. "You need to leave here and go immediately to Good Samaritan."

"I can't do that," Pablo protested. "The whole reason we come to you is because we can't go to a regular doctor."

"Sir, you've probably been exposed, too. If you can't think of your son, maybe think of yourself."

Pablo blanched. Susan hoped this would be enough, and to her relief Pablo softened and nodded. She gave him a detailed list of further instructions, then sent him to retrieve his son. When she went back in to see Federico, she almost thought she'd gone to the wrong room. He seemed to have aged several years in the few minutes she was away.

He knows, she realized.

Luis watched Pablo and Federico exit an unmarked door at the rear of the shopping plaza. The boy was the spitting image of his mother. He eyed the pair closely, looking for any sign that they might be infected with the virus that had killed Esmeralda. To his relief, he saw none, but he knew that meant little.

Climbing out of his car, he hurried over to the door but found no handle.

Huh.

Moving around the side of the building, he found a handful of other businesses, including a florist, a doughnut shop/deli, and a pet store that primarily focused on exotic fish. There was no sign of how to enter the doctor's office. That is, until he went down a side hallway and found another unmarked door by restrooms. He took the handle, found it locked, but then looked up and saw a security camera lens staring back down at him.

A small voice box came to life beside the door. "Can I help you?"

"I'm here to see Dr. Auyong."

The door buzzed and Luis entered. The waiting room on the other side was about the same as any other doctor's office he'd been to. Four people were waiting, including a mother and her young daughter. There were two televisions on, a number of magazines laid out, and a large kid-friendly fish tank in one corner with an advertisement at the bottom revealing that it and its contents were purchased from the store around the corner.

"Sir? Are you a new patient?" the receptionist asked.

"I am. But I just need to see her. I'm a friend."

The receptionist eyed Luis's collar and she nodded. Luis wondered if Father Chang had ever been here. When Susan appeared a moment later, several boxes in both hands, she looked at him with surprise. Then it seemed to dawn on her.

"You were the priest at Good Samaritan, weren't you?" she asked over the receptionist's desk. "With Esmeralda Carreño?"

"Yes."

"I suppose I should thank you," she said.

"I think we can skip that," Luis replied. "I'm afraid I need to talk to you for a moment."

"I'm just on my way out," she said, opening the door from the waiting room. "So you'll have to make it quick."

They filed back to Susan's office. She loaded bags with boxes of drug samples and vitamins.

"I found out a few things about Father Chang's death," Luis said. "I thought you'd want to hear them."

"I don't know if I do," she admitted, piling the bags on a chair. "I'm sure there'll be plenty to say at the trial, but I have time to get ready for that."

"You don't know?"

"What do you mean?" she asked.

"Yamazoe's dead. He died sometime last night. They think it was poison."

Susan went very still. Then she smacked her desk and looked back up at Luis. "Good. Who did it?"

"Depends on who you ask. A lot of the foreign papers that ran it already say it was suicide. Guilt over Father Chang's death."

"And now the truth?" she asked.

"I think he was killed by the LA triad."

Luis explained about everything he'd learned in the past forty-eight hours. Susan's jaw dropped lower and lower. When he got to the part about Michael Story, Susan stopped him.

"You're friends with some kind of prosecutor?" she asked.

"'Friends' isn't the right word. Collaborators, I suppose."

"I hope you didn't say anything about me."

"Not a word," he assured her, glancing around. "Did Father Chang know about this place?"

"He did."

"Was he your patient?"

"No, we actually met off-site. One of the ways we get the state medical board to look the other way is through charitable work. We hit the streets, look for people in need of care, and take care of them. I ran into Father Chang when he was doing the same thing."

"Where exactly?"

Susan considered her response for a moment, then nodded to the door. "I'm heading there right now. You want to ride along?"

———

"César Carreño was a drug dealer?" Michael asked the assistant, one of the newer young women whose name he'd actually made the effort to remember—Naomi Okpewho—who'd come in with the news. "I thought he was some kind of construction worker."

"Yeah, they think even the daughter didn't know," Naomi replied. "LAPD has him selling drugs on work sites all around East LA and the San Gabriel Valley for the past three or four years. Sold to a lot of people on the street."

Michael nodded. Since the SARS announcement that morning, the day had become a flurry of paperwork. There were extrajudicial health screenings of prisoners to be done, warrants for welfare checks to be brought to the right judges to sign, and now this—raids on places César Carreño's customers might frequent. As a possible patient zero, every detail of Carreño's life had been scrutinized. He hadn't traveled recently anywhere there had been an outbreak, he hadn't visited any farms or slaughterhouses, so the belief had quickly crystalized that he must've been infected by someone else.

Finding that someone else and quarantining them, if they were still alive, and anyone else they'd come in contact with was the city's top priority. Keeping the suddenly terrified populace from boiling over into outright paranoia and flight was a close second.

"So, are we talking raids? Or just hitting the shelters and asking if anyone's had a bad cough?"

"Raids. I think the city knows it doesn't have the time to be polite," Naomi replied. "No one wants to be the bureaucrat who put up red tape as more people got infected."

Michael felt the memory of Jeff Lambert's grip on his bicep and the crush of his handshake. He put his laptop bag back down on his desk and took off his suit jacket.

"Good point," he said. "Put the word out. Anybody who needs anything smoothed through the DA's office can find me—me, personally—right here on this desk. Let's get out in front of this. You game?"

"Are you asking me as someone you hope organizes your campaign staff, or somebody in an actual position of power once you win the election?"

Michael looked at Naomi with new eyes. "Both."

Naomi nodded. "Let me get back to my desk."

As she left, Michael considered that his steadfast refusal to leave his post might be seen as a cynical play for attention and possible advancement. But if there was even the slightest chance that it could work in his favor, he knew it'd be worth it.

And no one's expecting you to actually hit the streets, so it's all phones and e-mail.

Michael sank back into his chair. Naomi had left his door slightly ajar, and he could just see Deborah Rebenold's office in the corner on the opposite side of the floor. It had never seemed so close.

XIV

"How did it happen that you were at Good Samaritan?" Susan asked as she drove Luis deep into the San Gabriel Valley.

"My pastor is sick," Luis said, realizing this was the first time he'd actually said as much aloud. "He gets his chemo there."

"How bad is it?"

"Stage Four. They don't think he has much longer."

"Is he fighting it?" she asked.

"That's a good question. I think he is because of his friends. But I think his beliefs make it easier for him."

"Ah," Susan said, tapping the steering wheel. "He believes he'll be on the right hand of God five minutes later."

"If not the right hand, then he'll at least have a few answers," Luis allowed before changing the subject. "Have you been in touch with the CDC about the Carreños?"

"I relayed all of the relevant information anonymously," Susan said. "But don't think it's because I'm afraid of getting arrested. That's no problem. If we get raided and our records seized, however, the confidentiality of my patients could be compromised. I'm not going to inflict that on people who may already be in tricky situations."

Luis nodded. "What about other patients the Carreños could've infected in your clinic?"

Susan scowled. "Wow, I'd never thought of that," she shot back sarcastically. "Maybe we should assemble a list of at-risk patients and schedule in-home visits with them. Wait, maybe we should do the same for nurses and staff!"

"Point taken," Luis replied sheepishly.

"Just because we're unlicensed doesn't mean we don't care really, really deeply for our patients," Susan explained. "The good news is, contrary to its popular conception, SARS is actually rather difficult to pass from person to person. If it wasn't, the entire human race might've been wiped out years ago."

"But they're sure this is SARS? It couldn't be something else?"

"Without question. The signature of SARS-CoV—coronavirus—is as distinctive as the Taj Mahal. This is SARS." Susan looked Luis over for a moment, then shook her head. "The collar is too much. We're going to have to do something about that."

She turned around and dug through the backseat, though she was still hauling down the block at almost fifty miles per hour. Luis stared through the windshield in terror, but she was back a moment later holding a UCSF sweatshirt. She thrust it at him.

"This'll have to do," she said.

"Did you go here?" Luis asked as he pulled it over his head.

"For my residency," she said. "I did my undergrad at UHK in Hong Kong and med school at Peking University Health."

"How did you end up in California?"

"Would you believe I followed a guy? Met him as a resident, came over after I finished in Beijing, thought I was going to marry him. Turned out he already had a fiancée. I couldn't face the shame of going home, so I stuck around."

"I'm sorry," Luis said.

"I'm not! I love California. Hong Kong's expensive. Beijing's over-populated and way overpolluted, like, 'if your lungs aren't accustomed to it, you're sick for a week after you leave' overpolluted. But here in LA I've got my apartment, I've got my job, I've got my friends. It's perfect."

"So, you're legal?" Luis ventured.

"Uh, *technically* no?" Susan said. "I was on a student visa and then an H-1B visa after that. But that one means you have to leave and reenter the country every couple of years. The last time I did it they were real dicks about it and said they wouldn't renew it the next time. So I just stayed. That was four years ago."

"You haven't been home since?"

"Nope. And I don't miss it," Susan admitted. "It took me a while to get used to American life. Now it'd be hard to go back to China. It'd be like reverse culture shock."

"How did you end up at the clinic?" Luis asked.

"I had the medical education but not the license, so I couldn't work at a regular hospital. I was going to try and start the process when I heard about all the 'medical repatriation' that happens in California. Say you're an illegal immigrant and you get in a car wreck and go to a hospital. There's a chance you'd wake up back wherever you came from, with none of your money, possessions, or even family members. Happened just last year to two comatose patients in San Francisco. They were put on a medical plane and shipped. I think it discourages people from getting help when they need it, and that makes everything worse. When I heard about these clinics, I hunted one down through a friend of a friend and got a job."

Luis didn't know how to tell her that he admired this a great deal without sounding like a sap, so he kept his mouth shut.

"What about you?" she asked. "How did you become a priest? Were you like the third son in some landed aristocracy?"

Luis laughed, then sobered a little as he recalled the real reason.

"It was my mother's doing. My brother was the religious one and had been training to go into the priesthood. He was killed in a random shooting near our house. Our mother went a little nuts fearing I'd be next and convinced the local bishop to let me take my brother's place. She was just trying to keep me safe."

"Wow. And I thought you guys were called by a higher power."

"We are. I just didn't recognize mine until later. Once I began learning, God's plan, which had always been there, finally made itself known to me."

"A miracle," Susan pronounced.

Luis shrugged. "Are you religious?"

"It's so, so different in China," Susan said. "I'm into Buddhism and Taoism—which I still believe in—but it's more tradition than a faith-based religion like you guys have. You guys go to extremes with fantasy land crap—no offense."

"'Fantasy land crap'?" Luis asked with a grin.

"You know, infinite fish and water into wine," Susan said with a shrug. "Dead men returning to life. Carpenters walking on water. People turning to salt."

"Yeah, and Taoism has *yāoguài*."

"You get that from a Wu-Tang album or watching kung fu movies growing up? That's folklore stuff."

Luis laughed. "Didn't Father Chang grow up in China?"

"Yeah, but whenever he talks about it—sorry, *talked*—he described it as he was just looking for something to convert to. When the missionaries got to him in his teenage years, it was a way of getting out from under all the Communist Party nonsense keeping him back. I kind of think he converted as a screw-you to everyone around him."

"How so?" Luis asked.

"Christians in China are such a strange group. For a long time they were viewed almost like a kind of cult. 'Why would you want to be Western?' was the question, rather than 'Why would you believe in the Bible?' Still, Christians never rode in on horseback trying to conquer us as they did everywhere else, so maybe the modern Chinese are able to have a more prosaic, live-and-let-live view. Just in recent years Christianity's exploded to the point that the government started to remove crosses from the tops of buildings and arrest priests. But even then, when people arrive here it's one of the few symbols everyone recognizes."

"That's how we get you," Luis explained. "We're like the McDonald's arches. You know what you're going to get when you walk in our doors."

Susan giggled so hard it almost sounded like she was crying.

"You sound like Benny," she finally said. "He loved God, saw him as a friend, somebody to communicate with, and so on. But he thought the whole evangelizing bit was a crock. He was terrible at it. He just tried to lead by example. The idea was that if people saw how much joy he got out of being a Christian, they might follow."

Susan's cell phone rang. "That'll be Nan," she said. "I'll call him back. He's having a hard time with Benny's death. He doesn't have many friends. Father Chang was his whole life."

"They were that close?" Luis asked.

"Oh yeah," Susan said. "They were together what? Three years? Four? Nan's family practically disowned him when he came out. Father Chang and I were his new family."

Luis didn't know how to react to this. He hadn't even remotely considered that Father Chang was a homosexual. Not once. When he looked over at Susan, he saw that she was scrutinizing his reaction.

"So that's how you knew he didn't molest Yamazoe's daughter," Luis said finally.

Susan's face clouded with anger. She jammed on the brakes and spun the wheel, sending the car to the side of the road. She looked Luis right in the face, and he thought she might hit him.

"No, I knew he didn't molest Yamazoe's daughter because I knew Father Chang. His being gay has nothing to do with that."

"Why didn't you just tell the police?" Luis asked.

"You don't think it would just make things worse? I'm not going to use something that's none of anybody's business to defend a man who shouldn't need defending. Also, he's dead. I'm not going to use that as an excuse to say anything he didn't want said. Got it?"

"Got it."

Susan scanned Luis's face for a moment longer as if to assure herself he really did. Then she put on her left blinker and moved back into traffic.

Luis fell silent in the passenger seat. He now knew exactly what Father Chang had seen in Dr. Susan Auyong.

———

Tony arrived at Wanquan Yang's house just after dark. He parked a couple of blocks away and walked over, always reluctant to add to the number of vehicles around a Dragon Head's home. Billy Daai was waiting for him on the driveway, a cigarette in one hand, a cell phone in the other.

"There's been another death," he said. "This one all the way out in Sierra Madre. Just heard it from our contact in the sheriff's department there."

"Sierra Madre?" Tony asked, surprised. "That's miles from the other cases. How on earth did it get all the way out there?"

"No one knows," Billy said, pocketing the phone, then immediately pulling it back out to check something else. "But now the whole city's panicked. Before, people were writing off three of the cases as being in East LA, and the little girl was some kind of anomaly or accident. But when they announce Sierra Madre in a couple of hours, people are going to know that nobody's safe from this."

"You're right," Tony agreed. "There's going to be mass panic."

Billy leaned in close to Tony. "You were right, by the way. The Sierra Madre case is this little old man who never left the house. Had his groceries delivered; postman and neighbors say they never saw him leave. He hadn't taken his car out for months. Said he'd called 911. The paramedics got there and put on their masks, knowing immediately what they were dealing with."

"How was I right?"

"The media showed up and started looking around once they realized how far he was from the other cases. You know what they settled on? There's a Sunrise Asian Market directly behind his place. A bunch of people they talked to said it must've come from there. Infected food, rats, mosquitos. They told the news crews they'd call the police and ask for it to be temporarily shut down."

"But those are just local crazies," Tony said, lowering his voice as he nodded to a couple of his other triad brethren walking up the driveway for the meeting. "That doesn't mean a thing."

"It means something that the news crews put them on the air. They knew it would keep folks at home glued to their sets. They love whack-jobs. It's going to air and re-air all night."

"They have no idea how SARS is spread," Tony pointed out.

"Since when does that matter?" Billy asked ruefully. "But you said you might have a way to fix this."

"I do. At least, I have begun moving us toward a solution. I am anxious to hear what our brethren think."

"I'm sure they can't wait to hear it."

The pair entered the house together, old men already lining the ornate sofas in the house's large living room. A handful of wives moved from room to room, passing out drinks and hors d'oeuvres. There was only one woman sitting with the men: Jing Saifai. Tony considered introducing himself to her but thought it would appear nakedly ambitious and refrained.

From the outset the rhetoric was all fear, particularly of harsher inspections of Asia-originating ships hurting their bottom line. Everyone's concerns were self-centered and self-interested. Everyone thought they were the right one to deliver their grievances and fears to the mayor's office. Everyone believed they had the right plan to see them through this or even improve their standing. Why not use this moment to get the unions to help roll a few of the tougher regulations back even? But no one had any plan that took the needs of their brethren into consideration.

Tony stood aside and let these windbags air their grievances and then deflate. He, like Beaumarchais's Figaro, would need only to wait for his cue to save the day.

"Zhelin Qi has a suggestion."

It was Billy who'd stepped forward. Though he was far younger than everyone else who'd spoken and only two days before made a Blue Lantern, he wasn't ignored, out of deference to his father. Eyes turned to Tony, and he was glad he'd worn his one bespoke suit to the meeting. He looked like one of them and hoped he sounded like one.

"I have consulted with a partner of ours in the tourist business about—"

"Who?" demanded an older deputy. "Who did you consult?"

Don't forget that the knives are out.

"His name is Oscar de Icaza," Tony said calmly. "We were discussing another aspect of our business when this calamity came to light. Some of you know de Icaza from his auto trade with Hong Kong. He is a native to Los Angeles. He is—"

"Who does he report to?" another man asked.

"No one," Tony replied. "At one point he was affiliated with the Alacrán street gang of East Los Angeles. But that was in his youth. Mr. de Icaza operates his dealings with our organization independently out of the auto repair centers he owns."

"A businessman! Like us!" someone chortled. Others followed suit.

"Why are you talking to a boss? Why not one of us?" someone else said.

"As I said, it came up in conversation. Also, it was an opportune moment. I didn't want it to pass by."

"Okay," said Dragon Head Wanquan Yang, fluttering his hand to suggest he'd allow these words to be spoken in his house, though mostly out of courtesy.

"De Icaza has proven to be a good and trustworthy man," Tony explained. "And he is connected to other good and trustworthy men. If our problem is temporary and cosmetic, one solution could be to expand our partnership with him. Rather than have restaurant owners turn our deliveries away, our drivers and deliverymen will be replaced by his. Our trucks by his trucks. Maybe we even dummy up some claim about businesses having been sold. It'd be like using a shell corporation or a front. I mean, it's only about perception."

The room fell silent for a moment. Then a rotund onetime Red Pole named Hu got to his feet and shook his bamboo cane inches from Tony's face.

"Give away our business to these *lǎowài*?" he said, spittle flying with the words. "What gives you the authority? What audacity. How dare you? We haven't even met this man."

Tony didn't flinch, but he didn't respond, either. He couldn't break the man's gaze to cast around for support, and Billy Daai wouldn't be enough.

"We built these businesses," Hu continued. "How can you expect to simply capitulate? We are not our ancestors and not filled with fear of, or beholden to, these local magistrates. We belong here. We have rights!"

Tony could feel the support of most in the room lining up behind Hu. But then a new voice rose over the others. Tony didn't recognize it at first, but everyone else did and turned. A tall, thin man rose from a piano stool and moved toward Tony. Tony realized who it was and immediately bowed low.

His name was Den-yih Zeng, and though the Los Angeles triad had only limited connections to their distant brethren's organization in Hong Kong, Zeng was an exception. An elegant gentleman of ninety who could still pass for a spry sixty-five glided from underworld to underworld, imparting his wisdom and taking tribute as he went. He was not affiliated with a single triad per se but was respected by all for his deep connection to the oldest Hong Kong triad, the 14K, which he'd been a member of since its inception in 1945. Despite his dapper appearance and affable demeanor, he'd also been a ruthless enforcer in his day. It was said that his body bore a road map of scars, from the base of his skull to the soles of his feet.

When he spoke, people listened.

"You are suggesting, Mr. Qi, that these businesses go underground?" Zeng asked. "That is correct?"

"I am, Master Zeng."

"Pick up any Western book on Chairman Mao, and they'll inevitably make the same paternalistic joke," Zeng said quietly. "'Mao's only success, it is widely understood, was that he drove the triads out of Singapore.' People believe this as one day they were there, the next they weren't. And now that Mao is gone, they have returned in force. But as we know, this isn't only untrue, it's almost comedy. We *flourished* under Mao. We made more connections and did more business than we ever had before. Privation meant demand. Demand needed supply. That was us. We had merely gone underground."

Tony knew that Zeng's emphasis on "we" wasn't lost on the men in the room. What they knew of street fighting came from relatively minor Chinatown turf battles in the seventies. Zeng, on the other hand, had literally crossed swords with Chinese government troops, run ships with a smuggler's ransom in goods through blockades and into unfriendly ports, and, as a teenager, had even fought for Chiang

Kai-shek's Nationalist Army in the final battles of the Chinese Civil War. Everyone felt like something of a paper gangster next to a man like Zeng.

"The very nature of our society is based on survival," Zeng said. "The five monks who founded our order did so to combat a corrupt emperor and fight for the people. They didn't stand on ceremony. They *survived* so that our order might, too. Mr. Qi's words are born from that same spirit. Your ego is not what's most important. It's that our triad may continue to do the work that is its eternal purpose. When we fought Mao, we accepted weapons from the British and the Americans. When we were outlawed, we did business with the Koreans, the Japanese, the Burmese government, and even factions within Ho Chi Minh's leadership in Vietnam. We have always prospered during moments of oppression by making fortuitous alliances. Mr. Qi has brought that thinking back to the present. Thank you, Mr. Qi, for thinking of the triad first and the individual second."

As Zeng bowed to him, Tony bowed back, perhaps the lowest he'd had to for a decade or more. He felt as if he were being blessed. He'd barely known Zeng, yet he'd found in him a surprising and staunch ally.

The Vanguard who'd overseen Billy's initiation ceremony rose next and bowed toward Tony.

"Thank you, Mr. Qi."

Several others rose now and bowed, thanking him as well. Tony bowed back as humbly as he could. Hu waited for all of the others to bow and then followed suit.

"I apologize for my shortsightedness," Hu said. "And thank Mr. Zeng for correcting this."

Tony bowed deeply to him. When he rose, he looked for Billy, but the young man was gone.

Ah well.

XV

It didn't take long for Michael to regret staying downtown. There was work to be done, sure, but it was nothing Naomi couldn't handle and actually made Michael look silly. He could hear it in people's voices. *Why is he there instead of doing something more important?*

And the answer was clear: *Ah, to score cheap political points.*

Still, he kept at it like a crazed information desk docent. He handed out phone numbers, answered questions, signed forms, and became a veritable rubber stamp. The one thing he couldn't do, which frustrated more than a few of his callers, was approve overtime or free up additional monies from the city budget. If he hadn't known where the powers of the district attorney's office began and ended before, he certainly did now.

"So what're they doing about it?" Helen asked when she called.

"Right now they're just trying to contain it. But they've got epidemiologists coming in from DC, a couple of experts from the Mayo Clinic, and then there's the surgeon general from Canada, who handled the Toronto outbreak, coming in to consult on all things we haven't thought of. By the way, did you know being surgeon general is an actual military rank up there?"

Helen said that she did not. The kids were in bed, so she'd been watching the news. Everyone kept saying the same thing: that the virus wasn't spreading in a predictable way.

"Yeah, that's why everyone's spooked," Michael said. "The only way it could get out to this many people spread this far and wide is if there are a great number of carriers that no one's discovered yet. You couldn't have staged anything more perfectly to inspire fear. We'll get to the bottom of it, but right now it's doing its job."

"Well, I hope the source is discovered quickly," Helen replied. "I know there are a lot of frightened people out there. I'm still not sure why they need you there."

Michael hesitated. He hadn't mentioned the Jeff Lambert conversation to Helen at the science fair. There just hadn't been the right moment, and he didn't want to do it in front of the kids.

"Well, that's nebulous," Michael admitted. "I kind of had an interesting talk with Jeff Lambert last night."

"I saw him at the science fair," Helen said. "A skeevy guy, right?"

"Definitely," Michael agreed. "But pretty connected with the Democratic Party. He wanted to talk to me about running for district attorney."

Helen let out a bark of a laugh so cruel, so tinged with incredulity, that Michael almost hung up the phone. It was ugly and petty. Worse, there was no mistaking it for humor. She'd known he was serious, and this was her response.

"Thanks for the support, Helen."

"Sorry, Michael, but that's a little bit out of left field. What about Deborah?"

"They don't think she can win. The challenger has a massive war chest, and it doesn't look good."

"And somehow you're the fix for that? Michael, are you sure you're not being set up as some kind of sacrificial lamb? Like, Deborah knows she can't win, so she's bowing out rather than taking a loss, but they still have to run somebody?"

Now Michael was mad. She might not have believed in him, but she didn't have to be such an asshole about it.

"It's the Marshak case."

"Ah, of course it is," Helen said with a sigh. "What did you tell him?"

"I told him no. I told him even if I got elected, I didn't know if I could do the job. I told him that I didn't want my family to face the scrutiny of a political campaign."

This last part was a lie, but he wanted to hear Helen counter it.

"That's smart," Helen said instead. "The kids are too young. And I don't know if I trust this guy. What if he just wants to use you to raise money because of Marshak but then doesn't get you in office? Once you're a loser, people look at you that way. You only get one shot."

Exceptions like Reagan and Nixon popped into Michael's head, but even more examples to support Helen's assertion.

"This is something we've talked about for a long time, Helen," Michael said. "There were always going to be campaigns. When we first met, you said you fell for me because you'd always seen yourself as being a congressman's wife one day."

"I was twenty."

"But this is what I've been working toward for years. I've always seen us on this path. We can do a lot of good."

"'We can do a lot of good,'" Helen said, scoffing. "That's the best you got? Everything comes out during campaigns. Our children are too young to process that."

"You really think some scandal is going to come out of the woodwork?"

"Don't you?"

Michael froze. *Is she talking about Annie?*

"I thought this was what you wanted," Michael said lamely. "I thought we were in this together."

Helen didn't say anything for a long moment. Finally, she spoke, her voice a shrug.

"Maybe we're not."

———

Luis idly tried to determine if the horseshoe-shaped two-story complex had at one time been a small apartment complex or a motel. Every door and window of the building was boarded up. The grass around the exterior had been allowed to grow wild, and ivy crept up the outer walls. There was a rusty pole jutting up from the sidewalk nearby, but the sign that had once topped it was nowhere in sight.

It didn't matter much. In a part of town this bad, he couldn't imagine people wanting to live or rent there.

"We're protected here," Susan said, clocking Luis's concerns. "We don't even have to lock the car doors."

The car bounced up into the overgrown courtyard parking lot and pulled to a stop in a space closest to the street. Luis glanced back to the street and saw there was nothing but obstructed views. Nobody driving by could see them. Protected or not, coming down here was asking for trouble. There was always that one guy who didn't get the memo of who could or couldn't get jacked.

Susan popped the trunk and climbed out of the car. She hefted as many of the plastic grocery bags of bottles and boxes as she could and called up to Luis.

"Can you help me with this?"

Luis said a quick prayer and got out of the car. He tried to imagine Father Chang coming down here but figured it was during the day.

"How come we're here at night?" he asked.

"No one's here during the day," Susan said. "Everyone's out looking for a couple of bucks or trying to score. The only time anyone's here is when it's not good to be out on the street."

Luis nodded and took out a few of the bags. "What is all this stuff?"

"Vitamins mostly. A bunch of antidiarrheals. Some antacids. Some aspirin. A couple of boxes of antibiotics in case we run into any hard cases. Oh, and you'll want to wear a mask and gloves."

She indicated an open box of latex surgical gloves at the back of the trunk, as well as a bag of heavy cotton masks like the kind gardeners wore.

"It's cheaper to get the ones at Home Depot than from some medical supply company," she said. "And they're just as effective."

Luis slipped one over his mouth and nose. Susan moved to the door of the nearest unit and beckoned for the priest to follow.

"Don't say anything to anybody," she warned. "If people talk to you, look away. Don't make eye contact. You're not here to talk, make friends, or convert anybody. Cool?"

"Cool."

Susan eyed him one last time as if to let him know she wasn't joking, then knocked on the door twice before opening.

"You don't want to wait?"

"They knew we were here the moment we turned onto the block. I'm not looking to waste time with pleasantries."

Luis was expecting to have to go door-to-door. When they entered, however, he saw that the place was completely gutted. The roof, outer walls, support columns, and a few chunks of second-story floors that now acted as lofts remained, but everything else had been removed. It gave the place a cathedral-like feeling, particularly as the only light streamed in through narrow breaks in the ceiling and areas of the windows where the newspaper that covered them had been torn away.

Everywhere he looked, Luis saw the belongings of dozens of squatters. There were sleeping bags, cooking equipment, articles of clothing, a few suitcases, a couple of books, and bags of food hanging from the ceiling instead of on the floor, likely to keep rats and other vermin away. What was missing were people.

"Where is every—?" he began to ask, but then saw that Susan had no idea.

She was looking around, eyeing the corners and the lofts for any sign of people. It was completely empty.

"This is crazy," she said. "This is all they had in the world. They wouldn't just leave everything here."

Luis eyed a couple of the books more closely and saw that they were in Chinese. The labels on the suitcases and even some of the shopping bags were as well. The only things routinely in English were the boxes of pills Susan had brought on earlier trips.

"If the place had been raided, there'd be signs," Susan said. "There's nothing. Everything's intact."

There was a creak from upstairs. Both Luis and Susan froze for an instant before Susan stepped forward.

"Hello? Who's up there?" she asked in English before repeating in Mandarin and Cantonese. "My Spanish sucks. You think you could—?"

"*¿Quién es?*"

No one responded to any of it. The creaks, however, continued.

"Let's go up," Susan said.

"Up" meant taking a ladder to a landing in the corner of the building, then crossing what appeared to be a narrow catwalk to a second section of ceiling. Susan, who'd clearly done this dozens of times, hurried up the ladder and slipped across the catwalk as nimbly as a mountain goat. Luis, whose eyes were just now adjusting to the dark, was less sure of himself and almost toppled off a few times.

Finally, Luis crossed to where Susan stood in front of a large door that had been sealed off with tarp and tape.

"This isn't good," Susan said. "Something's very wrong here."

Luis stared at the door, wondering why someone would do such a professional job of sealing it off. An answer occurred to him and he blanched. Susan grabbed the doorknob but found it locked.

"We have to get through here."

No sooner were the words out of her mouth than a commotion erupted outside. Multiple vehicles came to screeching halts in the parking lot. Light flooded in from multiple directions. Heavy footsteps followed.

"It's now or never."

Luis kicked the door with such force that the lower half cracked and fell off. He kicked the top half, and it broke in two before falling out of the doorframe. The smell that poured out was so bad, Luis thought he might throw up. He took several steps back and almost tumbled off the ledge.

"Oh crap," Susan exclaimed, looking into the room. "What the hell?"

As Luis stood back up, covering his mouth with both hands, Susan took out her cell phone and turned on the flashlight.

"Father?"

Luis moved to the doorway and saw what she saw. Piled in one corner of the room were the bodies of at least five people. Luis had no idea how to tell how long they'd been dead, but it didn't seem like it could've been more than a few days.

"I recognize the girl," Susan said softly. "And that's her father. Holy Christ."

Luis stared at the bodies and for the life of him couldn't distinguish which one was a woman and which an older man. They were covered in heavy blankets, but this did nothing to obscure the smell. On the floor rats scuttled about, even as the air was filled with flies.

Behind them Luis heard heavy footsteps pounding up the ladder. Several sets in fact.

"ICE!" roared the first man up the ladder, an Immigration and Customs Enforcement agent clad in riot gear and wearing a gas mask. "Step out of the room! Hands where we can see them!"

Susan didn't comply. She was too busy throwing aside blankets as she attempted to identify the dead.

"Out of the room now!" roared the agent. "Or we will shoot!"

Susan ignored this order, too. Holding a glove over her hands, she checked the nose and mouth of the youngest of the dead, as well as the skin under the arms and torso.

"She's been dead about three days. Jesus Christ, Luis. We found our patients zero."

Before Luis could respond, he felt a hand on his shoulder. He was spun around, his eyes filling with bright-white light just before the butt of a rifle was slammed into his stomach. He doubled over and hit the floor. Hard.

"I'm a doctor!" Susan shouted behind him. "We were passing out medicine and found these bodies."

"Holy crap!" barked the agent, though his voice registered shock. "She's dead?"

"Yes, and judging by her mucus expression, you're going to need to quarantine everyone in this entire building. Including yourself."

Still doubled up on the floor, Luis stared up at the chastened agent. "What're you looking at?"

Before he could respond, the agent fired a boot strike into Luis's chin. Everything went black.

———

After his success at the triad meeting, Tony Qi felt like celebrating. He knew it was a terrible breach in protocol, but he thought he'd head up to the house on Grand View and see if Jun was awake and interested in hitting the Sunset Strip for another dinner. With Chen Jiang and Archie in tow, naturally, but even that would be okay.

It was ironic then that while he was on the way up Laurel Canyon Drive, he got a call from Dr. Soong.

"Tony? Um, I'm not sure what the protocol is here, but I think we need to get Jun to the hospital."

"What happened? Is it the baby?"

"No. It's, well, it's her. She's taken ill. Worse, her symptoms are not so far removed from . . ."

And the doctor said the name of the virus that was on everyone's lips. Tony couldn't believe his ears. It had to be some kind of a mistake.

"I'll be right there," he said.

Tony hung up and hit the gas. The canyon roads were winding and narrow, but he couldn't care less. The universe wouldn't let him crash. It couldn't. When he finally got to Jun's door, he barely remembered to put the car in park before launching toward the house.

"What's her condition?" he asked the first person he saw, Archie, when he entered.

"I don't know," Archie said. "But I don't think I can be here anymore. This isn't the job. You understand?"

Tony nodded. Archie took his leave and went to his car. Tony hurried to the bedroom, where he found Chen and Dr. Soong, both masked, standing over Jun. Her skin had paled, and her cheeks had gone sallow.

"Jun!" Tony exclaimed.

Everyone in the room turned. Tony was immediately embarrassed by his outburst. Jun sat up and smiled at him a little.

"I'm fine, Mr. Qi," she said, eerily calm. "Really. I'm fine."

As much as he wanted to believe her, her breathing was labored and her movements unsteady.

"I've done this before," she continued. "It's anemia. I'm so stupid. I don't eat right, and then I'm surprised when I fall apart."

But there was real fear on her face. She knew it was bad, and her eyes were pleading with anyone who caught their gaze to come up with a solution. Tony shot a look to Dr. Soong. He didn't move, but he obviously didn't think it was something as simple as anemia.

"Who has been here?" Tony demanded to know after leading Chen Jiang and Dr. Soong from the room. "There must have been somebody."

Chen shook her head. "Only you, Archie, and the doctor. That's it."

"No one that Kuo Kuang sent to check on her? No friends here in the States you don't want me to know about for fear word will get *back* to Kuang? I need to know, auntie. And I need to know now."

From the fear in Chen's eyes, he knew the old woman was telling the truth. There'd been no one. No friends. No secret lovers.

"How could this be SARS?" Tony asked Dr. Soong. "Unless she brought it over from China. And that seems very, *very* unlikely."

"I took a sample of her phlegm and had it tested. Then I sent a sample to a lab in Agoura Hills. The entire city's in an uproar, so it was expensive to keep the results quiet. But it confirmed it."

Dr. Soong handed Tony the results. Tony couldn't make heads or tails of any of it until the bottom of the list. There was no question.

"No one can know," Tony said. "They'll investigate the airport, and that means roping in Kuo Kuang. They'll tie it back to our organization. To our brethren."

The doctor blanched.

I must never bring trouble to my sworn brothers, or I will be beheaded by a myriad of swords.

"So you need to tell me right now what you can do for her," Tony concluded.

"Very little," Dr. Soong admitted. "People do survive SARS, but those few aren't already in as delicate a condition as she is. In fact, pregnant women are often hit the hardest."

"And the baby?"

Dr. Soong hesitated. He'd delivered enough bad news for one night. Tony nodded.

"She'll lose it," Tony realized.

Dr. Soong nodded. "We could try for a Cesarean, but it would surely kill her. All I can really do is keep her alive for as long as possible. This means putting her on a ventilator and potentially feeding her intravenously. I'll need to rent the equipment—"

"Do it right now. Don't wait. Now."

Dr. Soong nodded and headed out the front door.

Once he was alone, Tony headed to the rooftop deck. He now had to figure out what the CDC, law enforcement, and every doctor in the county and possibly even the state was deliberating at the same time.

How did Jun contract a disease if she didn't come in contact with a carrier?

XVI

It had been a lifetime since Luis had seen the inside of a cell. He hadn't seen what they'd done to Susan but assumed she was incarcerated as well. But despite Men's Central Jail being on high alert for SARS, the doctor who checked on Luis shrugged off his concerns.

"You can't get it from dead bodies," the doctor said. "Unless they sneezed on you, you're good."

"But it sounds like nobody really knows what the story is with this version of SARS," Luis replied. "What if it really is traveling some other way?"

"You know how many of you guys have already tried to use that to medical out of the cells? I'll give you a hint. Every one I've seen today."

You guys, Luis thought. *How quickly I'm nobody again.*

Anticipating bail, Luis was led to the common area still in his Roman collar and clerical clothes. Only his collar was now scarlet from the gash the kick to the face had opened on his bottom lip. At first, Luis worried that his being a priest could be trouble and attract the wrong kind of attention. Then he heard that everyone thought he was in for assaulting a cop and he knew he'd be fine.

"Are you really a priest?" one guard asked.

"I am," Luis said as he settled into a chair.

"Priests usually go around fighting cops and resisting arrest?" the guard said, loud enough to be heard by the other prisoners.

Luis didn't say anything.

"Yeah, ICE plays it rough," the guard said, giving Luis a sort of half wink to let him know he was trying to be helpful. Luis didn't respond to this either.

Though a few people looked his way, Luis knew better than to acknowledge pests, especially ones that might be high. Instead, he zeroed in on the infomercial droning along on the common room television, cleared his mind, and began to pray. He prayed for the people who had died, those who might still be infected, and all their loved ones. He prayed for Susan. He prayed for Pastor Whillans, he prayed for Father Chang, and surprised himself by praying for Shu Kuen Yamazoe. He then prayed for Miguel.

It was the longest conversation he'd had with God in some time. As usual he didn't ask for answers, merely guidance in seeing how it all fit together. It wasn't a solution to his current problem, but it was the closest he'd felt to the Almighty in days.

It was during this prayer that he heard a couple of men gossiping nearby. It was just the typical jailhouse nonsense about mutual acquaintances, messages to be passed, and recitations of their lawyers' sincere assurances that they'd be out in no time at all. But when the conversation turned to the goings-on in county itself, Luis heard a familiar name. Keeping his eyes closed, he leaned for a moment longer as one wove a story for the other. The story was salacious, intimated secret sources and hidden knowledge, and ended with a murder.

In other words, all the hallmarks of a lie told to pass the time and impress whoever.

But Luis detected a kernel of truth, the one fact that the rest of the tale had been embroidered around. He returned to his prayer, added it to the things he requested guidance over, and realized how troubling the story would be to him if true.

"Chavez."

It took Luis a moment to realize the voice was coming from without rather than within. He said his "Amen," rose, and moved to the desk. He'd been praying for just under four hours.

After being processed out and having his personal items returned, Luis stepped out into the cool early-summer morning to find a very unhappy man waiting for him on the sidewalk. He shook his head in frustration as Luis drew close.

"You called *me*?" the man, Sheriff's Deputy Ernesto Quintanilla, asked. "Of all people, you called *me*?"

"There was no one else," Luis said.

"Your pastor."

"He's sick."

Ernesto looked down, having obviously forgotten. It wasn't as if Luis would've wanted to call him even if he were healthy. The only other person that made sense was Michael Story, and there wasn't a scenario in which the deputy DA wouldn't use it to his advantage later somehow. Quintanilla, on the other hand, the son of a homebound parishioner whom Luis looked in on from time to time, was sure to gripe about it, but Luis knew he'd show.

"What happened to your face?" Ernesto asked, pointing at the busted lip. "They said you mixed it up with an ICE agent."

Luis did nothing but return Ernesto's gaze. The deputy sighed.

"You know how amped those guys get when they go on a raid," Ernesto said. "If PCP was legal, they'd pop twenty before heading in. You have to get out of their way, or you get the horns."

Luis understood why Ernesto felt he needed to defend his fellow law enforcement officers. Didn't change his opinion of the incident one bit, however.

"Do you know what happened to the doctor I was with?"

"She was taken to Good Samaritan with the bodies to talk to the CDC," Ernesto said. "Samaritan's become SARS ground zero. They've got two whole floors dedicated to dealing with it. You know they found a new case out in Laguna?"

Dear Lord, what is going on?

"They still have no idea how it's spreading?" Luis asked as Ernesto led him to his squad car.

"No idea," Ernesto said, sliding behind the wheel. "Your little find gave them a starting place, though. They haven't announced it yet, but man, the rumors are flying about the squat houses."

"Houses plural?"

"They raided three squats altogether. Five bodies in yours, one in another, two in the one off skid row. All Chinese immigrants. All fresh off the boat."

Luis stared out the front window of the cruiser, wondering how these things were linked. There was no logical connection between the murder of Father Chang and a SARS outbreak. So why was God putting so many things that suggested there was one in front of him? If there was anything he took from divinity school when it came to prayer, it was that there were no coincidences. God put signposts in front of you for a reason.

Ernesto changed lanes to head up the entrance ramp to the 10. Luis shook his head.

"Can you drop me in Echo Park?"

"What's in Echo Park?" Ernesto asked. When Luis didn't respond, Ernesto shrugged and stayed on Cesar Chavez as it left downtown and became the far eastern tail of Sunset Boulevard.

Rather than have Ernesto drive him all the way to his destination, Luis got out at the corner of Sunset and Lemoyne. He thanked Ernesto again, then walked the rest of the way.

Make him be there, Lord.

Oscar's auto body shop was a stone's throw from Dodger Stadium and only blocks from the neighborhood streets Luis and he grew up on. If you were from the area, Oscar barely charged you a cent if your car needed repair. This made for a loyal customer base that kept an eye out for Oscar's other, more lucrative business of stealing high-end cars from the city's elite and racing them down to the ports to be shipped overseas almost before the real owner could file a police report. It was old-fashioned ward politics gangster-style, but Oscar was well liked and considered fair.

When Luis walked up the short driveway to Oscar's garage, he figured there'd at least be some of Oscar's homeboys around. Instead, he found only the shop's owner hunched over the engine of a decades-old Mercedes, a shop light hanging low from the ceiling.

"Is that a diesel?" Luis asked as he stepped out of the darkness.

"Yeah, a '76 240," Oscar said, barely looking up. Luis figured few got within a hundred feet of Oscar without appearing on his radar. "You ever fired one of these up?"

Luis admitted that he had not.

"It's a whole process, like starting a tractor-trailer," Oscar said, getting behind the wheel. "You turn the idle knob all the way clockwise. Then you key the ignition." He did both of those things. "Next you pull the second knob until the heating element glows to life. See? Once that happens, you yank it back like you're starting a lawnmower."

When Oscar did this, the engine chugged and chugged until it finally roared to life. Oscar gave it a little gas and it began to hum.

"No fast getaway with a car like this, huh?" Oscar said, smiling.

"What's wrong with it?"

"Air conditioner. Completely shot. I have to rebuild it. But it's worth it, since the cars last forever. This one already has over two hundred thousand miles on it. The Germans just don't understand the economics of building disposable cars."

"I'll bet they understand just fine," Luis offered. "They just fundamentally disagree."

Oscar grinned at his old friend for a moment while he looked him up and down. He pointed at the gap in Luis's shirt collar.

"Where's your dog collar?"

"Bled on it a bit. Gotta trade it in."

"How come the only time I ever see you is when you get your ass kicked?" Oscar asked, sounding like he was only half joking.

"You should see the other guy," Luis offered lamely.

"Your unscratched knuckles tell the tale, pal. Is that why you're here? You want me to exact some revenge?"

"No, but revenge brought me here. I just got out of county and I heard a funny story while waiting."

"Did you?" Oscar said, giving Luis his full attention now. "Nothing like guys trading 'stories' in county."

"There was a killing of a Chinese prisoner, Shu Kuen Yamazoe, out at Hollenbeck yesterday. Grim case. They got him with poison."

"Sounds like the Chinese," Oscar said, smirking.

"Right, but they were saying it was a contract. Paid for."

"Is that so?" Oscar asked.

"And you know what else?" Luis asked, pressing on. "They're saying one of the triad gangs was behind it, but since they couldn't do it themselves without it possibly being traced back, they got another gang to do it. Somebody they trusted. Somebody with connections inside law enforce—"

Oscar's hand shot out and gripped Luis's shoulder. It was a friendly enough gesture, but Oscar's strength was such that he could hold Luis in place if he wanted to.

"I'm going to stop you right there," Oscar said slowly and evenly, his eyes fixed on Luis. "I can't have you saying something with consequences, right?"

Luis went silent. Oscar waited a long moment before retracting his hand.

"You of all people should know that guys in jail love having something to talk about," Oscar said. "So whatever you heard or think you heard is nonsense. Got it?"

Luis stared at Oscar, wondering if his old friend would have killed him if he'd accused him of being the middleman for the Yamazoe poisoning. In truth, how could he be sure that was the case? It was just two guys talking a few chairs away. And Oscar was right. No bigger assemblage of liars than jail.

But something about Oscar's reaction told him that for once a couple of gossiping prisoners had it right.

"Got it," Luis said, stone faced. "Didn't sound quite right anyway. Murder? I don't know who the guy was trying to impress, but that's a room you can't walk out of."

Luis extended his hand. Oscar shook it.

"You watch your back out there, Father," Oscar said.

"You too, brother."

———

After the ICE raids turned up the seven bodies, any hope Michael had of slipping home even just to shower and change went out the window. This was the worst-case scenario everyone feared. Not only did it double the number of SARS deaths, it suggested that dozens more, the ones who had lived in the squats and handled the bodies, were potentially infected and running through the streets, possibly infecting more people.

The city was about to descend into abject panic.

So not only did Michael stay, but he had Naomi call everybody else in. He went three blocks over to his twenty-four-hour gym, showered and changed there, then hurried back. As he walked into his office, it was like the world had flipped a switch. Only hours before the calls were about warrants and favorable judges. Now they were about the legalities of shutting down whole sections of the city, targeting the ports, questioning and detaining people off the street, and even a few wanting to ban travelers arriving from China.

"If the virus is already here and came from there, all that does is say we think China has an outbreak and they don't even know it," Michael said. "It's xenophobia."

"I hate to disagree with you, Mr. Story," said the man from the TSA. "We're talking about the Chinese government here. They may have no problem getting people out of the country they deem contagious. Makes it our problem, not theirs."

"You sound paranoid."

"You don't sound paranoid enough," the TSA man shot back. "We've had a dozen deaths in seventy-two hours from a Chinese disease that we now *know* came from within the Chinese illegal immigrant population. They didn't come from nowhere. China knows *something* about this and they're just not saying what. Maybe I am firing one across their bow, but maybe they deserve it."

Michael said something noncommittal about needing to consult with the DA when she came in, then hung up. The next call was about shutting down Asian markets and burning the meat. The one after that was about quarantining the Chinese parts of the San Gabriel Valley, Chinatown, and Monterey Park, and banning public assembly.

"As that is literally against the First Amendment, I'm pretty sure it won't fly with Deb," Michael said, hanging up on the caller, this one a city councilwoman from El Sereno.

As he leaned back in his chair, incredulous at just how quickly those meant to lead the populace during a crisis could wind themselves up into a tizzy, Naomi knocked on the door.

"If this is about more coffee, I think I'll die if I have another cup."

Naomi poked her head in and nodded back toward the lobby. Though it was only six o'clock, the building was buzzing with activity.

"You have a walk-in," she announced.

"That doesn't sound promising."

"It's Jing Saifai," Naomi replied.

Michael sat up straight. "About what?"

"I have no idea. She was very apologetic and said she'd wait to work around your schedule. All she needed was five minutes."

Michael's mind raced.

What the hell does she want? This couldn't still be about Yamazoe, could it? That felt like ancient history.

"Put her in the conference room," Michael said. "Tell her I'll be fifteen minutes. Tell her we're out of coffee."

"Got it."

"Then come back and get me in thirty minutes."

Michael got back on the phone. Over the next half hour he had Naomi phone the assistant closest to the conference room to report back what Saifai was doing. It was always the same: nothing. No phone, no rifling through her bag, nothing.

Time to say hi.

"Sorry for making you wait, but I hope you understand," Michael said in his most unapologetic voice when he finally swept in a moment later. "It's a bit crazy here right now."

"Of course," Saifai replied. "I only want a few minutes of your time."

"What's this about?" Michael asked, disinterested as possible.

"There were a number of raids on buildings this morning," Saifai began. "They were allegedly being used for illicit activities."

"If you expect me to confirm this, I can't," Michael said.

Saifai waved these words away. "I represent the pool of owners of these buildings. My clients had nothing to do with this and were in all cases far removed from the process. In the case where the most bodies were recovered, the property was already being transferred, as it had become so troublesome. These are prominent businessmen, however, and it would hurt their reputations should they be associated with something like this."

Am I hearing this? Michael thought.

"Let me get this straight. You want me to strike names from potential indictment lists to shield your clients' reputations? I'm sorry, but that's cra—"

"We have been told that you're considering a run for district attorney next year," Saifai said, interrupting. "My clients have unique access to some of the largest voting blocs in the city. Your election would be guaranteed."

Michael knew who she meant, a handful of the largest unions in town, likely the dockworkers, the textile workers, and the hotel and restaurant employees union, but also the Asian-American community in general. He knew she couldn't deliver every one of those votes, but if she even brought in a fraction she was right about him winning the election.

"I need to inform you that you are attempting to bribe a public official," Michael said. "You can be arrested as soon as you walk out the door."

"'Can' suggests that we are past 'attempts' and entering into the negotiation phase," Saifai said. "If I remember correctly, when I presented the current DA with a similar offer before she ran eight years ago, she threatened me with arrest in the very courtroom I'd approached her in. She even called over a bailiff. Yet here we are."

Michael was blindsided by this revelation. Saifai could tell and almost cracked a smile. But when Michael thought about it a little more, his stomach knotted.

Is that how they knew when Yamazoe was set to be transferred? Did Deb set me up?

"Forget it," Michael said, getting to his feet. "If it was any other day than one where I'm dealing with a crisis like this, I'd throw the book at you. But right now I'm just too busy. Please show yourself out, and never try to pull that kind of thing with me or anyone else in this office again."

Jing Saifai rose from her seat and eyed Michael indignantly. Just as she was about to say one more thing, however, he turned and exited the room.

———

Luis awoke in the cemetery. It hadn't been by design. He'd meant to take a taxi back to St. Augustine's after he left Oscar's body shop and had walked a good half mile down Sunset looking for one. But every time a cab came along, his arms stayed by his side and his feet kept walking. He eventually found himself at the back gate of the cemetery where his mother was buried and crept inside. When he reached the plot she shared with his brother, he leaned against their headstone, closed his eyes, and fell asleep, warm in her imagined embrace.

He slept fitfully, his thoughts turning on the events of the past several days. When morning came, he prayed over the graves one last time before heading back out to grab one of the first crosstown buses of the morning.

Once on board he plucked out his cell phone, now almost completely drained of its battery life, and called Susan. Though it was six in the morning, he imagined she'd been up all night.

"Nan?" she asked, her voice spectral and exhausted.

"No, it's Luis," he said. "How are you?"

"Not great. There are two more dead in Encino. A husband and wife. The thin bit of good news is that we've started to have some who are merely infected coming into the hospital for treatment. While the prognosis is dire, we're at least able to map their interactions and reach out to others they might've infected or been infected by."

"The other two addresses, the ones where they found the other bodies—did you visit those, too?"

"Not me personally, but I think clinics that were closer probably sent people over."

"Do you remember how you first got the address of the place originally?"

Susan thought for a moment. "No, not really. Probably came from our administrator, Clover Gao. She might've been threatened by local enforcement over something, and she decided to cover her ass by doing something positive for the community."

"How's that covering her ass?"

"If it's a triad squat, it'd be her way of doing them a favor."

"But you don't know that."

"No, I don't know that for sure. What're these questions?"

"I only have one more."

"Fire away."

"Would Father Chang have visited all of these squats?"

"Oh God, you can't think he was infected, can you?"

"Hadn't he recently returned from Indonesia?"

"Weeks ago!" Susan cried. "But if he'd been sick with something as fast moving as SARS, I would've known it. He was healthy as a horse. You don't actually suspect that he infected anyone, do you?"

"All the doctors in the city can't figure out what the pattern is here, but I've found one. There is a link between at least a couple of them that couldn't have come in contact any other way."

"I'm all ears, Father," Susan said.

"You, Dr. Auyong," Luis said. "The squats, the Carreños, the man at the dry cleaner. You interacted with them all. *You're* the link."

PART III

XVII

The patient zero's name was Yanan Su, this according to a hasty investigation launched by the ICE liaising with the State Department. She was nineteen years old, born in Wuhan to a father who worked at the Wuchang shipyards and a mother who passed away when she was six. Yanan had come to America with her boyfriend, Xugang Sun. He left her two days after they arrived. She was dead four days later.

But the City of Los Angeles didn't mourn her passing. They made her a scapegoat.

Before the raid Tony knew his businesses and those of his brethren would come under attack. This almost wasn't a question.

Oh no, racist people are racist!

But stupid people were stupid and they fell for simple workarounds like new deliverymen and painted-over trucks. *Fronts.* Those were things that could be handled with a couple of conversations and a few handshakes. It was a done deal.

Now that the population had not one but several patients zero—all illegal Chinese immigrants, spread in three locations across the city—work-arounds were a thing of the past. The media had its scapegoat and it wanted blood. There was a tangible enemy now, whereas before it was simply a virus. Law enforcement agencies were leaned on, congressional representatives were called, and the media demanded action on illegal immigration.

See? It's not just about immigrants taking your jobs away anymore. It's your life, too!

And Tony knew it would work the moment it happened. The FBI, ICE, LAPD, and any number of other alphabet agencies had been waiting for a moment like this to come after, among other organizations, the LA triad. It was not going to be easy. The triad was entrenched, it had powerful friends, and even more importantly, the best lawyers. An incident like this, however, was like when it was a police officer's kid that got shot. *All* overtime, no matter how tangential, suddenly got approved. Need more manpower? You got it! High-tech equipment? Hey, let me fill out that requisition form for you! You want one warrant? How about fifty? In fact, how about I just sign a bunch and leave them blank so you can fill 'em out later?

It was open season. All Tony could do was hold down the fort at the Century Continental and wait for the revolving door to turn and usher four uniformed LAPD officers into the lobby with his name on their warrant. Until then he'd reassure guests, helpfully cancel reservations, and get his office affairs in order to allow a smooth transition once he was gone.

Of course, his mind wasn't entirely on himself. It was with the young pregnant woman somewhere overlooking the city with her jet-liner views and teetering health. He was surprised by how much he longed to be beside her. To be the one who would tell her that she was going to be all right. That the baby was going to be fine. Or even just to amuse her with funny stories until she felt better.

But he wasn't wanted there any more than he was needed. Part of him just wanted to leave the city, but the "and go where?" question wasn't easily answered. He settled on Geneva. He had the money. At least, money enough. That there would be no going back, that it would be the same as when he washed up on shore in San Diego so many years ago, a stranger in a strange land with no friends or references, kept him paralyzed and at his desk.

It was just past nine when his cell phone rang. He saw that it had the +852 of Hong Kong and was briefly relieved at the prospect of talking to someone Chinese. When it turned out to be Kuo Kuang—not a subordinate, not an adviser but the crime boss himself and father of Jun Tan's baby—Tony almost lost his composure.

Almost.

"Good day, *géxià*," Tony said, just the right amount of obsequiousness in his voice.

"Jun," Kuang said.

"She is at the house," Tony replied. "She is in the care of our doctor. There are no complications with the pregnancy. I'm sure you've heard of the outbreak here."

Four unimpeachable statements.

"Shen Mang, your man at the airport. He has called me. He has said that America's agents are at his airport asking questions, looking at flight logs, and viewing security footage. They think the disease came from China."

Tony wondered which agents these might be. *Homeland Security? FBI? ICE? INS? CDC? FAA? All of the above?*

"I have received no such reports," Tony replied. "And no one has come to see me."

"Does Shen Mang know where Jun is being housed?"

"He does not," Tony said, stretching out the last word. "Should he?"

"Shen Mang said that he feared arrest," Kuang continued. "And made it clear in clumsy terms that to ensure his silence about Jun and this operation, all I needed to do was send a first-class ticket for him back to Hong Kong as well as twenty thousand dollars in expenses money. Is that what it would take to ensure your own silence, Mr. Qi?"

"Absolutely not," Tony assured him. "There are no illegalities here. None at all. This is about the outbreak. All they can do is harass, but to get to Jun or even you—"

"They cannot get to me," Kuang interrupted.

"To get to Jun they'd have to get through me," Tony stated. "And I won't allow that to happen."

Kuang went quiet. Tony hoped this was enough to appease him.

"Do your assurances extend to this driver you've hired for them?"

So Kuang knew about Archie.

"They do. He's a trusted member of our organization and—"

"He is not Chinese," Kuang said.

"No, he is Samoan," Tony replied. "But he has done work for us for years."

"All right. But does your assurance extend to Shen Mang?"

Tony thought fast. Shen Mang should never have tried to blackmail Kuo Kuang. The next time he saw him, Tony knew he'd have to lay into him for such an impertinent move. Still, he had allowed Mang into the operation and couldn't pretend otherwise now for fear of looking like a poor manager.

"Of course," Tony said, but with a light touch. "He is the functionary of that airport and supports all our efforts there. He is of our brethren, so I consider him above reproach."

"Shen Mang is dead," Kuang said. "And if anything happens to my unborn son, you will die next."

The phone line went dead. Tony sat for a long moment thinking about his next move. No, he might not be able to keep Jun alive, but someone had infected her. At the very least he could discover who.

━━━━━

Chan Yip, Raymond Shaw, Kwok Kwong, Lo Kwan Deshuai, Moses Li, Chui Songwei, Wanquan Yang, and Chan Hui. These were the owners or co-owners of the three squats where the patients zero were found. Well, not *directly*. The actual buildings were owned by a number of shell and holding companies whose origins were obscured with carefully strung webs of red tape.

If Michael—or more accurately, his newly corporate-busting assistant Naomi—didn't know what they were looking for, it could've taken weeks if not months to decipher the real ownership. But as Jing Saifai had delivered a barely veiled inference on a silver platter, it took only half a day.

"They are all alleged organized crime figures," Naomi said. "And once you really start reaching for connections, you see how immigrants got there in the first place from the ports. You've got men who own ships, others who run import/export businesses, and still others that control swaths of real estate. If you are trafficking in humans, you don't need much more than that."

"How hard do we have to hit that 'alleged' part?" Michael asked.

"Not very. The papers will do it for us. You give them something like this at a moment like now, and they will write whatever you tell them to and thank you later."

Christ on the cross, Michael thought.

"Can you give me a moment?"

Naomi nodded and exited the office. Michael leaned his chair back and stared out the window overlooking the south end of the recently completed Grand Park. He remembered what Jeff Lambert said when they first spoke, that Deborah had tried to "use" the triad bust to keep herself in office. So either Jai Saifai was lying, or Deborah thought them toothless enough that she could turn on them without consequence.

He figured it was the latter.

Now that he had a real case linking SARS to the triad, starting with a bunch of dead bodies piled up in their dilapidated buildings, this would be front-page news, and he would be way out front. But there was no way Saifai wouldn't hit him back however she could. He'd need backup with political capital once the triad bosses began pulling the strings of everyone they had in power.

He checked his contact list for a number and hit "Call." Lambert picked up on the second ring.

"Hey, Story," Lambert said, sounding winded. "Wish I had time to talk shop, but everything's a bit in flux over here. People are in full-on panic mode, though I'm not entirely sure what they think their local political party reps will be able to do about it."

"The patients zero paid the LA triad to bring them over from China, they made the crossing on triad-owned ships, and they were put up in triad-owned buildings."

Lambert went so silent, Michael thought he might've passed out. But then he came roaring back, his exhausted tone all but gone.

"You're shitting me."

"Was just looking at the shell company records. They've got their fingers in businesses all over town."

"'Marshak Prosecutor Targets Triads, Saves City.' Jeez, Michael. When you decide you want to get elected, you really go all out, huh?"

"Yeah, but you know they're going to come back guns a-blazing."

"Good point," Lambert said. "Ideally you'd be on that podium between the mayor and the chief of police."

"I want the mayor to make the statement."

"Not you?"

"Too early. Let the mayor say it, then let the papers connect it to me. CNN won't run my face, but they will run the mayor's, and that's what we want, right? Even better, he'll owe me."

"You are a crafty bastard, Prosecutor," Lambert said. "But you're also right. I'll call the mayor right now. You gin up a briefing so he knows what he's saying. You ready to make any arrests?"

"Nah, I don't want old guys in their golf gear getting pulled out of their suburban houses with kids and grandkids crying in the background," Michael said. "We put the word out and we wait. The first one—and you know there'll be one—who tries to hop on a plane back to China we give the whole treatment to. News vans, big cameras, bewildered-looking guy in handcuffs frog-marched out of the terminal, the works. The kind of thing that shoots bail up to the stratosphere, as they're all known flight risks. The trial might not happen until after the election. We've got to get all the play we can out of it now."

Lambert laughed. "If I had ten of you, I guarantee I could get one of 'em into the White House in ten years. You're dangerous, Mr. Story."

"Don't you forget, Mr. Lambert," Michael said, then hung up the phone.

Luis sat opposite Susan in her clinic's tiny lab as she tested her own blood for SARS. Due to newfound interest from law enforcement in these unlicensed clinics as they related to the spread of the plague, Clover Gao had told the staff to take the next few days off. Most had already gone after the Carreños' deaths, but the last holdouts were now gone, too.

"Moment of truth," Susan said, checking the sample she'd taken from within her nasal cavity with a commercial polymerase test kit. "Ah, looks like I'm not Typhoid Mary. Sorry to disappoint you."

Luis was surprised. He'd thought the connection was too spot-on to be a coincidence. "But you're the only one who can tie your patients' cases to the squat house."

"That we know of," Susan said. "This could just mean there are far more unreported cases than we've seen so far."

"And you're sure it's not Father Chang?" Luis asked. "Could he have been a carrier but not gotten sick?"

"I don't think that's possible," Susan said. "Also, due to the sexual nature of the accusations against him, they would've taken tissue samples at the coroner's office—blood, seminal fluid, and so on. They would've found SARS."

"Are you sure?"

Susan took a moment and called a friend of hers working with the CDC team at Good Samaritan. She outlined Chang's potential involvement in the vaguest terms possible. The doctor on the other end said he would call over to the coroner's office and check. Five minutes later the phone rang again. The verdict was negative. Father Chang's samples were SARS-free.

"How long would SARS be present in the sample?" Luis asked. "Couldn't it have vanished?"

"The virus maybe, but not the body's response to it. But the samples were kept in inert substances that wouldn't absorb the virus. In a human the virus would alter, grow, change, or die. On something inert it could survive indefinitely, just waiting to be activated. Scientists have done biochemical weapons tests with viruses on spider webs. Someone trying to infect an enemy that may return to an area will spray a sample on the web and, the theory is, the bad guy could still get sick if they touch the spider web weeks later."

Luis puzzled over this for a moment. He'd been so sure there was some kind of connection here. Now they were back to square one.

"I should probably get some sleep before heading back over to Good Samaritan," Susan said, rising and patting Luis on the shoulder. "It was a good guess, but sometimes that's not good enough."

Luis nodded and headed out of the clinic. As he rode the bus back to St. Augustine's, he tried to put the pieces together, but the final image remained elusive. He had arranged for a substitute to teach his morning classes, a priest from Holy Trinity in Baldwin Hills, but Luis knew he couldn't keep doing this. He was either a parish priest or he was some kind of amateur sleuth gallivanting around the city, trying to do the job of the police.

For the rest of the day he threw himself into his work. He taught his classes, he graded papers, he prepared a test for the end of the week, and he actually, in long hand, began to write his sermon about Saint Peter Claver.

When he checked the local news on his phone in the early evening, he caught sight of Michael Story at a press conference, alongside the mayor, the chief of police, a representative of the ICE, and a few other groups. Without ever using the word "triad," the mayor succinctly explained that the outbreak resulted not from poor security measures at the airport but because of an unscrupulous criminal organization. He was careful not to cite "illegal immigrants," knowing what kind of backlash a statement like that could lead to. By tying it to a bunch of crooks, he turned fear into a rallying cry. The news story then showed one of these alleged crooks, a Chui Songwei, being arrested as he attempted to flee the country with his wife and two children from Las Vegas's McCarran Airport.

And then came the clincher.

"Deputy District Attorney Michael Story, who is spearheading the investigation, made headlines earlier this year when he took on a human trafficking—"

Luis turned off and pocketed his phone. He knew the rest. He also knew that Michael likely orchestrated the entire event down to the mayor's speech. He wouldn't have put it past him to have driven Songwei the five hours to McCarran just to make sure he looked guilty as sin for the cameras.

But it still didn't explain the killing of Father Chang.

With all of this on his mind, he headed to the chapel to help with evening Mass. Before he could reach the sacristy, Erna stopped him in the hallway.

"There's a delivery for you in the office," she said. "I would've brought it to the rectory, but it was too heavy."

Luis thanked her and moved to the admin office. He was surprised to see that the box came from St. Jerome's. He opened it and found what was described on a card as Father Chang's personal effects as taken from his car. It wasn't much. Just what Pastor Siu-Tung had described.

When Luis got to the bulk boxes of pills, however, he was surprised. They weren't the same as the ones he'd come across in Chang's medicine cabinet. In fact, they weren't for hypertension at all. The boxes were labeled "Glutide," with English-language instructions designating it as a product for diabetics. Price stickers on each seemed to indicate that, yes, they'd been paid for in Indonesian rupiah. Only the why was missing.

Unsure what to make of this, Luis called Susan.

"I'm looking at a stack of generic pharmaceuticals Father Chang had in his car trunk the night he was killed. Was he diabetic?"

"No, not at all. He was hypertensive and took Lozol for it. But diabetic? No. And yes, I would've known."

"Could he have been bringing them back for someone? A cheaper alternative to what's available here?" Luis asked.

"Can you read me the active ingredients on the box?"

Luis did. There were only two.

"That's identical to a number of products here. The cost of travel would wipe out any savings. Worse, it's the Wild West down there. A lot of what you find on the shelves isn't even what it says it is. You've got these fly-by-night drug companies making unregulated generics in India and China to compete with the expensive American and European brands. They claim to be the same stuff, but you never know the quality of the active ingredients or what's being used for the inactive ones, much less the conditions under which it was made. It's big, big business."

"Do people ever get hurt?" Luis asked, Susan's statement triggering something in the back of his mind.

"Yeah, all the time," Susan confirmed. "People even die. A few years ago it happened here. Nineteen people died because of some tainted pills they thought they were getting from a Canadian pharmaceutical company, but it turned out to be a totally unregulated fly-by-night outfit in China."

Luis's mind raced. He stared at the box in his hand, a theory beginning to form.

"What is it, Father?" Susan asked.

"If I wanted to know everything about Father Chang's travels, where would I start?"

XVIII

Tracking Father Chang's movements through Indonesia proved remarkably easy. At least, at first. Susan directed Luis to online editions of St. Jerome's church bulletin as well as ones from the churches Father Chang had visited overseas. There he was taking photos with locals, sampling the cuisine laid out for him, visiting parishes both urban and rural, and taking part in everything from dances to building projects to Mass. A clear picture was painted of everywhere he went, whom he saw, and the parishes he visited. It was practically a diary.

But peering at it through the prism of someone who was there for another purpose altogether, Luis saw it for what it was—a cover story.

There were gaps in time. Half days missing. A day missing. Nights missing. A weekend missing. Pulling up a second browser window on Erna's computer, Luis looked at a map of the sprawling, multi-island nation. Some of the gaps could be accounted for with travel time. The rest, however, were a mystery.

When he searched local news stories for instances of SARS, no results came back. When he switched that to cases of tainted pharmaceuticals, he hit the mother lode. The stories began with a handful of unusual deaths. In an early article it was suggested that an outbreak of some kind of infectious disease had claimed the lives of about a dozen men. Then there was a second article from a different part of the country saying much the same thing. In both cases the victims were elderly, poor, and male. Local fears centered on some new mosquito-borne disease that attacked a compromised immune system. The men had uniformly suffered from issues typical of their ages like heart disease and high blood pressure.

When no definitive cause was discovered and the deaths ebbed off, it seemed as if the story, too, would go away.

But when a third outbreak happened farther up the coast, a local blogger cum investigator named Kirk Asmara got involved. He'd known the family of one of the dead men and had begun putting the pieces together. After speaking to all the families, he learned that each of the men took beta-blockers for high blood pressure. More importantly, in each household he discovered the leftover pills were all of the same low-grade generic brand. These weren't the kind found in the finest hospitals and pharmacies so much as from street vendors or bodegas, where one could also buy anything from knockoff perfume that turned out to be colored water and vanilla to bulk cases of shampoo that turned out to be vegetable oil, dish soap, and food coloring.

One death from shoddy generics was easily swept under the rug. A pattern like this was harder to ignore. When Asmara gathered his findings and took them to Jakarta's largest daily, it ran the story on the front page. There was a minor outcry, prompting a government investigation. The drugs were discovered to have come from a company in Hong Kong, which quickly admitted its guilt, made payments to the families of the dead in the amounts of 70 million rupiah, or about $5,000, a piece, and shuttered.

As far as Asmara could tell, no one was ever charged.

A few months later there was another outbreak of deaths Asmara tracked back to tainted pharmaceuticals. He began reaching out to activists in other areas around the Indian Ocean and discovered even more victims. In each case the pharmaceuticals could be traced back to shadowy companies in China or India that would often close up shop or outright vanish as soon as improprieties were reported. What Asmara seemed to realize, however, was that with this intricate a web of distribution and such high profits to be made, there had to be at least some kind of major corporation backing it from somewhere.

Luis couldn't tell exactly when in the timeline Father Chang got involved, but once he did, his travels to the region coincided with Asmara's web articles outlining clandestine visits to distribution centers and dealers. He seemed to know he was getting close to the big story, and Father Chang was helping.

Then it came to a swift halt. Six months back Asmara died when his motorcycle collided with a guardrail on a lonely stretch of road outside Makassar. There was no suggestion that it was anything but an accident, except the detail Luis discovered that Asmara didn't actually own a motorcycle. On a memorial website set up by the families of those he was trying to help, Luis found a note from Father Chang. It was short and anguished and in the end said only that the fight against "Fanrong" would go on.

Fanrong?

Fanrong, it turned out, was the name of a drug manufacturer and subsidiary of an outfit called the Jiankang Holding Group. Though *jiànkāng* meant "health," it had a worldwide reputation for promoting the exact opposite. It was also a billion-dollar enterprise and rumored to be linked to the Hong Kong triad.

And there it was: the big monied corporation behind the cheaply made and occasionally fatally tainted pharmaceuticals.

Luis shook his head. Of course, organized crime was involved in the mass production of knockoffs going way back, from Louis Vuitton suitcases that fell apart after two usages or Chanel suits that became discolored when exposed to even a droplet of rain. Only these knockoffs killed people. If all these outbreaks really were linked together, *thousands* of people.

Like the SARS outbreak in Los Angeles was doing.

It's not an outbreak at all, Luis realized. *It's contaminated pills.*

He had to find Susan.

————

Tony Qi was no investigator, but he knew when things didn't add up. He mapped and remapped the route they'd taken with Jun from the John Wayne Airport to Sunset to the Beverly Hills Hotel and then to the house. There was no way possible for her to have come into contact with anyone on the list of the infected or the dead. Either she had come over with the virus, which would have been the coincidence of all coincidences, or she had picked it up some other way.

Which is when he thought of Dr. Martin Soong.

"I've been tested and retested for the disease," Martin said when Tony drove over to his mid-Wilshire office. "There's no one I've come in contact with who I know to have been infected, but that doesn't mean much. That said, the gestation period of the disease does match up perfectly with when I first saw her. So yes, I've been concerned. But I would've expressed the symptoms of the disease by now, so the timing is a coincidence."

No such thing, Tony thought.

"Could you be a carrier without being infected yourself?" Tony asked.

"No. For some diseases, yes. For SARS, no."

"What about your equipment? Could it have carried the virus in?"

Martin shook his head. "It's all sterilized. Besides, if she was infected from it, it would mean another patient had it, and that hasn't happened. She's the only one, I'm afraid."

This answer didn't work for Tony. He'd actually called Oscar after leaving the house the other night to get the gangster turned real estate baron to assign a couple of men to watch the house and make sure no one else entered. When he'd rung back several hours later, Oscar reported that no one had entered or exited except Dr. Soong.

Could it have been Archie?

When he called the big man's home, Archie answered, apologized again for quitting, but reported that his health was just fine.

On the drive up to the house, Tony tried to think of other points of intersection between Jun's world and Los Angeles at large and couldn't come up with a one. The house had been vacant before they'd moved in. The house to the left was unoccupied; the house to the right was home to an elderly couple, who seldom left. The postman drove by, but there was no mail.

He was only a hundred yards from the house when his cell phone rang. Surprised to get reception, he discovered the caller to be Bo Xu, one of the warehouse managers who was overseeing the switch from the triad deliverymen to Oscar's crew.

"Mr. Xu? How are you?" Tony asked as he answered.

"There's an issue with these men you've sent me," Xu complained. "Their delivery times are shot to hell. I even had one group leave their truck half-full of perishables out on Sawtelle. They just left it there! I had to find a second crew to take over. They'd run out of gas."

"Whose job is it to fill the trucks?" Tony asked.

"The driver."

"Were they told that?"

There was a pause. "I'm sure they were."

"Well, let's make double sure, and I'll have a word with Oscar."

"That's not the issue," Xu said without thanking him. "An entire section of deliveries is going undelivered."

"Section? I'm confused. What do you mean?"

"They're refusing to deliver to the hospitals and clinics," Xu said. "They've bought into the bull about it having come from China and figure if they walk into a Chinese-owned clinic, they'll catch the virus."

"But taking money from Chinese bosses in Chinese warehouses is just fine, huh?"

"Seems to be."

Tony considered this problem. He knew the triad controlled the supplying of linens and cleaning supplies to a number of hospitals and urgent-care facilities around Los Angeles that would fall under the Oscar arrangement. But all the Chinese-owned unlicensed clinics they supported wouldn't need temp deliverymen.

"For the unlicensed clinics, just send our regular drivers. I'll talk to Oscar about how to handle the hospitals."

"Great," Xu replied, then hung up.

Tony parked at the house on Grand View and headed inside. Chen Jiang was seated in the living room drinking tea and watching television.

Why wasn't she *the one to get sick?* Tony scoffed.

But the thought stopped him in his tracks. Why *wasn't* Jun's constant companion sick? There was nothing Jun did away from her. She ate the same meals, had stayed in the same rooms, had shaken the same hands, had breathed the same air.

So why wasn't she sick?

It couldn't be the pregnancy.

"Hello, Tony," Jiang said. "She is sleeping, but I have to wake her up soon for her pills."

"Which ones? I'll wake her up."

"The ones in the bathroom," Jiang said. "The prenatal vitamins I'm still giving her, but also the ones Dr. Soong left for her symptoms."

Slipping a mask over his face, Tony entered the bedroom and was mortified. The Jun he'd seen even hours before was spectral now. If he couldn't hear her ragged breathing, he might imagine she was dead.

He didn't even want to think about the status of her unborn child. He turned to move into the bathroom when he heard his name.

"Mr. Qi?"

"Tony. Please."

"All right. Tony, can you come closer?"

He moved to the bed. The voice was as unrecognizable as its owner. Jun held out her hand to him, and he only hesitated for a moment until taking it.

"I know I can't ask you to do this, but will you lie down with me for a moment? Just long enough to tell me another of your stories."

Tony looked down at her. What had come before felt like prologue. She had an easy charm and a flirtatious streak, which had likely served her well as an actress and television presenter. He'd let himself be seduced like any viewer might. Rather than money, what she wanted from him was likely the odd favor, the knowledge that he'd come when called, and so forth.

But things were different now. Now she needed something but wasn't sure how to get it so was falling back on whatever had worked in the past.

"Ms. Tan," Tony said carefully. "I fear we're in danger of crossing a line."

And like that the artifice momentarily vanished from her face. It looked like she'd been caught out, her condition preventing her from coming back with the perfect witty deflection. She nodded but then found her way back to a serviceable response.

"I understand if you're worried about getting sick," she said evenly. "But if you fear Kuo Kuang, you should know he won't learn of any of this."

Telling himself that he was doing this only because the extreme situation demanded it, he moved to the other side of the bed and slipped in next to her. With arms so weak they felt like a child's, she wrapped his arms around her and moved her body close to his. He put his head on the pillow next to hers as her hair grazed his nose. He inhaled, smelling both her illness and traces still of the scent he'd found so intoxicating when she'd emerged from the plane for the first time. He held her, and she gripped his arms tighter.

"If you could take me anywhere in the world, where would it be?" she asked in barely more than a whisper. "If we could board a plane tomorrow, what would I see when we landed?"

"You've seen Paris, but have you seen the Val-d'Oise?" he asked.

"What is that?"

"It's the great forested river valley about an hour north of Paris. It's all rolling hills, farmland, rich forests, and lakes. It's a magical place. If you go far enough east, you reach a place many still swear is the location of Merlin's tomb and the underwater castle of the Lady of the Lake."

"I thought King Arthur was an English story."

"It is. But if you ever saw this place, called Brocéliande, you would understand its reputation. They say that if you pierce the surface on just the right day, you will see the Lady's great castle in the depths below. But if you swim to it, the distance will remain constant until you've exhausted yourself and drown."

"Goodness," Jun said, her voice fading. "Tell me about our journey."

"We'll leave here by car and be at the airport in an hour. We'll board an Air France flight, settle into our first-class seats, and be airborne in seconds."

"My passport? Won't we be stopped?"

"But of course we'll have new ones."

"Ah, of course."

Tony wound a story of cycling through an empty countryside of tall, interwoven trees, of long-forgotten battlefields and the warm summer sun. He invented cafés to eat at, trains to take, an abbey they'd take refuge in when it rained, and the sights they'd see. They'd visit the grave of Van Gogh and tour his last apartment. They'd go to the castle at Montmorency. They'd visit Chantilly.

By the time he was explaining where they'd stay for the night, she was asleep again. He watched her ragged breathing for a moment and realized that maybe he'd seen the real Jun the whole time. He hadn't been seduced by the image but his subconscious recognition of the person within. And maybe, just maybe, that was something she found appealing, and not simply as a novelty.

It could be nice to be known.

He rose as gently as he could, allowing her to settle back onto the bed with little fuss. He realized he hadn't delivered her the pills she needed but decided they could give them to her when she woke. He went to the bathroom and found them where Jiang had said they'd be.

And that's when he realized what had come into the house for Jun that wasn't shared with anyone else.

———

It took Luis ten minutes to finally get someone at Good Samaritan who knew who Susan was.

"Dr. Auyong? Oh, she went back to her clinic a little while ago," the voice on the line said. "I have a cell number for her if you want to try her there."

When she didn't answer her phone, Luis got in his car and raced over as fast as he could. He pounded on the door for almost ten minutes before a bleary-eyed Susan opened up.

"You scared the hell out of me," she said. "What do—?"

"The virus is being spread by pills," Luis announced, barging in. "The victims are all taking tainted medications. That's the link."

"That's not how SARS is spread," Susan said after getting over her initial shock. "It's through person-to-person contact. You can't get it from a pill."

"What if you could? You said yourself it could live on an inert surface. If the pills are generics from China or somewhere, they could've been infected overseas, then come here. I think this is what Father Chang was investigating when he was killed."

Luis explained about Father Chang's secret trips to Indonesia to track down Jiankang knockoffs and interview victims with Kirk Asmara. How he brought back samples, and how the whole thing was controlled by the various Southeast Asian triad organizations. He also laid out how many people had died.

"So, tell me. Of the victims you interacted with—Rabih Chaumon, César Carreño, and the girl in the squat house—were any of them taking these kinds of generics?"

Susan thought this over for a second, then led Luis to the receptionist's desk, where she accessed patient files. She started with César Carreño. The file came up immediately.

"Jesus Christ," she said. "He was on Hasix for hypertension."

"Hasix is what Father Chang brought back from Indonesia. Is that Jiankang?"

"Yeah, but they call themselves Bumblebee Vigor or something in America," Susan said, already typing in the next name. When Rabih Chaumon came up, she found the same thing. "Hasix."

"That can't be a coincidence. What about the stuff you took to the squat houses?"

"I'd bring Asozide, a generic diuretic, but also a compound vitamin called Biox with iron, folic acid, and so on—same thing I had the receptionist give to Esmeralda Carreño," Susan recalled. "Two of the most harmless drugs imaginable."

"Both made by this Bumblebee Vigor?"

"Yeah," Susan said, leaping to her feet. "Come with me."

Luis followed Susan down the hall to the supply room. There she opened cabinet after cabinet, revealing dozens of boxes with the logo for Bumblebee Vigor on the side.

"The turnover on this stuff is high, so it's all recent stuff," Susan said, grabbing a number of boxes. "Put on a mask and gloves. You're going to help me with this."

Luis said a prayer and did just that. Over the next fifteen minutes they batch-tested eighty pills using PCR kits Susan had on hand from Good Samaritan. The first seventy-nine came back negative. The eightieth, a pill that had been hermetically sealed inside a blister pack until three minutes before, tested positive for SARS.

When Susan tested the rest of that twenty-pill pack, three more came back positive.

"That's it," Susan said. "The smoking gun. And just this many pills means they could be all over the entire city by now. That's literally hundreds of thousands of people at risk. Maybe even millions."

"Time to call the cavalry," Luis said.

XIX

Michael's heart beat a mile a minute as he listened to first Luis then Dr. Auyong lay out their doomsday prediction on the phone.

"Is there any chance it can spread to those who haven't taken the tainted medication? A carrier passing it like a normal virus?" he asked, unsure he wanted to hear the answer.

"We haven't had a case like that yet, but that doesn't mean it can't," Susan said. "If we don't isolate the infected fast enough, that's the doomsday scenario we could be facing."

"How many people could someone unknowingly infect? Just themselves?"

"Entirely dependent on their daily social interaction," Susan replied.

Michael estimated that people might interact with between ten and twenty others a day if they worked outside the house. If the distribution of the pills was as widespread as the doctor suggested it was, with up to a hundred thousand people potentially becoming carriers, the result was no less than an outbreak capable of wiping out every human being in Southern California.

"Can I speak to Luis again?"

The phone was passed. "Hello?" said the priest.

"I don't know how you did it, but I appreciate the heads-up."

"I didn't do it for you," Luis said.

"I know," Michael admitted. "But if this is why they killed Father Chang, I promise you that our office will make sure that angle is front and center when we start handing down charges."

"Great," said Luis, then hung up.

Michael sat at his desk practically hyperventilating for a moment before grabbing the edge of his desk, as if to keep himself from falling off the earth. He had to think fast.

"Michael?" Naomi said, her voice full of alarm as she stepped into his office.

"I don't even know the right person to call about this one," he finally managed to say. "I think it's going to have to be the mayor."

"It's getting late. I'm not sure—"

"Find him," Michael demanded, his voice rising. "Right now. I need him on this phone within a minute. I'm not kidding. This needs to happen right now."

Naomi hurried from the office. Forty seconds later Michael's phone buzzed.

"The mayor's on line one."

Michael picked up the phone and got right to the point. "There's no easy way to say this, sir, but we have to figure out a way to tell everybody taking prescription medication in the City of Los Angeles that they may be in serious danger without setting off mass panic."

There was a long pause. Then the mayor asked to hear the whole story as he added his aides to the call. Michael repeated exactly what Luis had just told him, relieved now to have only carried the burden of the city's fate for less than five minutes. When he was done, no one said a word.

"If this is true, Michael," the mayor began, "it's not Deb who's got to worry about you taking her job, it's me."

Michael wasn't sure whether to laugh or vomit that the mayor's first thought was to his political future.

"Before I make any kind of announcement, we need to test—"

"Dr. Auyong is having a mobile team from the CDC come to her clinic to test the pills. We should have confirmation within the hour. They're calling me directly."

"Well done, Michael," the mayor said. "That's really good news. Let me know the moment you hear. I'll have my deputy call you right back to begin prepping my statement. The city is in your debt."

The city is in my debt?

The line went dead. Michael shook his head, wondering if he hadn't properly expressed the danger to the population. His head was still swimming.

But then one thought knifed through all the others.

My children, he thought. *If anything happens to my children . . .*

———

It wasn't the biggest house Oscar had seen. Not the house with the highest resale value. Not the place with the most perfect amenities, greatest views (though the view was spectacular), or even the most easily accessible.

But it was the best house.

When Helen had texted Oscar about meeting her up on Outpost, overlooking Hollywood, to see a house that night, he'd kept it in his mind all day as he oversaw the recruitment and placement of a hundred of his local crew guys, men and boys who were used to the high-adrenaline thrill of boosting cars and getting them out of the city, into jobs as glorified delivery boys. Though the pay was more than fair, the work was *boring*, and the guys got unruly fast. They thought it was a joke having to do this kind of shift. They were crooks specifically because they *didn't* want to put on a uniform and do wage work. Time and again Oscar had to bring the hammer down and get the guys in line.

But the day was finally over and he got to see *her*.

Even as he checked the address on his GPS, Oscar feared he'd get a text from Helen begging off for whatever reason. A babysitter, something at work, her husband. But it never came. Instead, only a quick text asking him which wine he preferred, with an accompanying photo of different bottles.

When he arrived twenty-five minutes later, the place was completely empty, the owner having already moved out, save for a large dining room table with two chairs. Candles were burning on the table, and a beautifully catered meal was set out from one end to the other. Helen came out of the bedroom, turning off the lights as she did. The house was soon dark, except for the two candles and the moon visible out over the city.

"How are you?" she asked, giving Oscar a peck as he wandered in.

"Good," he said. "Great."

If this had been one of his old girlfriends, she would've been waiting for him in, say, four-inch heels and nothing else. Helen wore a blouse and pants. She might've thrown on lipstick, too, but he couldn't tell.

"Have a seat before it gets cold," she said, sitting opposite him. "And tell me about your day."

They talked for two hours. It was maybe the longest conversation they'd ever had. Maybe the longest conversation he'd ever had with anyone, Oscar thought. Sure, he was still thinking about the moment at which he'd lift her from her chair, kiss her like mad, and carry her to the balcony, where they'd have sex, but there was something else, too.

"I love you, Helen," he said as they split a dessert.

Her fork stopped just above the cake, then continued its trajectory through the frosting. When she didn't say anything, Oscar figured he'd screwed up. But then she took a bite of the cake, leaned over to him, and kissed him on the mouth.

"I think I love you, too, Oscar," she said.

She took his hand now and led him away from the table. At first, Oscar thought they were heading to the bedroom but then saw the large hammock swaying in the light breeze on the balcony.

"We can see the stars better out here, don't you think?" Helen asked, taking off first her shoes before moving on to her blouse.

Ah, Oscar thought. *I do.*

An hour later, with Helen tucked into the crook of his arm, Oscar finally looked up to the dark sky and saw the stars. Up here away from the lights of the city, there seemed to be millions more.

Just for the rich, Oscar thought.

"We forgot the dessert," Helen said.

Oscar laughed and kissed her. Then he kissed her again.

In the living room Helen's cell phone began to ring. She let it go for a moment, then finally broke away.

"It might be the babysitter," Helen said, rising from the hammock. "Don't move."

Oscar watched as Helen went to her purse, took out the phone, rolled her eyes at the caller ID, then answered with an annoyed-sounding "Hello?"

Husband, Oscar realized.

But her features turned serious after that. She spoke for only a moment more before hanging up and hurrying to the balcony.

"I need to speak to you about your work," she said, her mind clearly racing. "I know that's off-limits, but this is an emergency."

Not what Oscar expected to hear.

"I don't want to say, in case you have to lie about it later," he protested.

"This is so much more important than that," Helen said. "Michael was calling to warn me that we should get the kids out of town, as the outbreak might be worse than everybody thought. Then he told me *why*. You mentioned that you'd taken over some deliveries for your Asian partners, which includes deliveries to hospitals and pharmacies, right?"

"Um, yeah," Oscar replied unhappily. "What's that got to do with Michael?"

"I need the list of places where the deliveries were made. All of them. And I need to get them to my husband as soon as humanly possible."

"Wait. Why?" Oscar said, getting defensive. "That's hundreds of stops. He's not busting people, is he?"

"The pills are spreading the disease," Helen explained. "He's going to need to know where the boxes went and who took what. You're only the delivery system, so no one's going to care about your connection to this. What he'll need to know is who else took possession of them. That's all."

Oscar didn't like this at all, beginning with Helen getting off the phone with her prosecutor husband, then coming over to tell him what he was or wasn't going to do.

"*Oscar,*" Helen insisted. "There are thousands of lives at stake, maybe even millions. People will die, and others could become infected. You do this and you're saving people. No one will ever have to know where the information came from, but this city will owe you forever. You will be bulletproof. If you stay away from violent crime and narcotics, there won't be a cop in LA who gives you a second glance."

"I'd be ratting out my partners."

"They are going down already," Helen said. "It wouldn't be anything you did. But imagine if you did nothing and a week from now it comes out that, say, their drugs killed a thousand people. They'd all get the chair. You're saving them, too."

Oscar still didn't like it, but Helen's words rang true. She took his hand.

"You trust me, right?" she asked. "This is the right move. I promise."

———

When Luis got off the phone with Michael, Susan grabbed her car keys.

"Come on," she exclaimed.

Before he could ask where they were going, she pulled him out of the clinic and toward the parking lot. Ten minutes later they were racing toward Chinatown.

"Once word gets out, the clinics will put their stock on lockdown, which is great. All that stuff will be burned immediately," she said. "What we have to make sure is that the supply line gets quarantined, too. No more pills leave any of the warehouses, and if there are any still on ships in the port, they've got to go down, too."

"We're just going to barge in and seize all these pills?" Luis asked. "Shouldn't we leave this to the police?"

"Time is of the essence," Susan said. "That, and I don't think these distributors will just hand over their stock when LAPD rolls up. Besides, customs was supposed to be checking all this stuff, and they missed it. Worse, since the outbreaks of a few years ago here in America, the FDA has been flying over to China to test their factories there, and they missed it, too. If we want to stop this, it might be up to us."

"That's what I don't get," Luis said. "If there was a SARS outbreak in China, wouldn't we have heard about it? These people weren't infected by one pill. They got it from diuretics, vitamins, beta-blockers, and their diabetes medication. How do *all of them* become infected with SARS?"

Susan stared through the windshield, slowly shaking her head. "I don't know."

The warehouse took up two blocks in a south corner of Chinatown. Susan circled once, then parked on the street.

"We're not protected here," Susan warned Luis. "I don't know who's here and who isn't, but I guarantee you the triad wouldn't like us snooping around. Especially now."

Luis nodded. He followed Susan as she checked various side doors, finding them all locked. The only way in was through the large open garage doors of the loading bays. Luis couldn't imagine these would be unattended.

But as Susan peered toward a group of workers milling around in front, she lightened.

"I know that guy," she said.

Ushering Luis to a concrete ramp leading into the warehouse, she waved down one of the men.

"Hey, you deliver to my clinic, right?" she asked.

The young man, who'd been pulling on beers with his friends, rose from an upturned bucket and eyed her through the dark.

"Yeah, that's me," he said. "What're you doing down here?"

"My boss has the place locked up tight because of the SARS scare," Susan lied. "But patients need their pills. People are getting sick without them. I just wanted to grab a couple of boxes from our supply."

The deliveryman looked skeptical.

"Who's this?" he asked, nodding to Luis.

"He's helping me with home visits."

Luis waited for this to be the deal breaker. Then Susan peered at the young man.

"Didn't you . . . didn't you used to live on Woosung?" Susan added. "In Yau Tsim Mong District."

"Um, yeah, I did," the deliveryman said, surprised. "How'd you know that?"

"I grew up on Kwun Chung," she said. "I thought you looked familiar the other day."

"Yeah, that's me. Jordan, huh? Small world."

"Small world."

She waited. He finally nodded to the warehouse. "Make it fast. Seriously."

"You got it," she said, flashing him a winning smile.

Luis followed her in, not missing the fact that the other three workers drinking with the young deliveryman were watching them like hawks.

God, please guide us in our search and let us be fleet of foot.

The warehouse was a dimly lit labyrinth. To make things even worse for Luis, much of the writing was in Chinese *hanzi*. He looked around for anything with the Bumblebee label on it, but there was nothing.

"Is this something?" he asked, discovering a box that looked likely.

"Party favors for a kid's birthday," Susan replied. "Try again."

Luis kept moving, staying in a state of prayer, hoping for divine inspiration, but nothing presented itself. A few of the boxes were open, others had silhouettes of what was contained inside printed on the exterior (cutlery, headphones, etc.), but no boxes of drugs.

So it was with relief that he heard Susan's cry from the back of the warehouse.

"Here we go," she announced.

Luis hurried over to find Susan in a valley of cardboard boxes piled high over her head. On both sides he saw nothing but the now-familiar Bumblebee Vigor label. The labels indicated a broad range of contents, but they were all pills.

"What now?" Luis asked.

"Look for the shipping forms," Susan said. "See if you can tell which factory they came from or ship they were on."

Luis nodded and turned the boxes over, looking for anything that fit the bill. When he found nothing on the boxes, he noticed a nearby pallet still wrapped in cellophane, with its forms in a folder taped to the side. He tore off the packet, saw they were written in Chinese, and took them to Susan.

"Bingo," she said, sifting through the pages. But just as quickly her countenance darkened. "Wait, this doesn't make sense. These forms are for export, not import. Where did you find them?"

Luis walked her to the pallet. Together they tore through the cellophane and opened a few of the boxes, discovering not Bumblebee Vigor pills in these, but ones featuring the red letters of Fanrong.

"I thought those were only available in Indonesia," Luis said.

Susan looked over the forms again. "They are." She picked up one of the boxes and read the label. "It says they were manufactured in China. So what are they doing all the way over here in Los Angeles?"

Luis didn't have an answer. At least not immediately. But then something on the packing boxes caught his eye. He picked it up and turned it over.

"Those pills were packed here," he said, handing over the box. "Look at the bottom. The shipping boxes say they're in inches and made by a box company outside Fresno. It's in English." He pulled down a box of party favors nearby and turned it over. "This shipping box is sized in metric, and the thickness is completely different. Also, the writing's in Chinese."

"But why would the triad import these to America, only to then export them back to Indonesia?" Susan asked.

And that's when it all came together in Luis's mind. He saw the whole scheme from beginning to end. Even so, he couldn't quite believe it.

"Everything I read said that all these crackdowns force the counterfeit pharmaceutical manufacturers to close up shop and move somewhere else each time," Luis said. "What if this time they came to America?"

Susan gasped. "That's why Father Chang brought those pills back from Indonesia. He was trying to prove they were coming from here. That's what got him killed."

There was a sound from the other side of the warehouse. Two vehicles squealed to a stop, and several car doors opened and slammed shut, followed by volleys of loud Mandarin going back and forth between the workers and the new arrivals. Susan blanched and nodded to Luis.

"Time to go."

They hurried away from the pallets of pills as the lights all went on overhead.

Lord, please help us to—

"Whoever you are, stop right there, or we'll shoot on sight!" barked an angry voice now in English. "You are trespassing, and we are well within our rights."

Too late.

XX

The next command was for Susan and Luis to emerge with their hands held high. After a moment's reluctance the pair was prodded forward by a gunshot as a bullet was fired into the ceiling.

"Now!" came the command.

Luis nodded to Susan and led them out from the boxes. The new arrivals were eight young men, most barely in their twenties. They were skinny, well dressed, and held automatic weapons. The workers, including the deliveryman Susan had charmed, were long gone. Like the men in the casino, these fellows seemed to be the triad's version of *sicarios*. Whereas in some organized crime cultures, hit men made sure to fade into the background, in the cartel world they were the flashiest dressers and stood out, as if to dare anyone to take a shot. Luis figured the same might be true of triads.

"Another priest?" their leader said. "You've got to be kidding me."

"And I'm a doctor," Susan announced. "What's that in currency for you?"

"Not a thing," the young man said. "Get out of there. We're taking you to the office."

"To call the police?" Susan asked.

"Of course. This is a place of business. We're security guards. Who else would we call?"

But the sneer in his voice suggested the opposite was true.

The warehouse's office was tiny, but there were two faux-leather-backed swivel chairs that were perfect for Susan and Luis to be dropped into, their arms zip-tied to the armrests and their ankles zip-tied together. The young man indicated for two of his crew to keep watch as he stepped out and made a call.

"You know what's going on here?" Susan asked the two gunmen. "That outbreak? The SARS? It's coming from those pills down there."

The gunmen eyed each other for a second, decided this wasn't true, and turned their attention back to looking impassive.

"It's true. You've got SARS right here in your warehouse. All I'm trying to do is save your lives."

Luis admired Susan's guts but didn't think these guys had the authority to do anything with the information she was filling their heads with. He prayed silently, but not for his or Susan's freedom. Rather, that if any of the pills in the warehouse below were tainted, his intervention tonight might keep them from killing anyone else.

The leader of the young men ducked his head back into the office and looked from Susan to Luis. "The police are running a little late, but I have a friend coming. He'll want a word."

They waited twenty minutes. The two gunmen at the door got noticeably bored, but Luis wasn't about to give them the excuse to shoot him down right there by making a break for it. He glanced to Susan and was glad to see that she seemed to favor the same course of action. When the headlights of another vehicle flashed through the office window before going dark, Luis felt goose bumps rise on his arm.

What if he just shoots us as intruders? Am I ready to see you, O Lord? Is my mission here on earth complete?

The young leader of the "security guards" entered with a middle-aged man wearing a suit. He was tall and gaunt and also Chinese. He looked from Susan to Luis's collar and then to the pile of blister packs the leader had dropped on a nearby desk. The young man spoke to him in Mandarin for a moment, but the newcomer waved him away.

"Leave us alone," he said, nodding to the gunmen as well.

The lead guard looked surprised, even perturbed, but the middle-aged man insisted. Once the room was empty save for him, Luis, and Susan, he closed the door and introduced himself.

"I am Zhelin Qi," he said. "You can call me Tony. I apologize for Billy. He can be overzealous. It's a touchy time right now. There's been a lot of negativity toward Asians in the press here and we've come under siege a bit."

"So what?" Susan shot back. "You thought we were saboteurs or something?"

Tony raised a silencing hand. "Yes, but you were here in our warehouse under ridiculous and patently false pretenses. You had in your possession these pills, which, to any officer of the law, suggests drug-seeking behavior. If you were junkies, we can be forgiven for fearing you might be violent."

Tony sat back. Luis could tell he felt comfortable. He didn't like that.

"Two of those men are carrying fully automatic assault rifles with high-capacity magazines, both illegal in California," Luis said. "These zip ties? That's illegal detention. Meaning: kidnapping. Those pharmaceuticals out there? We have reason to believe they're mislabeled and their customs forms forged in some way. We'd get misdemeanor trespassing *maybe* with intent. Even if you talk your way out of discharging an illegal weapon, you're still looking at a string of penalties that gets worse the more verbal and implied physical threats you make. So keep talking."

Tony didn't reply for a long moment as he seemed to regard Luis with new eyes.

"What's your name?" Tony asked.

"Father Luis Chavez. I'm a priest at St. Augustine's parish."

"I don't know it," Tony said, turning to Susan. "And you?"

"Dr. Susan Auyong. I'm a doctor at Go Fuck Yourself."

Tony nodded as if he'd somehow expected her to say this. He extracted a blade from his pocket and sliced through the zip ties. As soon as he was free, Luis got to his feet. Tony, however, raised a hand indicating for him to stay seated.

"I . . . I think we can help each other," Tony said, reaching into his coat pocket. "In fact, I'm sure of it. You see, you may have been here for the same reason I was on my way here this evening."

He took the box of Jun's prenatal vitamins out of his pocket and handed them to Luis.

"Is this a part of it?"

Luis took the box and tapped the Jiankang label. "What do you know about this company? At least, their operations in Los Angeles?"

"In China they're huge," Tony said. "But here they're just one more minor manufacturing concern. They have two warehouse-sized facilities just off downtown. I think they make toys. Cheap stuff like little plastic saxophones and pianos."

Luis handed the box back to Tony. "If I'm right, they're making a lot more than that."

———

Michael flipped through the list of addresses, but his eyes refused to focus for some reason. The street names that on any other day would be as familiar as his own socks and shoes looked like references to faraway planets. Maybe it was the hour, the comedown from the amount of caffeine he'd ingested of late, or simply the stress of the day.

Or maybe it was that his wife had arrived at his office to deliver the list with known Echo Park gangster and chop shop artist Oscar de Icaza in tow.

"What is this again?" Michael asked, handing it to Naomi.

"A list of every location to which the Jiankang drugs are regularly delivered across the city," Helen said simply.

"Where on earth did you get it?" Michael asked.

"Is that important?" Helen asked, her tone imperious in a way Michael had never heard it before.

"Yes, of course," Michael said. "Before I acted on something like this, I would need to know if it carried any weight whatsoever, wouldn't I?"

"I gave it to her," Oscar said, stepping forward.

That was another thing. Naomi was young, attractive, and wearing a form-fitting skirt and top combo. Helen was in jeans and a T-shirt. But Oscar couldn't take his eyes off Helen.

"And where'd you get it?" Michael asked.

Oscar shrugged. "Showed up on my doorstep this morning with the *Times*."

"And you just decided to give it to your, what, realtor?" Michael asked.

"My realtor, who happens to be married to a deputy district attorney, yes," Oscar said. "If I gave it to LAPD, they'd probably bash my head in for my trouble. So yes, this seemed like the most reasonable and responsible course of action."

Michael hated that Oscar was probably right about that.

"How do you know it's authentic?" Michael asked.

"Oh, I don't," Oscar said, raising his hands. "For all I know the LA triad could be in the business of making fake lists of drops to confuse law enforcement or their competition. But if you check even a handful of those addresses, you'll see what I did—they seem to be a lot of businesses that don't really exist. There are a few pharmacies and hospitals, though not exactly Cedars Sinai, but the rest? They're just delivering to a bunch of back doors somewhere."

And given the current climate, it would take nothing to get a warrant for LAPD to check one of them out, Michael thought. *How perfect.*

"How perfect," Michael said aloud.

"Right?" Oscar replied.

Helen shot Oscar a harsh look. Michael had seen that look before, but only ever aimed at him. He caught Helen's gaze and saw the whole sordid tale written in her eyes.

Why him? He wondered. *Why him? Has she really picked this man, knowing how it would look? Or does that look say there's something real between them?*

"You're telling me that if I do this, if I send out the dogs, this ends now?"

"I'm telling you that if you want to get all the potentially tainted drugs off the streets right now, then yes, this is what you want to do."

The speaker this time was Helen. Michael felt Naomi's eyes flit to him and then flit away just as fast.

"All right," Michael said finally. "I'll send a couple of cars to these addresses and call the mayor back. I think the bulletin is going out within minutes."

"This'll prevent a lot of panic," Helen said encouragingly. "And, of course, make you look like the guy who saved Los Angeles. Nothing will keep you from being elected DA."

"Meaning 'nothing including the fact that my wife is sleeping with a known gang leader'?"

It was the kind of thing Michael would never, ever say aloud no matter how much he believed it to be true. So why had he said it now? Did he want to show up Oscar for stepping into his office like this? Or show Helen that he could still surprise her?

Helen stared long and hard at him as a thin smile formed on Oscar's lips. Naomi just looked embarrassed to be there.

"Yeah, that," Helen said simply before heading out the door.

Oscar lagged behind, eyeing Michael curiously. "You think you just humiliated her? Or yourself?" he asked.

When Michael didn't respond, Oscar exited as well.

Tony left Susan and Luis in the warehouse office and went out to speak with Billy. He wondered if he could be honest and say the brethren might be responsible for the plague it was currently wrestling with. But then he'd have to bring up Jun, and there was no way he wouldn't look foolish.

But could he really lie to his brethren?

"They're not junkies," Tony said to Billy after leading him out. "And they're not cops. In fact, it seems the woman is a doctor at one of the San Gabriel clinics we supply to."

Billy scowled. "We know all that. She said some crazy stuff about how the pills are causing SARS."

Oops.

"Yes, she said that to me, too, but I think she's just been driven a little mad," Tony lied. "People are dying, and she doesn't know how to save them. So she's blaming the pills. I think the priest is trying to keep her from hurting herself."

Billy eyed Tony as if he didn't believe a word he said. "What do we do then?"

"I'd like you to let me handle it," Tony said carefully. "I can get them away from here. I can speak to the priest about what influence he does or doesn't have over her. And most importantly, if there's a need to call the police and have her arrested, it won't happen at one of our warehouses."

This resonated with Billy exactly as Tony knew it would. Everything else aside, having the police show up and ask questions at one of their warehouses was bad news.

"So, will you let me take them off-site?" Tony asked. "I'll make the problem disappear."

"Yes," Billy said, bowing. "And thank you, Mr. Qi."

"You're welcome," Tony replied. "I am most happy when I can be of service."

As he walked away, Tony felt a pang in his heart. The first of many, he imagined, as the result of his interaction with Jun. He wished he could write her off and put her behind him, but even now he was acting in service to her.

So be it if the outcome is the preservation of life, he thought.

———

Luis and Susan didn't have to wait long for the man who'd called himself Tony to return.

"Time to go," he said, indicating for them to follow him out.

As they passed Billy, Luis could see from the young man's expression that he disagreed with the way Tony was handling the situation but could do nothing about it. Tony was the man in charge.

"Follow me in your car," Tony said. "It's not far."

Once they were alone in the front seat of her car, Susan turned to Luis in surprise. "Should we follow him? Or just get the hell out of here?"

"It's not like I trust him, but he did show up with that box," Luis said. "And he's not the one who's pregnant. So there's somebody out there he's doing this for."

"But he's triad. They killed Father Chang for investigating the pills. Why won't he do the same?"

"Not this guy," Luis said. "*Those* guys. The one he called Billy. You heard what he said, right?"

Another damn priest.

"So maybe this 'Tony' just saved our lives," Luis continued. "And if following him means we might save others and stop the outbreak, then it's a chance we have to take."

Susan nodded and put the car in gear. She shot a glance back to the warehouse one last time, then pulled behind Tony on the way into downtown.

Los Angeles's so-called Toy District was among its most unlikely named areas. Though it conjured images of a Santa's workshop–type neighborhood, it was really storefront after storefront of cheap merchandise wholesalers—in this case, party supplies, toys, and, of late, accoutrements for the numerous marijuana dispensaries springing up around the city—above ground parking lots, and off-the-street sweatshops, where hundreds worked but few for a living wage. The left-turn blinker came on Tony's car, and he rolled off the street and up a ramp to a rooftop parking lot. Susan followed.

Once on the roof Susan parked alongside Tony's car. Luis climbed out and looked up to the forest of skyscrapers immediately in front of the building. He wondered if anyone was looking out at them from above. He said a silent prayer and turned to Tony.

"Follow me," Tony said.

He led them to a stairwell and descended to the first floor. Rather than go out into the street, he approached a side door, plucked a key from his pocket, and unlocked it. He pushed the door open, and the three of them were immediately greeted by the roar of machines. A handful of workers toiled away at molding machines, keeping them pouring out disposable-looking plastic parts for toys. They barely looked up as Tony ushered Luis and Susan inside.

"What is this?" Susan asked.

"One of our brethren's local manufacturer's spaces," Tony said. "The largest one, in fact. If they were in the business of mass-producing pharmaceuticals, it would be done here."

Luis moved up and down the rows, eyeing the plastic dolls currently being made by the molding machines. It was a surreal sight, dozens of miniature bodies without heads in one row, others without arms or legs on another. The line for the heads was even stranger, eyeless faces with hollow sockets all staring in the same direction, as if accusing the passersby of an unspeakable crime.

But no matter where Luis looked, there was nothing to suggest any of these machines could have much to do with the manufacture of pharmaceuticals.

"Could they have facilities you don't know about?" Susan asked over the noise.

"Doubtful," Tony said. "Particularly one large enough to make pills in any real volume. Besides, the manifests at the warehouse said those pallets came from here, no? It must be here or in an adjacent building."

Luis stepped into the center of the room and looked up. He stood there for a long second before turning back to Tony.

"Is there an emergency stop switch?"

Tony glanced around and found it. "Why?"

"Just shut off the line."

Tony hesitated a second longer, then flipped the switch. A loud buzzer rang out as a red light strobed overhead. Now the workers looked at Tony. He raised his hand and shook his head.

"Just a precaution," he said.

What surprised Luis was not the sudden stillness of the room now that the vast assembly line was shut down. It was that the cacophony, though muted, continued from underneath the floor.

"What is that?" Tony asked.

Luis moved around the room looking for a door, a hatch, *anything* that might lead down. Finding nothing, he walked back outside, Susan and Tony trailing after. Moving down the sidewalk, he glanced through every window, checked every service door and access hatch, and even went back onto the roof to see if there was another stairwell that maybe bypassed the first floor.

When he looked across the street, however, he realized he was barking up the wrong skyscraper. He waited for a taxi to pass by, then jogged across the street.

"Where are you going now?" Susan asked.

"Every abandoned doorway in downtown is someone's territory," he said, then pointed to a narrow vestibule across the street. "Except that one."

It was an old residential building that once had a bank and, according to the hand-painted signage still on the windows, a men's clothing store at the street level. A rusty accordion gate blocked the entrance but was bowed at one side. When Luis tried it, it was easily pushed aside.

"In here," he said.

The trio entered what had at one time been a spectacular Art Deco lobby, with green and white stones and the tail of a peacock stenciled onto a large mirror over the elevators. Only the mirror was mostly shattered, with just the peacock's head and pieces of its tail visible. Half the stones were now missing as well.

But the dust and grime left behind meant a trail leading across the red carpet from the entrance to a stairwell alongside the elevators was perfectly visible. Luis led his comrades to the stairwell and down. Dim naked bulbs lit the way like in a service tunnel. When they reached a T, Luis recalibrated himself to where the street was overhead and moved in the direction of the toy factory.

Soon they could hear the sound of the machines again. Coming to a thick steel door, Luis tried to open it, to no avail. He saw a small security camera in the upper corner and nodded to Tony.

"Up there."

Tony stood in front of the camera and looked up. A voice speaking Mandarin came through the door.

"Zhelin Qi," Tony answered. "We need to be let in. Now."

There was silence. A few more seconds passed, and then the door slid open. An officious-looking man in khakis and a polo shirt eyed Tony with surprise.

"Can I help you?"

But Luis was already past the man and into the vast underground manufacturing floor behind him. There were eight assembly lines, each beginning at one side of the room, where workers fed raw materials into large heating canisters. These were then poured into mixers that expelled the ingredients into small slugs and sent them onto a mesh screen. A lubricant was added; the ingredients were formed into pills by a punch machine. The finished pills were then shoved down the assembly line, where they were either poured into bottles or dropped into blister packs that were then automatically sealed. The bottles and packs continued down the line, where they were boxed and the boxes sent through taping machines. The finished boxes were then placed on pallets to be shipped off.

Almost immediately Luis saw that the labels on the boxes were of all kinds. He recognized the Indonesian Fanrong but also the domestic Bumblebee Vigor. In addition, there were several others, including a few in Spanish and Portuguese and then another in lettering Luis recognized as Korean.

"What is all this?" Susan asked the man at the door.

"What does it look like?" he responded. "Manufacturing."

Tony strode to the front of one of the assembly lines and inspected the chemicals being poured into the heating canisters. He then checked the labels at the other end, with Luis looking over his shoulder.

"What does that say?" Luis asked, pointing to a line clearly not referencing ingredients at the bottom of the label.

"'Manufactured in Hong Kong under the regulations of the CFDA,'" Tony translated, practically shaking as he did so. "It's counterfeit. The triad is counterfeiting pharmaceuticals. And it looks like they're shipping them all over the world."

From Tony's reaction, Luis could tell he hadn't known about the enterprise. Even more than that, it seemed to shift his understanding of where he stood in the triad not to have been informed.

"If the pills were infected with SARS here in Los Angeles, people could be getting sick in every corner of the globe," Luis said. "This isn't just a police matter anymore. We have to alert the FBI. Any shipment that went out of here, no matter where it is in the world, has to be stopped."

"But the brethren," Tony said vacantly. "It will expose everything."

The words landed flat. Even Tony didn't seem to believe that mattered, as if airing the concern out of some misplaced sense of duty.

"If Father Chang was right, triad-made pharmaceuticals have already killed dozens if not hundreds of innocent people," Luis challenged. "You want to make that thousands?"

Tony hesitated only a second longer before reaching in his pocket for his cell phone. "Of course, you're right," he said, the cool, unflappable edge returning to his voice. "Will you allow me one phone call before calling in the dogs?"

XXI

For the next three days Michael felt like a cartoon character. All he needed was a tommy gun and a car with a running board and he would've been a throwback to the days of LAPD's take-no-prisoners Chief William Parker. That Michael wasn't a detective, federal agent, or even had any kind of authority at a crime scene seemed to rankle those that did, but as his office coordinated the busts for the most part, he made sure he was there as raids were conducted at all points along the drug-delivery chain.

His convoy would pull up to a warehouse or depot, hospital or free clinic, manufacturing plant or packing facility, the proper warrant would be served, and everything seized.

"Boxes with the Bumblebee label," he shouted as his team poured into a free clinic in Northridge that seemed to have been abandoned days ago. "Also, Jiankang Holdings. Anything that looks out of place."

The men knew the drill and swept in. It was like a training exercise, Michael occasionally pointing out to officers what was or wasn't within the scope of the warrant.

"These are on the FDA banned list," an officer would say, bringing up a stack of boxes like a hunting dog happily carrying a pheasant to its owner. "We can get them on all of this."

"Outside the scope of the warrant means fruit from a poisoned tree," Michael would reply. "Could unravel the case. Put it back."

Disappointed, the officer would return the items and carry on. Michael made a mental note to investigate what else the triad was trafficking in to get a better warrant next time.

They'd found eight drug-manufacturing facilities across the city so far, but only the one downtown in the Toy District had turned up trace amounts of SARS. Michael was cautiously optimistic that this would remain the case and limit the exposure of the virus to the pills made on that assembly line.

So, where's the infected worker? The patient zero?

This was the question that spurred Michael on. As he entered every squat and factory, he fully expected the cinematic reveal of a bloated, blistered corpse. This would be the body of the worker at the Toy District plant, likely a recent undocumented arrival, who had infected the line.

But this missing piece remained frustratingly elusive.

"No one at the plant is willing to talk?" Naomi asked as she joined Michael on his way to the Chinese consulate one morning to discuss what was going on with the obviously concerned representatives of the Chinese government. "They must've seen something."

"From what I gather, they had a different lineup almost every day," Michael reported. "The triad brought people over, put them up in those squats, gave them a zero- or low-paying job at the plant, but as soon as they could they moved on. We're trying to pull traffic-camera footage from the area once we narrow down around what dates the pills were tainted, but that may be a couple more days."

"They're probably dead, though, right?" Naomi asked.

"Yeah," Michael said, hoping that was the case. "Just praying they didn't infect others out there before they died."

Naomi nodded. "You know they found some of the tainted pills at a couple of the big chain drugstores. The customers had no idea their generics were being bought from these shady distributors."

Yeah, and the lawsuits are going to be record breakers, Michael thought. *Big class-action affairs that keep first-years grinding their gears for months on end and partners getting rich off the billable hours. Ain't America great?*

He felt a hand on his knee. Naomi was leaning forward.

"So, how are you doing?" she asked pointedly.

Meaning, Michael knew, *with the whole being humiliated by your gangster-loving, soon-to-be ex-wife thing.*

"I'm good. Glad to have a case like this to throw myself into, but good all the same."

"Your kids?" Naomi asked. "I mean, if you don't want to talk about it—"

"No, it's fine," Michael said. "We haven't discussed it with them yet. I haven't been home, but they think it's because of all this. A bridge to cross down the road."

Naomi nodded. "If there's anything you need, just let me know."

"Thanks," Michael said, then realized the gratitude he felt was real. "Thanks," he said again.

"Ma'am, this is Tylenol," Luis said, holding the pill bottle up to a terrified parishioner. "It expired eighteen months ago. I know I'm saying that you shouldn't take it anymore, but that's because of the expiration, not because I believe it's infected with SARS."

"But, Padre, I took two this morning!" the old woman said, her hands shaking as she sat back down on her bed. "Will I die?"

Luis sighed.

If he'd thought the discovery of the manufacturing plant in the Toy District would calm things for a while, he'd been very much mistaken.

The mayor's announcement about the tainted pharmaceuticals caused a minor panic within the St. Augustine's community. While most in the city checked their cupboards and medicine cabinets against the labels flashed on TV screens and printed in the paper, others had called the church in alarm.

Knowing that neither the police nor paramedics nor the CDC would respond to the requests to do home visits to check prescriptions, Luis dutifully divided them up among St. Augustine's priests and began spending every evening going from house to house to quiet nerves. Though he didn't find a single pill he could remotely tie to the case, he did find several parishioners with potentially dangerous, even narcotic pills in their possession.

Oh, that? Those were the painkillers they gave Frankie after he came home from the last trip to the hospital. What do you mean they're powerful enough to kill a horse?

I never finish antibiotics. It's good to keep a few for the next time you get sick. Saves a doctor's visit.

I don't know. The pills just make me feel so good. Every time I go to the pharmacy they fill the prescription. If there was a problem, the doctor would've limited the number of refills, right?

In the case of the eighteen-month-old Tylenol, Luis simply produced another bottle he'd brought from the drugstore with him.

"How about we just trade, Mrs. Jiminez?" he asked. "This has more in it anyway."

The old woman looked over the bottle and finally shrugged. Luis pocketed the expired pills and headed out.

When he got back in the car, the radio was blaring the latest news. Shipments of pills from Los Angeles had been blocked at various ports around the world and had actually become something of a political football. Local drug manufacturers who'd for years competed with the supposedly above-reproach American brands suddenly had a foothold. The politicians they owned looked for ways to score even points.

Luis turned off the radio.

The one positive thing out of all of it was that indeed Michael Story had kept his word. The chief deputy DA was very much the hero of the hour and was soaking up the attention. Luis had been surprised, but not surprised to hear the rumor that DA Rebenold might not be seeking reelection and that Michael Story was seen as the heir apparent. But in interview after interview, he deflected credit from himself and laid it at the feet of the martyred Father Chang.

"This was a godly man who'd discovered that local criminals were responsible for unsafe business practices that had led to a number of deaths in Indonesia already," Luis had heard Michael say on one news program. "He was about to ring the alarm bell here. He had the pills in the trunk of his car, but they killed him first. Father Chang is a hero."

Rather than being ostracized as a pedophile, Father Chang was suddenly being talked about as someone whom churches, parks, and intersections were to be named after. There were calls for canonization. Luis even saw a quote from Pastor Siu-Tung in the *LA Times* celebrating Chang's sterling character and action.

It was all too much.

"I had a phone call from the archbishop," Whillans said, finding Luis in the chapel late on the Saturday night before Luis was to deliver his sermon for the feast day of Saint Peter Claver. "He wishes to speak to you when he returns from Rome. While I did not detail your involvement in the revelations concerning Father Chang, he seems to have plenty from your friend in the prosecutor's office. It sounded like he was ready to elevate *you* to sainthood. Or at least to bishop."

Luis shook his head, bemused. Whillans clasped a weak hand on his shoulder.

"You must see that this isn't normal, can't you?" Whillans asked. "Whether God is working through you or you just have some sort of preternatural ability toward investigations, you're doing the Lord's work. I suppose, why can't it be both?"

Luis stared down at his hands for a moment. Something had been troubling him for days, but he hadn't been able to pinpoint it. In the moments between Tony Qi calling his triad bosses to let them know all hell was breaking loose until the first police officers arrived at the scene, Luis had spent some time looking around the various assembly lines, trying to puzzle out how a single SARS-infected worker could've tainted the supply of so many different drugs.

As everything was cleaned during a changeover, it meant that the worker had to repeatedly reinfect their own line but also the adjacent ones. There were six different counterfeit generics, including Glucoxan and Asozide, found to be infected with SARS. That meant the worker had to come in contact with both. But if SARS moved through people so swiftly that they were incapacitated within a day or so, that meant the line or whatever shift they were on switched at least five times. If the shifts were twelve hours long, and the infected person might've been contagious long enough to last two shifts two days in a row, that meant almost constant switchovers. The ingredients had to be changed over; the labels, boxes, and instructions had to be changed. The lines had to be sanitized.

It meant that what, *maybe* a few thousand pills went out for each drug a night? And if the SARS-tainted pills numbered in the hundreds, it meant direct contact with pill after pill. So why didn't anyone else in the factory get sick?

But the CDC didn't seem to want to focus on that. The infections had ground to a halt, and Luis figured this was all that mattered. It was only when he thought about it that all the probabilities didn't work out.

"What's troubling you, Father?" Whillans asked.

"In our vocation we're hardly unaccustomed to feeling an invisible hand behind the workings of things," Luis began. "I am feeling one here, but it's not God's."

"What do you mean?"

"As Father Chang discovered, and as Michael Story informed me, it's impossible to take down a member of the LA triad. But now in one fell swoop the entire organization is brought to its knees in a matter of days by a plague which led to the discovery of a deadly counterfeit pharmaceutical ring. Father Chang had spent months pursuing leads on this, going so far as to fly to Indonesia and beyond. One of his contacts, an investigating blogger named Kirk Asmara, was even likely murdered over this, and he kept going until he was silenced as well. But then—"

"But then God stepped in," Whillans said. "*God*, so offended by the murder of his own priest, stepped in."

"You believe that God would kill a few dozen of his own beloved people out of revenge for the murder of a priest?"

"I am saying that what came to pass came to pass. You may never know the great cost in lives that might've come if not for the sacrifice of those people."

Luis stared at the old man in surprise. "That feels like the church's response, not *your* response, Father. How is that the God we've discussed at length?"

"The God who has never allowed terrible things to happen before? *That* God?"

"You seriously expect me to believe that God gives that much of a damn that, no, not the extermination of indigenous peoples, not a Holocaust, not mass starvation, but the murder of one of his own priests is enough to wake him and begin playing a more active role in human affairs? That's bull. And if you weren't so high on painkillers right now, I think you'd agree."

Even as the words came out of his mouth, Luis was shocked by their bitterness. To his surprise, Whillans was not. The pastor leaned across to Luis, putting his forehead against his.

"You are right," Whillans said quietly. "I am on immeasurable amounts of painkillers. I know you believe my relationship with Bridgette puts me outside of God's grace. And I know, most importantly of all, whether you will admit to it or not that you are furious with God for taking me away from you."

Luis said nothing, but real and honest tears began to form in his eyes.

"But spare a thought for the Almighty," Whillans continued, his words barely a whisper. "His name is cursed ten times as much as it is praised. Yet still there is great beauty, kindness, fellowship, and love in this world. And that is his doing just as much as the pain. My body is on fire. I have the smallest window into the torment of the Nazarene. Forget not that God loved his son more than any others, yet still he stayed his own hand and made his child suffer to benefit mankind."

Luis nodded, two slow streams of tears sliding down his face. Whillans kept his forehead against Luis's for another second, then leaned back and rose.

"You may be right in all of these things you believe, but you must also believe that God, for whom you are an imperfect instrument, will reveal all to you in time."

With that, Whillans offered Luis a weak smile and exited.

For three days Tony had sat at Jun's bedside on Grand View as Dr. Soong helped her cling to life. For three days he'd hidden out as his entire life and the lives of his brethren crumbled to dust.

When he'd called the Dragon Head to announce that he'd been present when a priest and a young doctor with a tenuous link to the CDC discovered that SARS-infected pills had been found in one of their own facilities, he'd hardly expected acclaim. What he hadn't expected was indifference.

"Is that all?" Yang's assistant had asked.

"Yes," Tony had replied.

"Thank you, Mr. Qi. We are very grateful for the information."

Which meant that they weren't grateful at all.

He'd gone up to Grand View to do whatever he could and fallen asleep there. The next morning he got a call from the general manager at the Century Continental informing him that they were cutting back staff due to the outbreak-related cancellations and he'd be among the first to go. He'd thanked the general manager and then decided to add he was "very grateful for the information."

The real problem was that at some point Chen Jiang had reached out to Kuo Kuang and informed him how dire the situation had become for the woman carrying his son. He'd told her to tell Dr. Soong to perform a Cesarean section to save the baby. When he'd protested, saying that this was unconscionable, likely even murder, Kuang told Soong in no uncertain terms that he would have a doctor flown in from Hong Kong to do it if Soong refused. Soong reluctantly agreed.

"What we need to do now," Dr. Soong told Tony, "is to get her as strong as possible over the next day or so. We can buy her eight to ten hours more before Kuang gets so frustrated he really sends that doctor. The flight is sixteen hours. That gives us almost another day. By the time we do the operation, she just might be fit enough to live."

But Tony spent those next hours watching Jun deteriorate, not recover. At one point he wished he'd pushed Dr. Soong to operate immediately, as Jun might've survived an earlier operation.

But how could I have known?

When Kuang's wrath did boil over and a doctor reportedly sent, Dr. Soong went to Tony and announced that they'd have to do the operation, or it would likely cost both their lives.

"I'm sorry, Tony," Dr. Soong had said.

It put it in perspective for Tony. He realized he'd actually believed when he slayed the monster that put Jun in this condition—in this case the facility that had made the tainted pills—it would have some kind of magical curative effect on Jun. Instead, she just got worse and worse, likely to become the outbreak's final victim.

Dr. Soong arrived on Saturday night with an anesthetist Tony had met before, as well as a nurse. The baby was to be taken from the house immediately and brought to a safe location, where it would be treated until it could be flown back to Hong Kong.

Like a prized orchid or specially bred hound, Tony thought.

"Jun? Can you hear me?" Dr. Soong asked the patient. "We need to give you some medication right now. We're worried about the baby."

Tony looked at Jun's face for any sign of understanding, but she didn't respond. She'd been in and out of it for days, unable to eat or drink, kept alive with intravenous feeding, saline, drugs, and machines to preserve her failing organs for a little while longer. Tony wondered if she knew it was palliative care rather than any attempt to get her better.

She must, he thought.

"Let's get started," Dr. Soong said to his team.

The operation itself took less than fifteen minutes. Jun wasn't put completely under but felt no pain. For Tony it was one of the strangest things he'd ever witnessed. He hadn't really known what to expect but thought it would be like those anatomy models that allowed a user to take apart a body by layers until they reached a baby. Instead, the Cesarean was much like opening an envelope, reaching in to pull out the child, then resealing it after.

Rather than be disgusted, Tony marveled at the science of it.

The baby was in perfect health as far as Dr. Soong could tell. Phone calls and texts were exchanged. Dr. Soong's team, the baby itself, and Chen Jiang left. Tony was a little surprised to see Jiang leave Jun's side, then realized that of course the baby, not Jun, had been Auntie Jiang's charge the whole time anyway.

Once they were alone with Jun, Dr. Soong took Tony aside.

"At this point it's a foregone conclusion," he explained after reeling off Jun's vital signs. "She'll be gone in a few hours."

Tony nodded dumbly as if of course he knew this to be the case.

"So, I have to go now, but call me when it's over and I'll come back," Dr. Soong continued. "I'll take care of everything. Okay?"

"Okay," Tony managed to say.

He wondered if Dr. Soong knew he had a thing for Jun. Maybe the doctor wanted to give them a few last hours together. Or maybe being threatened with his life had caused Dr. Soong to reassess his involvement in Tony's ongoing enterprise.

Whatever the case, as soon as he was gone, Tony climbed back into bed next to Jun. She was a mess of bandages, tubes, and sweat-soaked sheets, but Tony wasn't going to let her leave the world on her own. If somewhere in her drugged-into-unconscious mind she could still feel his hand around hers or his breath on her neck, he would be there with her. It was only seconds before he was asleep, too.

Three hours later he awoke to her moaning in pain.

"Tony, the stitches itch so badly. I feel like I'm going insane."

"I'm sorry," he said. "Do the painkillers help?"

"Since we're not worried about the baby anymore, I say we just load me up. Wine's probably out of the question, isn't it?"

"Yes, I think so," Tony said, getting out of bed to retrieve water and the heavy prescription painkillers the doctor had brought over from Hong Kong.

He refused to hear the lightness in Jun's groggy voice. The bounce that had been missing for days that was suddenly back. It was obviously a false positive, that moment of clarity before she fell off the cliff. He would not allow himself hope.

She fell back into a stupor moments after taking the pills. Then two hours later, just before daybreak, she awoke again saying that she was hungry. This time Tony didn't know what to make of her request and called Dr. Soong.

"Are you sure you're not imagining this?" the doctor asked.

Tony held the phone up to Jun so she could ask herself. This time Dr. Soong replied, saying he'd be right over.

"How do you feel?" Tony asked as soon as Dr. Soong hung up.

"Weak," Jun said. "You stayed."

"I did."

"Is that why I'm alive?"

"I doubt it. You're very strong."

"Is the baby healthy?" she asked.

"I think so," Tony said, having no real idea.

"Do you know what Kuang named it?"

"No."

Jun fell silent for a moment. Tony took her hand.

"Jun, I—"

Jun slid her hand from his grip. "Tony. I will stay with you for a while if you'd like. But we are not actually compatible. I have known men like you who want to adore 'someone.' It wears off. Your needs, whether you realize it or not, are bottomless. I could try to fill them for a while, but it would be temporary, and I would grow resentful. You would wonder why I was pulling away and pursue me twice as hard. But you'd be looking for something that was never real in the first place, a false face. I say this to you because I am so very grateful to you for your care. And I think the best thing I can give you in response is my honesty. I think that deep down you are a good man, but you are also a broken one, again whether you know it or not."

Tony had never been more embarrassed in his entire life. He rose from the bed, bowed deeply to Jun, mumbled something in apology even as she protested, and walked out of the room. He waited for Dr. Soong to arrive. Smiled and let him know how relieved he was. Then walked out the front door, never to return.

XXII

When Luis woke up on Sunday morning, he did so with his sermon fully formed in his head. He wrote a couple of notes to himself on the first piece of paper he found but then hurried on to prayer and breakfast. He was energized, his worries concerning the SARS outbreak from the night before diminished as his focus was solely on Saint Peter Claver. It was now four days following the discovery of the manufacturing facility, and there had been no more cases. It was all over. Time to move on.

When Luis reached the chapel, he found Father Pargeter and Father Passarella already setting up.

"Where's Father Whillans?" Luis asked.

"In his office," Father Pargeter said, but in a voice that told Luis the pastor wasn't looking well. "Good luck today, Father."

"Thank you, Father," Luis replied.

Luis hurried to the administrative office and found Whillans behind his desk, with Bridgette seated beside him. This was a surprise, as Bridgette generally used the time that Whillans was presiding over Mass to get other work done.

"She wanted to hear you speak," Whillans said, gauging Luis's confusion. "We're hoping to make you as nervous and uncomfortable as possible."

Luis would've laughed if his pastor's appearance wasn't so changed in the few hours since he'd seem him. His skin was the color of a birch and he hadn't shaved, which he never failed to do. He'd lost so much weight that he looked as if he could wriggle out of his too-wide Roman collar if he tried.

"Thank you," Luis managed to say.

"People know," Bridgette said quietly. "About you, that is. I've been asked a number of times if it's true. 'The priest who rescued the workers in Camarillo this past spring. Is he the same man who stopped the plague?'"

As Luis reddened, Whillans raised a hand and laughed. "You make him sound like Moses. Are you Moses, Luis?"

"Swaddled in back issues of *La Opinión*, dropped in an empty case of bootleg DVDs, and shoved down the Los Angeles River—that's me," Luis said. "Blood of my ancestors in the foundation of Dodger Stadium."

Whillans laughed now, as did Bridgette. "It's not funny, though," Whillans said. "That last part is probably true."

"Probably is," Luis agreed.

"Not to make you more nervous, but you may see a few more cassocks than usual out there this morning," Whillans said. "A few pastors from surrounding parishes are coming. If you needed more reasons not to screw up, well, there you have them."

Luis laughed for real now and headed out.

As the parking lot began to fill, the celebratory atmosphere of the Sunday Mass took hold throughout the campus. The relief everyone felt at the termination of the plague was palpable. There were more parishioners than usual. Luis caught several eyes watching as he moved between the chapel and the rectory, now in his cassock, and realized they weren't looking at just another man in the collar. They were looking at him.

He was by a window when the first clergy from the other parishes arrived, but he stepped away before they emerged from their vehicles. The moment felt heady, and he swelled with unwelcome pride. He found a corner in the sacristy and knelt in prayer, though he couldn't quite find the words.

Lord, please guide me through whatever this is.

Then it was time. The organ played, the choir. Whillans led his priests in and took his position at the pulpit to welcome everyone. He'd used a walker to get from the office to the sacristy but had set it aside to make the final twelve steps across the altar. Luis envisioned him toppling over, cracking his head, or a dozen other mortal scenarios, but Whillans seemed to pull strength from the parishioners and always moved with confidence.

The greeting was followed by the first reading, which was followed by the psalm, then the gospel. Finally, it was Luis's turn.

Without introduction Luis rose and moved to the pulpit.

"I'd like to direct you to Ezra 9:9," Luis began. "'For we are slaves. Yet our God has not forsaken us in our slavery but has extended to us his steadfast love before the kings of Persia, to grant us some reviving to set up the house of our God, to repair its ruins, and to give us protection in Judea and Jerusalem.'"

The congregation waited for context in silence. Ezra was hardly the most common book cited on a Sunday. Luis took a breath, then went on.

"Today is the Feast of Saint Peter Claver," he continued. "If you have heard of him, it's generally because you know he baptized hundreds of thousands of African slaves in Colombia in the early to mid-1600s. If you know anything else about his story, it's that when he was old and infirm an unknown ex-slave was hired to look after him but instead abused him horribly. Peter Claver, however, never spoke up and said, 'Don't you know who am I?' in an attempt to win favor or gratitude."

There was uncomfortable movement among the congregants. Luis found himself looking at Father Siu-Tung from St. Jerome's, his face colored with a hint of distaste.

"My sermon today," Luis continued, "is about that unknown ex-slave."

There was active discomfort now from both the assembled clergy and even, Luis could tell, the other priests of St. Augustine's nearby. When he caught sight of Father Siu-Tung again, the parish pastor gave a loud cough.

"Many of the lives of saints are parables," Luis said. "So let's ask ourselves, is this true? Or is this a parable? What we know to be true is that, yes, Peter Claver baptized hundreds of thousands of slaves, seeing it as his duty despite the Vatican's ongoing support of the transatlantic slave trade. The part about the abuse—well, if that's been added, let's ask ourselves *why*. Why does the church, after anointing Peter Claver as a deeply holy man for his commitment to African slaves, then invent a story of how he was abused by a former one? References to the abusive ex-slave go back centuries. I find it convenient. Too many Catholics at the time believed wholeheartedly in the subjugation of blacks for the church to actually take a stand and suggest all people were equal in the eyes of God, as Claver did. By adding the ungrateful ex-slave who didn't recognize the saint in their midst, you maintain the status quo. The priest is good. He helped when his fellow man needed it. The Africans took the help when they needed it, then didn't reciprocate. That's the takeaway."

Multiple coughs from the pews now, including Siu-Tung's familiar one. Luis glanced up once and was surprised by what he saw. Other parishioners, the nonclergy, were engaged. Even the kids who more often had their heads down as they stared at their phones. Whether they were interested or wondering where on earth this blasphemous lunatic was going, Luis didn't know.

Go big or go home, he thought.

"Now, let's imagine that the ex-slave story is absolutely true," Luis said. "This is still someone who has been ripped from his home in chains, likely torn from family, friends, and ancestral land. He's endured hardship and misery. And now in this foreign land he's been granted his freedom but is still servant to an old and dying man of the same nation that brought him there in the first place. For one moment put yourself in that man's shoes. Feel his anger. Now, imagine if somebody told you, 'Oh, wait. This is a man who baptized slaves. Who has brought his image of God to replace yours. If you accept it, he'll allow you water and maybe even food.' Has your anger abated?"

The chapel, with over a thousand people in it, was so silent that Luis could hear a bird singing outside.

"So on this feast day of Saint Peter Claver, I would like to invite you to remember the man and not the story. All we know is that he was born in Catalonia in 1580, arrived in Colombia in 1610, and spent every moment of his life ministering to slaves, to the sick and destitute, on the quay, in hospitals, and even on the plantations after the slaves were moved from the docks and were already baptized. Whether this was wanted or not, Claver expressed his revulsion for the slave trade in the only way his age made him think possible. He did the best he could. He tried. He thought about his fellow man. That's all anyone can do. And I invite you to do the same. Let us pray."

As Luis led the congregation in the Lord's Prayer, he heard the voices of the multitude rising as one. He wasn't sure if the increase in volume was due to his standing at the pulpit and thereby being the focal point of all the voices aimed in his direction, or if his sermon had inspired such a—

But his thoughts were cut off by the coughing of Father Siu-Tung. Luis momentarily lost his place in the prayer and cursed Siu-Tung in his mind, something he immediately regretted and chalked up to another sin of pride.

Luis waited a half second for Siu-Tung to finish his protest, odd and antiquated that it might be, but the coughs did not stop. A voice said, "Father?" and there were gasps.

Father Siu-Tung stood up, staggered past the three other clergymen between his seat and the end of the pew, and continued to cough. Luis saw now that he was in distress. His eyes were watering and his nose was running.

Oh God, Luis thought. *Oh dear Lord no.*

Luis hurried down from the pulpit. A woman screamed as Father Siu-Tung stumbled toward Luis. The pastor's hands clawed into Luis's vestments. He stared up at him with wild eyes.

"Bless me, Father," Siu-Tung said. "Absolve me before God."

Luis stared into the priest's desperate eyes and knew the truth. There'd been one last person, either guilty or at least complicit in the death of Father Chang, who'd escaped the dragnet of the police.

Luis turned to the nearest gawker. "Call 911. Right now." He then turned to the nearest clergyman. "Get everyone out of here that was more than three rows away. The rest stay to be looked over by the CDC."

The priest nodded, though with the face of a terrified onlooker, not a man of God.

Luis turned back to Father Siu-Tung, but it was a second too late. The priest would go to his maker unabsolved.

―――――

An ambulance arrived within minutes, but Luis was already out the door. His worst fears had been confirmed right in front of him—a dying man in his arms who couldn't possibly have been infected by the initial strain of the disease. Yes, it might be a coincidence, and Father Chang's pastor was the one man in Los Angeles who hadn't thrown away an old prescription and had taken tainted pills, but then Luis remembered his words.

Our insurance, as you must know, requires us to receive anything we have for ongoing conditions through bulk mail order.

Taking one of the parish cars, Luis raced across the city as fast as he could, lazy Sunday morning traffic allowing him to whip through intersections and past stop signs without hitting anyone.

"Susan?" he said after she groggily answered her cell. "There's been another case. At St. Augustine's. Father Siu-Tung died in the middle of Mass."

"Oh my God," Susan replied, quickly rousing. "I'm on my way."

"Not there," he said, then told her where he was headed.

"See you there in five minutes."

St. Jerome's Chinese-American Catholic Church was nowhere near as full as St. Augustine's that morning. The chapel was maybe half-full and the congregants uneasy. As Luis scanned the pews, he realized the double whammy of the murder of their priest and the outbreak that swept the Chinese community in Los Angeles might've kept anyone from services.

He finally spotted a priest and headed straight toward him.

"I need you to unlock Pastor Siu-Tung's room in the rectory," Luis said when he reached him. "That needs to happen immediately."

"Um, I'll need to consult with Father Siu-Tung," the priest stammered back.

"The father is dead," Luis said simply. "I'm sorry. Come with me now."

The priest was so shaken, he could do nothing but as Luis commanded. The pair exited the chapel to the stares of congregants and clergy alike and found Susan waiting by the rectory. Luis saw that, likely unbeknownst to her, she was standing in the exact spot where Father Chang had been murdered.

"Does he have keys?" she asked, nodding to the priest.

"If he doesn't, we'll break the door down," Luis replied.

The priest gave him a stricken, how-could-you look. Luis shoved him forward.

"This is a matter of life and death," Luis said. "Just get us to his room."

Unlike the other priests in the rectory, the parish pastor had his own small bathroom within his room. When the priest Luis had plucked from the chapel opened the door, Luis and Susan saw that it was almost as empty as Chang's had been. The bathroom door was open and the light carelessly left on.

Or was he already sick when he left this morning? Luis wondered.

There were three prescription bottles in the cabinet, none of them generics, all of which were brands that seemed outside the reach of Jiankang. Luis was about to open them when Susan's hand shot forward.

"You're being too cavalier now," she said. "If these really are infected, you can't touch them."

Realizing the truth of her words, Luis backed down. Susan extracted a pair of latex gloves from her pocket, as well as a face mask, put everything on, then dropped the three prescription bottles into a specimen bag. Once it was sealed, she took out her cell phone and called the CDC rep at Good Samaritan.

"I have the drugs here," she said. "They're contained. But we need a decontamination team over here, as well as a group to test the other priests." She covered the phone with a gloved hand and sent the priest who had let them in a shrug and a smile. *"Sorry,"* she hissed.

When she hung up, she nodded to Luis.

"We have to test these immediately."

"Your lab?" he asked.

"Hell no," she said. "CDC lab at Good Samaritan. The outbreak is supposed to be over. If it's not, everything is by the book. Even one life, including either of ours, is too much to risk. Got it?"

Luis did.

Forty-five minutes later in the lab at Good Samaritan, they had their answer. Two of the bottles were contaminant-free, as if they had never once been touched by human hands. In the third bottle, in a total of thirty pills a single infected pill hid among the others. Almost by a fluke the technician who tested it said that it had been on top, the first pill to come out of the bottle. When the inside of the bottle was tested, SARS was not discovered *except* at the very top.

As if the infected pill had been placed there on purpose.

"It appears the virus was introduced," the visibly shaken lab technician told Susan, Luis, and a small assemblage of his colleagues that had gathered as word began to spread of what was happening. "If that's the case, that makes the St. Jerome's rectory and possibly even St. Augustine's a crime scene."

Introduced.

Luis could tell that no one could quite process this. After dealing with SARS as a viral infection for so many days, the idea that it could be used as a weapon did not compute. But to Luis, in a flash it suddenly all made sense.

"They were all murders," he said. "Every last one of them. And I think I know who did it."

XXIII

Oscar awoke to light streaming in through the still curtainless windows overlooking the city from their perch on Outpost. There was a bed now, but aside from the table and chairs it was still the only furniture in the place. Even though he'd known his arrangement with Tony Qi could well be fragmenting, he'd impulsively bought the place the morning after he and Helen had made love on the balcony for the first time. Now that it was clear there would be no more birth houses for the triad for the foreseeable future, he figured he should be free to work on any renovations to be done and get it back on the market as quickly as possible.

When Helen walked back into the room carrying breakfast but wearing nothing, Oscar was shocked. He thought she'd left hours ago.

"You're still here?"

"No, I woke up early, was home in time for the kids to wake up, got them ready for school, dropped them off, and came back. You hadn't stirred."

Did you see your husband? Oscar was dying to ask but didn't.

"It's a nice place, isn't it?" Helen said, glancing around.

"Yeah, it is. It's away from everything but close," Oscar agreed. "And those jetliner views. Can't beat that."

"During the summer when the Hollywood Bowl is going, apparently you can hear all the concerts. To make it up to residents here, you're given free tickets."

"Smart," Oscar said. "Gotta keep your neighbors on your side."

Helen knelt beside the bed and placed a hand on Oscar's shoulder. She met his gaze, and he knew exactly what she was about to say. So he said it first.

"What about this place for us?" he asked. "Room enough for your kids. If they stay with their dad during the week, they're still going to their same schools, but then weekends and, say, all summer up here. What do you think?"

Helen kissed him. She then pushed herself against his body, effectively lowering him back onto the bed, and kissed him again. She put her arms around his torso and laid her head on his chest.

"Is that a yes?" he asked.

"Yes."

"What changed between now and 'Don't tie me down with all your rules'?" he half joked.

"It didn't feel right then. It felt reckless and impulsive. But it feels right now."

Oscar realized that she was right. He ran his fingers through her hair and kissed her lightly.

"You talk to Michael about a divorce?"

"He brought it up. Because of the campaign. He either wanted a long, quiet separation or a very quick and painless divorce."

"And you chose?"

"The latter. And no, not because of you but because maybe I owe him that."

Oscar didn't like the idea that Helen thought she owed anything to Michael but kept his mouth shut. That's when his cell phone rang. He considered not picking up but figured being off the grid for as long as he had been already wasn't smart.

"Hello?"

"Mr. de Icaza," said a voice he didn't recognize. "I am a representative of Mr. Wanquan Yang. We need a word with you."

"I don't know any Wanquan Yang," Oscar said with a hefty helping of bravado. He had a pretty good idea of who Yang must be affiliated with.

"Be that as it may, you have accepted his money this past week after entering into an arrangement with his organization. That arrangement was demolished by the intercession of the city's prosecutor's office. The catalyst of this dissolution, however, came from within."

The list, Oscar realized. *Oh crap.*

"Hey, I'm kind of busy right now," Oscar said. "Maybe in a day or so?"

"We have a car waiting in front of your house," the man continued. "Please have Mrs. Story accompany you."

For the first time in many years, Oscar felt fear. It appalled him, but he knew why it had come. If it had just been him, he would've been fine. The cost of doing business. If it had been any other woman, he would've also been okay. Again the cost.

But this was the woman he loved. And only seconds after they seemed ready to plot a future together, he'd put her in grave danger.

"And if I don't?" Oscar snapped.

"Please, Mr. de Icaza," the voice said sternly.

Before Oscar could respond, the line went dead. He turned to Helen, who'd clearly heard his half of the conversation. She looked terrified but nodded anyway.

"I'll get dressed."

━━━━━━

Luis didn't need to return to St. Jerome's and search through the security camera footage to know who had poisoned Pastor Siu-Tung. He knew the police would, however, and hoped it would buy him and Susan enough time to confront the killer and make him turn himself in.

Not that he was optimistic.

The University of Southern California campus was one of the largest in the country. Stretching over more than two hundred acres, it was bordered on three sides by neighborhoods no one would mistake for anything like a cozy university community, and a museum district on the other. Students were routinely told to stay on campus after dark or limit their excursions into the surrounding area. Police and campus security were everywhere and vigilant about outsiders.

It was a warm Sunday in fall, which meant many students could be found laying out in the grass between buildings, chatting on the numerous benches or low walls, or just in general walking or cycling or skate- or hover-boarding between destinations.

Luis had left his cassock in the car but was still in his black clerical pants and shirt and Roman collar as he stalked onto campus with Susan in tow. They'd parked in a shopping center across the street after having been denied access to the university grounds in the car.

"It's an emergency," Luis had said. "A matter of life and death."

"Did you call 911?" the security guard asked.

Luis had rolled his eyes and reversed out.

He was angry now. He understood the plot, but more than that realized that in order for it to work somebody had to be manipulated into coming along and tripping the dominoes. So even though he'd stopped the SARS outbreak and helped to line up what looked like an endless string of indictments against the LA triad, he'd still just been a puppet on someone else's strings.

The dorm itself was as secure as the campus, as only students were allowed access to the elevator banks that went up to the rooms. Susan led Luis to one of the stairwells, however, and they simply waited for someone to exit before heading up to the eleventh floor.

"Is Nan here?" Luis demanded when a sleepy-eyed young man finally opened the door to Room 1142.

"Um, no," the young man said, glancing over his shoulder to an empty bed on the opposite side of a narrow room.

"Any idea where he is?" Luis asked.

"The labs probably," the student said, then spotted Susan. "Oh, hey. What's going on?"

Susan pushed past Luis and into the room. Luis followed as she sorted through the piles of paper on Nan's desk. Luis recognized a handful of the articles printed out immediately as ones relating to Father Chang's visits to Indonesia. Also, a handful more from Los Angeles papers focused on business dealings in the Chinese-American community over the past several years. Luis saw the names of prominent business leaders circled, men who in recent days had been outed as members of the LA triad. He also saw a photo of Jing Saifai.

Are you going to kill them, too, Nan?

The solution had been staring him in the face all week; he just hadn't been able to see the whole picture. The triad had killed Father Chang and covered it up. Not only that, they'd provided the police with the shooter and a motive that most believed without question. That should've been the end of it. What they hadn't known was that someone out there not only had loved Father Chang but would be so incensed by their act that he'd concoct a revenge scheme capable of bringing them all down.

"Call the police," Luis said to the roommate. "And when they come, show them all this."

"Um, the police?"

"Now," Susan added as she followed Luis out the door.

As he strode across campus, Luis found his cell phone again and dialed the same number he'd been ringing all week.

"The priest who died just now—that was your parish?" Michael said the second he picked up.

"It was Father Chang's pastor," Luis said. "I think you're going to find a monetary connection at least between him and the triad. You need to seize his bank records and perhaps those of his parish."

"Done. Are you okay?"

Luis brushed off the question. "The guy who did all this is named Nan Tiu. He was Father Chang's partner."

"Partner?" Michael asked. Luis remained silent. "Got it. Wait. What do you mean, 'did all this'?"

"There was no patient zero from China. Father Chang was investigating counterfeit pharmaceuticals when he was killed and discovered that some of the latest were being manufactured right here in Los Angeles. Before he could report it, though, the triad had him murdered and covered it up. Only they didn't realize Chang's partner had a way to beat them at their own game and the access to do it."

"Access to what?"

"I just asked the CDC where someone could get ahold of a sample of the SARS virus," Luis continued. "They said it's very difficult, in fact. There's the CDC itself and its secure holding facility in Atlanta, or the VECTOR Institute in Koltsovo, Russia. But then there are the biochemistry labs at universities across the country. You can't keep it in storage, but you can request copies of it for study. Nan Tiu is a biochemical engineering student at USC. And just like the papers believed Father Chang was a child molester because of the other priests that came before him, Nan knew they'd believe the Jiankang-linked pharmaceuticals were tainted because the same company had been guilty of so many violations in the past."

Even as he said it, Luis couldn't believe how clever a plan it had been. The deaths of Kirk Asmara and Father Chang could be ignored and the real perpetrators allowed to go free. What couldn't be ignored was a full-on outbreak in a major American city tied directly to the triad's counterfeit drugs that looped in their unlicensed pharmacies, slums, and illegal immigration operations. It'd bring the whole thing down in one fell swoop, possibly even taking down his only other friend, who worked in an unlicensed clinic, in the process.

"That's insane," Michael said, his voice distant and incredulous. "Can you prove it was him?"

"LAPD is about to find his face on the St. Jerome's security tapes," Luis said. "And I'll bet there are enough security and traffic cameras around the manufacturing facility in the Toy District that you'll be able to place him there, too. What worries me is where he is now. He must've known he'd be caught after Father Siu-Tung's death. If he has other loose ends to tie up, I'll bet he's doing it right now."

It suddenly occurred to Luis that if he had come to this conclusion, the triad probably had, too.

"I have to go," Luis said.

"Wait, where are you? You're not going after him yourself, are you?" Michael protested. "Father Chavez—*Luis*. Come on!"

Luis hung up.

The organic chemistry lab was in the Seaver Science Center on the west side of the campus. When Luis and Susan arrived at its front door moments later, they found four Asian men in suits idling around out front, looking anything but inconspicuous.

"How'd they know?" Susan asked. "Do you think they saw the security footage from their warehouse?"

"If so, this could get bad," said Luis, perplexed. "We've got to get up there."

Circling to the back of the building, Luis and Susan entered and hurried to the stairs. There were labs on every floor, but Susan pointed out that only on the third floor were there indicators of potentially biohazardous material with attendant safety regulations.

As Luis took the hard concrete steps two at a time, he prayed.

Lord, I don't know what I'm walking into, but please guide me to do your will. And please comfort the soul of this killer so that he might be receptive to my words.

Two steps from the third-floor landing, they heard screams and a commotion from down the hall. Students and faculty members alike ran from a lab on the far end of the hall as if they were running away from a bomb.

"Get out of here!" one of the faculty members shouted at Luis and Susan. "We have to evacuate the building!"

Luis ignored this and pushed through the crush of students onto the third floor. Where there had been sound and fury moments before, there was now silence. Then the breaking of glass. Luis hurried in the direction of the sound and found an open lab door. When he stepped inside, he found Nan holding a label-less aerosol can and a syringe as he stood in front of a terrified-looking Jing Saifai, huddled in the corner. There were two men dressed similarly to those outside lying on the floor, their faces contorted and discolored, clearly dead.

"Nan," Luis said calmly.

Nan whipped around and, to Luis's surprise, his face softened when he saw Luis.

"Father Chavez! My God. You found me."

"You led me here," Luis said.

"No, I led you to them, not me," Nan offered. "Have you called the police?"

"They're on their way," Luis said.

"Then I guess this is the last one," Nan said, turning back to Saifai.

"Nan, stop it!" Susan protested, stepping past Luis and into the room. "What are you doing?"

"Dr. Susan Auyong, this is Jing Saifai," Nan said casually. "She's the chief counsel for the Los Angeles triad. She also negotiated trade agreements that allowed unregulated generics to not only be manufactured here but keep being made even after they'd killed people in Indonesia. Lose enough factories and you start looking for a permanent solution. And who'd think to look for tainted pills coming out of the States? Turns out you can cut corners anywhere these days."

"Nan," Luis said, raising a hand.

"No, you listen," Nan said. "I'm just getting to the worst part. Even after they knew the product was bad, they kept shipping it. You know how they knew? Because Benny told them. But when you've already had to put a percentage on what you deem an acceptable death rate for your product, what's one more death? Isn't that right, Ms. Saifai?"

The lawyer, visibly shaking, said nothing. She stared at Luis, as if begging him to save her life.

"I'm not going to try and talk you out of it," Luis said, sitting on a lab stool. "If it makes any difference to you whatsoever, go ahead and kill her. God knows she's done terrible things. But if she stands trial, what you know and what I know become public record. There'll be more investigations into every last business dealing she ever made. Villains we don't even know about will be taken down here and abroad. You kill her and she's just another victim of your 'reign of terror.' Heck, she'll probably get a whole day's worth of laudatory praise in the press about being this great upstanding lawyer for her community. Perception is everything. Which is why they knew destroying Father Chang's reputation was just as important as killing him."

Nan hesitated. He glanced from Saifai to Luis to Susan.

"They killed him, Susan," he said. "He tried to save people and they killed him."

"Do you know how many people you've killed already?" Susan snapped back. "You killed a little girl. You killed poor people who couldn't afford better medicine. You killed people who were just trying to provide for their families. They didn't do a thing to Benny. Not. A. Thing. And if he were here—"

"You think he'd yell at me about it?" Nan screeched. "You think he'd do what you're doing?"

"No, he'd weep," Susan stated. "The people you killed and the people the triad killed in Indonesia are the same. They're victims. He'd go after you the same as he did them. You would cease being the man he loved and be just one more faceless enemy trying to bring more pain into an already painful world. That's what he'd say."

Nan looked stricken by these words, as if he'd never thought of that. His face contorted and he looked like a child. He turned to Luis.

"And if they catch me and put *me* on the stand, everything about my relationship with Father Chang will be in the public record, too."

Susan grabbed Luis's arm to keep him from walking into a trap. Luis shrugged and replied anyway. "That's true."

Nan nodded and turned back to Saifai. "Let's go for a walk."

This wasn't what Luis expected. "What're you doing?"

Nan took hold of Saifai's arm and held the aerosol can in front of her face. "Perception is everything, right?"

Luis rose and stood in front of Nan, but he waved the can in front of Susan's face next.

"This isn't SARS," Nan warned. "It's strychnine. Works faster in a pinch. Now get the hell out of my way and don't follow me."

Susan touched Nan's arm. For a moment Luis thought she would try to stop him, to deliver the magic words that would yank him back from the brink. Instead, she simply nodded, as if realizing he was beyond the point of no return.

"Bye, Nan," she said quietly.

"Good-bye, Dr. Auyong."

Nan led Jing Saifai out of the lab. There were shrieks as a handful of people who'd snuck back into the hall scrambled away again. Luis went to go after them, but Susan reached out a hand.

"We should go."

Luis looked at her, perplexed, then realized what Nan intended to do. He was right. His plan wouldn't work if he was brought to trial.

"There's another stairwell in back," she said. "If we hurry, we can be out the door and away before anyone gets here."

"Okay."

As he hurried after Susan, he recited the Lord's Prayer.

Our Father who art in heaven, hallowed be thy name.
Thy kingdom come, thy will be done, on earth as it is in
    heaven.
Give us this day our daily bread. And forgive us our tres-
    passes,
As we forgive those who trespass against us.
Lead us not into temptation, but deliver us from evil.

Several shots rang out. Susan hit the door at the bottom of the stairs and shoved it open. Sunlight streamed in, followed by screams from around the side of the building.

"Let's go!" she shouted.

For ever and ever, amen.

XXIV

Michael arrived on the scene so fast that the bodies of Nan Tiu and two of the gunmen who'd shot him were still on the pavement in front of the Seaver Science Center. The campus police had taken the triad hit men down, but not before they had killed Nan. The two gunmen had been covered with yellow sheets, but they had held off with Nan, fearing the toxicity of the items in his hand. His heavy-lidded eyes stared straight up but didn't seem focused on sky or sun. More like he was still processing a thought and had stopped a moment to consider it fully. Blood leaked from beneath his body in three narrow streams that puddled at the base of the steps.

Exit wounds, Michael thought idly.

He took out his cell phone and rang Luis for the tenth time in so many minutes. It went straight to voice mail, as it had each time before.

Dammit, Luis. What happened here?

"Sir, you're going to have to step back."

The words came from a uniformed LAPD officer. When Michael looked over, he saw a hint of recognition on the man's face but complied anyway. He wasn't a detective, and this wasn't his crime scene.

That's when he spotted two female campus security officers—one sitting, one standing—next to Jing Saifai. She was kneeling in the grass off to the side as if about to pray. Her face was marked with trails of tears. It didn't look as if she'd been harmed. Seeing that she was safely on the neutral side of the cordon, Michael headed over to her. But before he got within fifteen feet, DA Rebenold appeared in front of her, similarly kneeling and taking her hand. The two of them spoke quietly but then fell into mournful, companionable silence.

Michael was so shocked that he had no idea what to do. Should he take a photo? Should he approach and say, "Gotcha, I knew you two were in league together"? Or should he do the human thing and turn his back to walk away?

He was considering all of these options when Saifai pointed at him, and Rebenold turned. When she made eye contact with him, her features seemed to gray and age. She seemed to nod to herself, as if his presence closed a door there, then turned back to Saifai.

Michael found a detective he was friendly with, Shannon Piriczky, and followed him back to Nan's dorm room.

"He didn't exactly leave a manifesto, but he might as well have," the detective said, picking up several of Nan's printouts with a gloved hand. "He was tracking triad activity across the city. He knew exactly how the counterfeit generics were delivered and where their source was. He also knew a lot about disease."

"Where'd he get the SARS?" Michael asked.

"We don't know that much yet, but he's a biochemistry grad student at a major research university. With the right accreditation, he could've ordered it from somewhere. More likely, however, it was already here. Hell, I was surprised walking into my son's high school chemistry lab once and seeing all they had on their shelves. There was enough chloroform in one barrel to knock out half the city."

The detective opened a drawer and pulled out a photograph of Nan and Father Chang. He raised an eyebrow as he angled it over for Michael to see.

"What do we think of that?"

Michael studied it for a long moment and nodded. "Father Chang was this young man's mentor. This was definitely revenge for Chang's death."

"'Mentor'?" Detective Piriczky asked.

"Yeah, you know I have my guy on the inside, right? That's the story there. The whole story."

Detective Piriczky regarded Michael for a moment, then nodded. "You got it, Story."

Michael looked around Nan's side of the dorm room but found little. There were a few odds and ends—a playbill from a musical, a program to a concert, a museum's exhibit guide—but not a thing backdated more than a couple of years. No indication whatsoever of a past. It seemed as if Nan's only focus had been on the present and future, which was all Father Chang. When this, too, was taken from him—well, he made the world atone.

"Michael? Can I see you a moment?"

Michael wasn't sure how long DA Rebenold had been standing in the doorway, but it looked as if she'd been dreading this confrontation. He nodded, excused himself from the detective, and followed her out. Rather than speak in the hallway or the dorm, she led him outside the building and into the law school, heading up to the library on the second floor. Michael was surprised to see that despite books and backpacks on a number of the tables, it was otherwise completely devoid of students.

Deborah indicated the exits.

"There was an active shooter on the grounds," she said. "They were to shelter in place and then be evacuated by campus police as quickly as possible. Did you know they go over all that during orientation now?"

"That sucks," Michael said limply.

Deborah fell silent again until they reached a small alcove in the foreign and international law section. She then hopped up onto a windowsill like a twentysomething coed and swished her feet back and forth.

"I did a postdoc year here," she said. "Bet you didn't know that."

Michael did but shook his head anyway. He knew she needed to tell whatever she was going to tell her way.

"This was the part of the library where no one ever, ever came. It was perfect to study, to write, to grade, everything. The students here— a lot of them at least—came from superwealthy families. I came with a chip on my shoulder about that. But they'd been well trained. They knew better than to come off as entitled, particularly when their last name was on the side of this building or that. So they treated me with artificial deference. So polite, so obsequious. Just enough to make me know that in any other context I wouldn't even exist to them. But as their professor, who might be interviewed one day about them, it had to be all shining marks across the board."

"Okay," Michael said.

Rebenold's eyes narrowed. "You don't have to include me in the indictments. I can campaign for you. I can write editorials. I can put you in contact with every major political donor in the state, even the ones Jeff Lambert doesn't have access to. I'm talking about people you may need for next year but will definitely need down the road. My word is golden with them. And then I'll be in DC. You know how many times I've needed a friendly ear in Congress? It's more than you think. I'll never not answer my phone. I'll—"

"Deborah."

"I'll meet with whomever you need me to meet with," she continued, already beginning to tear up. "I'll be your ace in the hole. Permanently. Anything you need. *Ever.* For example—"

"*Deborah.*"

This time she fell silent. Michael leaned back against one of the shelves.

"It's going to be fast. They're already seizing the bank accounts. Even if someone didn't talk about payments, there'll be transfers or payoffs. We won't even need to look at your bank statements, because we'll have the money heading there from theirs."

"Michael, you know how this works. Nobody has to look there—"

"Yeah, but when it comes out anyway I go down, too, for being the guy that didn't look there. At best I look stupid and incompetent. At worst, complicit. You come in now and do things the easy way, and it'll be a fine and a slap on the wrist. No jail time."

Deborah stared at Michael, her face slowly twisting in anger.

"You're not kidding," she said, incredulously. "You're offering me what I wouldn't even offer my worst enemy. A fine? A slap on the wrist? The second this comes out, it's my career. Do you even understand what that means?"

"I do."

"No, I don't think you do," Deborah shot back. "What the hell am I supposed to do for the rest of my life?"

"You have money. Pick a beach. Write a book. Hell, find a university somewhere they've never heard of you and soak up some more of that artificial deference."

Deborah's jaw dropped. Michael realized he'd gone too far. It wasn't a requirement that he be an utter dick about this. So why was he twisting the knife?

"Rot in hell, Story," Deborah said, shoving past Michael on the way out of the library.

He watched her go but then took out his cell phone. He dialed Naomi, who was already at the office.

"Hey, so I need you to get somebody in financial fraud to put a warrant together for Deb's financial accounts. Checking, savings, retirement, every last thing. Got it?"

"Deb? You mean *Deb* Deb?"

"That's right. When you're done with that, hit the e-mail and phone records, too. All correspondence relating to Jing Saifai, cross-referencing any names in Saifai's office, as well as any of the other triad-related warrants. Cool?"

Naomi didn't say anything for a second, then seemed to pull herself from shock. "Cool. Yeah. You got it, Michael."

"Thanks." When Naomi didn't hang up, he asked, "Something else?"

"It's that bad?" she asked.

"Yes," Michael said hoarsely. "But we'll make it right."

———

A Chevy Tahoe had been waiting for Oscar and Helen in front of their newfound residence on Outpost. A second Tahoe was parked in the cul-de-sac at the end of the block, with a third just down the street already angled back down the hill. A young man stood beside the first SUV, a tight smile on his face.

"Mr. de Icaza, Mrs. Story—"

"Helen," Helen replied evenly. "Just Helen, please."

"*Helen.* I'm Min Hsiao, an associate of Wanquan Yang," Hsiao said with a clipped bow. "As I mentioned on the phone, Yang has requested the pleasure of your company at a meeting place a short distance from here. I hope you don't mind."

"Not at all," Helen said. "Our own cars aren't sufficient?"

"A courtesy," Hsiao replied, indicating the backseat of the waiting Tahoe. "If you would."

Helen nodded and entered, sitting in the back as if she were sitting in a cab. Oscar wanted to make a run for it but knew he'd be gunned down in a heartbeat. Also, he'd look foolish in front of his much braver counterpart. He entered the car as well, the door slamming shut behind him. He stared back out at the house and wondered if it would be his last view of the place.

"Oscar."

He turned to Helen as Hsiao climbed into the passenger seat and spoke to the driver in Mandarin. Helen, making sure the two men saw her quick movement, leaned over and kissed Oscar on the lips.

"Screw these guys," she whispered. "You're Oscar de Icaza. What the hell are you afraid of?"

The remark made him smile, and he kissed her back. When they finally broke apart, he saw Hsiao looking at him in the rearview mirror. Oscar shot him a smug grin, sank back into his seat, and took Helen's hand in his.

I'm Oscar de Icaza. And I fear nothing.

The distance was anything but short. They wound out of Hollywood, through Studio City, past Burbank, and out toward Pasadena. It took Oscar all that time to realize where they were going. Over the course of the entire drive, Helen's eyes stayed fixed ahead, just as her hand held Oscar's in a tight grip. It wasn't one of worry, however, but resolve. Oscar was bemused for being so turned on by her even as they were being driven to their deaths.

If only they were allowed one last tumble in the hay. He'd make it worth it, something to remember all the way to hell.

If there was a hell, of course.

The paved road gave way to the gravel one, which gave way to dust as they approached the tree where Tony Qi had made his offer of a partnership with Oscar only days before. Rather than one car waiting there now, there were several. The lead Tahoe broke away from the caravan and circled around back as Hsiao indicated for their driver to slow to a halt up ahead.

"We will wait here for just a moment," Hsiao said.

"Of course," Oscar said.

A few men idled between cars, chatting and smoking cigarettes while others spoke on cell phones. The driver kept the engine running but also scrolled through his own cell phone. A man barely older than

Hsiao exited a nearby SUV and came over to Oscar and Helen's. Hsiao hopped out and opened the back door. The young man extended a hand to Oscar, who shook it. He then nodded to Helen.

"My name is Billy Daai. I regret to inform you that your former contact, Zhelin Qi, has been removed from his position within our brotherhood due to an inexcusable insult made against the father of one of his brethren. After he was presented with these charges, he confessed that he had passed a list of delivery sites relating to your business along to Deputy District Attorney Michael Story. To your knowledge, is this true?"

Luckily, the question was directed at Helen and not Oscar. If it had been, Oscar feared his incredulity would've given away the game. Why would Tony have covered for them? How could he even have known what they did? Then he realized that of course he'd have known. There was probably only one person other than him who'd had all that information.

Helen simply shrugged. "I have very little knowledge or interest in my husband's affairs."

The answer surprised Oscar, but Billy didn't seem fazed. He nodded and turned back to the assemblage of vehicles. He nodded to one of them, and the back door opened. Two men escorted Tony Qi from the back of the vehicle, bringing him to the side of the tree. They forced him to his knees.

"Whose father did he insult?" Oscar asked.

"It's not important," replied Billy.

Both gunmen drew pistols and shot Tony in the back of the head. His dead body flopped forward, dust rising as he hit the ground. Oscar stared at the corpse in grim bewilderment. Helen put a hand to her mouth but said nothing.

"We would like to continue our partnership," Billy said as the gunmen returned to their car. "In the short time it was operational, it proved fruitful. Mr. Qi was a man of vision in this respect."

Three other men now moved to the body with blades, and a fourth unloaded what looked like fifty-pound bags of lye from the back of one of the other trucks.

"I agree," Oscar said. "We are plugged into the city in ways you are not, and vice versa. I see no reason for the expansion of our cooperation to be temporary."

"Excellent, then I—"

"I would like to add something, however," Oscar interrupted.

"Anything, please," Billy said, though his subtly clenched jaw suggested he meant the opposite.

"I've been looking to expand my business away from simply mechanic's shops and custom parts and into dealerships," Oscar said. "The cars sell themselves, but visibility and location are everything. I would like three large parcels of commercial real estate in the wealthiest areas of San Gabriel and financial backing for this venture."

Oscar felt Helen's hand tighten around his own. He knew the first question she'd ask when they were alone: *How long had you been keeping that idea from me?* But the truth was, as usual, he'd simply reacted to the opportunity and made it up on the fly. It seemed reasonable enough, given they'd just made him and his woman bear witness to a capital crime so their complicity and silence would bind them together.

"Agreed," Billy said. "But it's not a loan. It's a partnership. Will you agree?"

"Absolutely," Oscar said, realizing he might have just signed his death warrant.

"More importantly, is there a place for Ms. Story in this venture?" Billy asked.

"Of course," Helen announced. "I'll be the general manager of all three and liaise directly with you and your brethren."

It was Oscar's turn to squeeze Helen's hand. He relaxed into this vision of the future, the two of them tied together in something that might actually add up to something else, and he was happy. Then he caught sight of the men with the blades carrying the pieces of Tony to an open grave and reminded himself how easily that could have been him and Helen.

Going to have to kill all these bastards one of these days.

———

Though Susan wanted to be driven back to Good Samaritan, Luis told her she should go home. After a couple of rounds of protest, she finally agreed, as if realizing she was in shock. By the time they got to Luis's car, she was almost paralyzed, and he had to buckle her into her seat like a child. Before they were even out of the parking lot, she was in tears. Luis tried to speak to her, but she shook him off. They drove together in near silence, her sniffles and occasional cry the only things breaking the quiet.

"What's going to happen now?" she finally asked as Luis pulled up in front of her house.

"I don't know," Luis admitted. "They're going to keep making arrests and building cases against the triad leaders based on the evidence that's been discovered, I guess. Once it comes out about Nan, public anger will turn to him and away from the triad, but that doesn't mean the cases won't lead to indictments. There's too much evidence for it all to go away."

"But without righteous indignation fueling things, they're guilty of what? Counterfeiting generic pharmaceuticals?" Susan asked. "That's a fine at best. A big one, but so what? They'll never get anyone for Benny's murder now. Heck, the public might even celebrate the dead triad gunmen who killed Nan as the real heroes who stopped the outbreak and got revenge for the victims. And the triad won't stop making cheap counterfeit pharmaceuticals. They'll just take it back offshore, and sooner or later they'll taint another batch with industrial solvents or chromium or even hydrogen cyanide like they found in Tianjin, and more people will die. So what was it all for?"

Luis thought about this. Sadly, Susan's words didn't ring so untrue.

"That deputy DA Michael Story is a real bastard," Luis said. "He's a careerist and a liar and a self-aggrandizing weasel. He loves power more than justice and likes seeing himself in the paper. And through this case, he just got enough evidence to subpoena the financial records of every last one of those people identified as members of the triad. He will go after them not because of what they've done, but because of what going after them can do for him and his career. It may be an odd thing to have faith in the corrupted, but Michael will make them hurt. I guarantee it."

As soon as he said the words, Luis realized he believed them. He hoped Susan did, too. She exited the car with a nod and moved up to her house. Luis was about to pull away from the curb when she turned back to him.

"I hope you're right."

Luis took his own leisurely time getting back to St. Augustine's. The radio was nothing but reports on the shooting at USC, so he turned it off and went for a drive. He hit Sunset, wound it up through Hollywood, and took Laurel Canyon high up to Mulholland Drive, from which he could see all the way to the ocean in one direction and out to the desert in the other. He drove west, finally stopping when the road ended at a grassy trail. He parked the car and walked it until he was overlooking the ocean over an hour later.

When he finally returned to his car, his cell phone, long out of reception range, showed several voice mails. He picked the first, from Bridgette, and listened.

"He's gone, Luis," she said between sobs. "He's gone."

Luis didn't listen to any more of the message. He tossed the phone into the car, climbed onto the hood, stared out toward the sun, and screamed as loud and as long as he could. There were no people around, and the sound didn't even seem to warrant a glance from the passing birds.

XXV

Michael sat alone in his empty house, reading the newspaper from his iPad. A week had gone by since the shooting at USC and things had moved quickly. Coordinating with the FBI and the US Marshals Service, LAPD had descended on the LA triad in force. There had been over 120 arrests, a vast amount of material seized, and, in the coup to end all coups, two cargo containers filled with over a hundred pounds of heroin, one of the largest busts in Southern California history, went down in San Pedro. It linked the SARS outbreak to narcotics in the public imagination, and at least some of the attention that had been diverted toward Nan Tiu was suddenly back on the big, bad dragon syndicate.

Michael knew the truth—or at least a version of it. There was somebody in authority down there, whether it was customs, TSA, DHS, or even the local sheriff's department, who'd likely been taking bribes to look the other way on the narco stuff. When everything began to crumble, they staged a bust to come out clean. Of course, the triad wasn't stupid, and Michael figured this particular member of law enforcement would be knocking on his door asking for protective custody soon enough once they realized they were marked men or women. Then his case would only grow stronger.

He was riding one of these highs when he called Deborah Rebenold at home and told her he'd had a change of heart. She was effusive in her gratitude and understood Michael's concern that if she ran for office the matter might come out. Chastened, she agreed to step away from public life. She'd already been made several offers in the private sector and was considering university positions in several states. She'd known that Michael had sent Naomi after her financial records and asked if there would need to be any remuneration. Michael told her that would only arouse suspicion. She was grateful all over again.

The truth was, neither Michael nor Naomi had found much that was actionable in Deborah's financials. The triad knew what they were doing and funneled money to her in ways that were difficult to track, likely with cash. While Deborah's bank accounts and credit cards revealed a very routine series of transactions, Michael knew of various vacations, cars, household renovations, items of jewelry, and so on that didn't appear on any statements. It would take half a department six months to get anywhere with it, and he didn't have that.

Better to avoid the scandal altogether, particularly given the one already on the boil for him at home.

Helen was gone. The kids, too. Though he had seen them during the week, the triad business had kept him at work late each night. So the children had been in the care of babysitters for a couple of days before Helen offered to take them in the short term to the place she was sharing with her new boyfriend. Michael had protested, figuring it was some gangster's hovel, but when he learned of its address he consented. When he talked to the kids, they told him how much they loved the new place. They didn't mention Oscar once, clearly by design.

Michael thought he'd miss Helen, or at the very least be jealous. He conjured the most depraved sexual images he could muster of his wife copulating with her new lover, but it didn't affect him at all. He just didn't care that much. Yeah, it would hit him in the bank account and couldn't help but affect his political ambitions, but beyond that? He was still young, reasonably well-off, and rising in esteem. He had a *future*. If that didn't result in primo tail, he didn't know what would.

Of course, he'd have to be careful. He couldn't exactly pick up a UCLA cheerleader at a Westwood bar and think she wouldn't raise a few eyebrows the next time he was on the red carpet at a charity event or political function. He had to find the right woman—smart, ambitious, beautiful, just cunning enough, and, he hoped, fun.

Like Helen, he thought.

His cell phone buzzed, and he checked the caller ID. It was Jeff Lambert. The two of them had been in almost constant contact over the past week as a decision neared on when exactly Michael should announce his candidacy. It couldn't look like he was using the triad busts for political gain, but he also couldn't wait until they'd faded in the public memory.

As of the night before they'd decided it should be leaked that Deborah wouldn't be running for reelection. The press would hem and haw over who her replacement should be, and with a little help Michael would look like the front-runner. They'd let a few days go by, as if the reports had taken Michael completely by surprise, as he was so buried in casework. Then he'd allow a reporter to ask him about it so that he could deflect attention. This would be all the loose thread they'd need, as they'd start asking him about it every time he gave an interview.

Finally, he'd give in, as if only to stop the questions in order to focus on his cases. It would almost be a joke.

Me? District attorney? Yeah, okay. Go with that. I'm in. See what happens. The voters are smarter than that.

And that's when Jeff's team would go into overdrive and sweep poor, unsuspecting, aw-shucks civil servant Michael Story into the district attorney's office.

"Good morning, Jeff. How are you?"

"I'm at your front door," Jeff said. "Can you come out for a second?"

Michael froze. This couldn't be anything but bad news. Had they found out about Helen and Oscar? That had to be it.

Goddammit.

Michael rose and moved to the door, checking himself out in a hall mirror as he went. He hadn't shaved yet and looked slightly disheveled. *Not* a politically viable candidate.

"Hey, you should've let me know you were on your way over," Michael said, opening the door. "Could've met for breakfast somewhere."

But Jeff, the king of pleasantries, wasn't having it. He handed Michael a large envelope.

"The Ramos campaign sent this over this morning," Jeff said. "They knew we were planning a run and wanted us to have this as a 'courtesy.'"

Michael opened the envelope. Inside he found several pieces of paper, photographs that had been printed off a computer. They were all of him and the late Annie Whittaker, the woman who'd been killed after recruiting whistle-blowers against the Marshak family. They were the same pictures the late Jason Marshak had tried to blackmail him with. After Jason was killed, the blackmail attempts had stopped.

Michael hadn't given much thought as to where the images might've ended up.

"What is this?" Michael asked.

Jeff rolled his eyes. "Come on, Michael. That's Anne Whittaker. And there's a time and date stamp. This comes out, the case you built your newfound stardom on is suddenly tainted, and you with it. You're out."

"Jeff, I don't understand. So I had an affair."

"*Michael.* You had an affair with a murder victim and never bothered to disclose that fact even as you brought down the people who killed her. I mean, go you. Way to get revenge. But wow, that's . . . that's an ethical quagmire a political candidate does not emerge from. The party had an emergency call this morning. We're going to beg Deborah to stay on and see what happens. But that's it for you. Keep those, by the way. I'd imagine there are plenty of copies out there in the world."

Jeff turned to walk away. Michael, his heart pounding, reached out to grab him. Jeff yanked away and looked at Michael as if he might bite.

"What the hell could you have to say to me?" Jeff asked.

"Did they tell you where they got them? Or from whom?"

Jeff scowled. "They didn't say. But it was Jing Saifai."

"How do you know?"

"You think anything that happens in your office is a secret?" Jeff shot back. "If I were you, I'd keep my head down for the next few months and then start looking for another job. Your name is going to mean jack in the City of Los Angeles."

With that, Jeff returned to his car. Michael walked back into the house, tossed the pictures and key drive onto the kitchen table, and sank into a dining room chair. He stared into space even as his cell phone buzzed and dinged and the house phone rang off the hook.

Pastor Whillans's funeral was on the Wednesday morning after he died. Luis had attended, hadn't said a word despite being asked to by several of his colleagues and friends of the pastor, and didn't remember a moment of it. He'd taken the week off from teaching, as had a couple of the other priests, and had spent much of his time off in his room on his knees and in prayer.

He'd prepared for this moment for months, ever since he'd heard Whillans's diagnosis. It was inevitable. He'd watched the pastor weaken and fall, but now he was gone. He went over and over their last interaction together, their jokey pre-sermon chat about nothing with Bridgette in the pastor's office. Luis had envisioned what their last interaction would be like—the pastor in bed, Luis praying by his side, a few words, a few last bits of wisdom imparted, and then a farewell.

But even as he'd stood in that office that Sunday morning, Luis had known and, he believed, Pastor Whillans had known it was to be their last meeting. So why hadn't they said more? Why hadn't that wisdom come? Why had they treated it as if it was nothing, that the more important moment was the sermon and who was coming to attend?

And if they'd known the night before, why hadn't they spoken of important things instead of this ridiculous murder case, the ins and outs of which were already escaping Luis's thoughts?

Because we didn't need to, came the thought. *Because we'd said it all already.*

Luis allowed this phrase to repeat in his head hour after hour, day after day, until he realized it was true.

Though the archbishop had flown back from the Vatican to attend Pastor Whillans's funeral, something Luis noted he hadn't done for Father Chang, he had barely had time to greet Luis before having to move on to the several other members of the diocese waiting for an audience. So when the archbishop arrived at St. Augustine's on Saturday morning, Luis was surprised that he was there to see him.

"Father Chavez," the archbishop said, embracing Luis. "How are you doing?"

"I'm all right, Your Eminence," Luis said. "I know that Father Whillans was suffering and was glad to soon be in the presence of God. That is a great comfort."

"Of course," the archbishop replied. "And amen to that. Will you come with me to the altar?"

Luis obliged as the archbishop guided him to the chapel. There, the archbishop knelt and indicated for Luis to do similarly.

"A few months ago Father Whillans made a request of me. It was something I knew right away I could not grant. It asked too much. I prayed on it, but the answer remained elusive. I didn't understand but do now."

"Yes?"

"Yes, Father," the archbishop said. "Father Whillans told me of how the spirit moves within you. What a true instrument of God you've proven to be. And following his death, he wanted you to succeed him as the parish pastor of St. Augustine's. I told him that was quite impossible, that you were far too young and inexperienced. That the congregation wouldn't have it. But by all accounts I've been proven very wrong indeed and am humbled to be in your presence."

Luis was stunned. He had never considered himself pastor material and even thought the diocese might reassign him to a different parish following Whillans's death. This was a bolt from the blue.

"Pastor?" Luis managed to say. "Your Eminence, I don't—"

"I know what you're going to say and I agree with you a hundred percent. But I ask you to do what Father Whillans asked of me. *Pray.* God will then tell you what he told me. Then I will have your answer."

Luis froze up. He had no idea how to respond. That's when he noticed what time it was.

"Um, I'm sorry, Your Eminence, but I have an appointment. Can we revisit this topic?"

"Of course, Father. But don't keep me waiting."

———

"Pastor?" Susan laughed. "You're going to be the guy in charge? Do they *know* you? Better yet, does their God know what you get up to, running around the city busting gangsters and all? They're nuts if they think you're suddenly going to be this choirboy for them."

On the other side of the glass partition separating the two of them, Luis laughed. He knew of all people that Susan would see the humor in it.

"What did you say?" Susan asked.

"I told him I had to come here," Luis said, shrugging.

"Here?" Susan said, indicating around.

"Well, not exactly," Luis admitted. "I said I had an appointment."

Here was the Mesa Verde Detention Facility in Bakersfield, a large campus for federal prisoners soon to be deported. Though thousands of deportees, generally those heading to countries in Central and South America, were housed in county, the lucky ones ended up in the federal facilities, away from typically more violent offenders. After several days of working with the CDC, Susan's visa issues came to light. Rather than fight, however, Susan turned herself in to authorities with a plan, she told Luis, to plead "no contest." Instead of the protracted court battle and endless delays she expected, however, she was arrested immediately and sent into federal detention to await a hearing.

Bail in those cases didn't apply, as the detainee could legally be rearrested the moment they exited the facility.

"So, how're you doing in there?" Luis asked.

"I'm bored out of my mind," Susan admitted. "I met with my court-appointed attorney for all of five minutes two days ago. She said that if I can get any letters of support from Good Samaritan, from the CDC, and so on, I might be able to fight deportation, but I think I'm done."

"I'd write you a letter," Luis offered.

"Thanks, but I think I'm ready to go back," Susan said, her attention seeming to drift. "My world here was the clinic, Father Chang, and Nan. All those things are gone now. What do I really have anymore?"

"What do you have in Hong Kong?"

"Are you trying to make me feel better or worse?" Susan shot back before softening a little. "To be honest, I don't think I'll end up staying in Hong Kong that long. I'll probably wind down to Sydney or Melbourne. I've always heard Melbourne is just really fun and laid-back. From there the islands maybe? Fiji, the Carolines, Micronesia. I don't know. Anywhere my education can get me in the door and my past is too far behind to kick me out."

"I hear you," Luis said.

"I'd been meaning to ask you," Susan said. "How'd you track me down after the incident at Good Samaritan? It didn't sound like Esmeralda Carreño gave you much to go on. Was that . . . God?"

"Not that time," Luis said. "That was a young man I tried to help before. Miguel. He's a good kid. But I can't seem to reach him right now. I keep trying and nothing works."

"The tests of this world are for the individual, right? Some people just need to get to wherever they're going on their own two feet. Have a little faith, Father."

Luis laughed. Maybe he should. "You want me to bring you any more books?"

"Absolutely!" Susan enthused. "My burn rate is about one a day. You don't even have to drive out. Just drop them in the mail. When I'm done, I give them to the library here. Thank you, thank you, thank you."

Luis nodded and eyed the young doctor, knowing he'd never see her again. Susan sighed.

"Don't look at me like that," she protested.

"Like what?"

"Like I'm not a stranger you got thrown in with. I am. It's an accident I was friends with a priest. An accident that we ended up having to fight back the triad *and* SARS *and* Father Chang's murderous ex-boyfriend. Go with God, Father Chavez, and keep kicking ass. I am retiring from that particular sport, and if you think of me, picture me somewhere sunny. Okay?"

"Agreed. Can I pray with you?" Luis asked.

Susan laughed so loud, Luis was afraid the guards would come get her early. "No, Luis. That's not me, either. I'm telling you. We're strangers. And that's okay. The earth's full of them."

"Okay," Luis said, nodding.

Susan leaned up to the glass partition and kissed it. "*Muah.* Take care of yourself, Father."

"Call me Luis."

"Take care of yourself, Luis."

Luis put his fist up to the partition, and Susan did the same. Then she walked away.

Luis sat for a beat before rising. As he headed for the door, he heard a woman calling out to him. He turned and saw a very large man he thought might be Samoan speaking to a lithe Asian woman on the deportee's side of the glass. She pointed at Luis and smacked her hand against the partition.

"Um, sir? You are a priest?" the large man said.

"I am," Luis replied. "Can I help you?"

"My name is Archie Salapu. This is my friend, Jun Tan. We are missing a friend and are hoping you might pray for him."

The carrel next to Archie and Jun was empty, so Luis borrowed the chair and slid it over.

"Is he in this facility?" Luis asked.

"We don't know. He may be incarcerated, he might not be. I've heard rumors that, well, that he might've met an accident."

"What's his name?"

"Zhelin Qi. Tony to his friends."

The man who saved us in the warehouse. The man who wanted five minutes to warn the triad leaders.

Five minutes was not enough.

"I will pray for him," Luis said. "Absolutely I will."

But when he turned back to Jun, he saw that her eyes had been boring into him since he sat. She saw everything he knew writ large across his face. She looked stricken.

"You know him," she said in halting English. "You know Tony."

"I met him," Luis said, surprising himself. "He stopped the plague. He saved hundreds if not thousands of lives. It was him. He found the drug factory."

In just-as-unsure Mandarin, Archie translated this back to Jun. But Luis could tell from the look on her face that she knew exactly what he'd said. Her face contorted, and it looked as if she might cry. Instead, she forced a smile and put her hand out to Luis.

"Pray for him, won't you?" she said. "Won't you?"

"I will," Luis said. "And I'll pray for you, too."

Jun smiled again, but this time couldn't stop the tears. Archie patted Luis's arm.

"God is great. He put you here to see us," he said, though his words were unsteady, as if two days later he might question if this conversation had even happened. "Thank you."

"God bless you and Ms. Tan," Luis said, then made the sign of the cross.

Archie nodded and mumbled something. Luis didn't think he could meet Jun's eyes again and walked away.

The air around St. Augustine's was fraught with tension the next day. So much had happened in such a short amount of time that Luis wondered if anyone would even show up for Mass. The death of Pastor Whillans was almost a tragic afterthought to the demise of Pastor Siu-Tung at the end of last Sunday's homily. What on earth would serve for an encore?

But this was the very nature of the priesthood. It was not about *him*. He was there to be God's vessel on earth, and the parishioners were just as distraught by the passing of their shepherd as he was. If he couldn't minister to them now in their time of need, when could he?

With a heavy heart Luis prepared for his first Mass as the new pastor of St. Augustine's Church. The announcement was to be made during the sermon, ostensibly a remembrance of Pastor Whillans that included stories sent in by congregants throughout the week. It only amplified to Luis what he already knew. Whillans was beloved and he touched the lives and hearts of so, so many.

Uneasy lies the head that wears the crown.

But as he looked out the rectory window, he saw the parking lot filling up. The tables of those selling food or religious icons lined the sidewalk, and everyone was talking and laughing and shaking hands and congregating around each other. A couple of older women even carried with them framed photographs of Pastor Whillans, but even they didn't look so much like mourners as celebrants. This was true fellowship.

He was seized with the desire to be out among them. He knew that the pastor was meant to maintain some reserve, some distance, from the parishioners, but maybe he could do that next Sunday.

He put on his cassock and hurried out of the rectory to the parking lot. He was greeted warmly but noted the surprise on the face of several. He was younger than so many of them. He couldn't be aloof if he tried.

So instead he introduced himself to everyone, committing new names and faces to memory, thanking people for coming, and blessing those who asked. Eventually, he was joined by several other priests, and the word spread. Parishioners who had already gone into the chapel returned to the parking lot. Members of the choir and even the laywoman who played the organ came out a few minutes later. The talk was not of Pastor Siu-Tung or Pastor Whillans but of God. How God would be with Luis and he would lead them. Luis said again and again that he would try.

But the doubt that had plagued the archbishop was absent in the eyes of everyone around him. Luis smiled and shook as many hands as he could. Someone brought up a chair and set it behind him. He stood on it and made a joke that some of the men were still taller than him.

People asked questions that he couldn't hear, made requests he couldn't fulfill, but he reached back to them regardless. There were so many people that no more cars could park, and traffic was backed up a quarter mile down the street. There were so many that Luis knew they wouldn't all fit in the chapel.

He raised his hands above his head. Everyone went quiet. When even the angry car horns were silenced and the air was still, Luis's voice echoed out over the crowd.

"Let us pray."

ACKNOWLEDGMENTS

The author would like to gratefully acknowledge the contribution of the many people whose time and talent went into putting this book together, including his editors at Thomas & Mercer, Jacquelyn BenZekry and Kjersti Egerdahl; his developmental editor, Charlotte Herscher; his agent, Laura Dail; and his Chavez comrade-in-arms, Lisa French, who is always the first eyes on anything he writes. He would also like to thank his wife, Lauren, and children, Eliza and Wyatt, for putting up with him.

ABOUT THE AUTHOR

Photo © 2015 Morna Ciraki

Born in Texas, author Mark Wheaton now lives in Los Angeles with his wife and children. Before writing his first Luis Chavez novel, he was a screenwriter, producer, and a journalist writing for the *Hollywood Reporter*, *Total Film*, and more.